SLOW DEATH

SLOW DEATH

by STEWART HOME

SERPENT'S TAIL
HIGH RISK BOOKS

NEW YORK / LONDON

First published 1996 by
High Risk Books/Serpent's Tail
4 Blackstock Mews, London N4 2BT
and 180 Varick Street, 10th floor, New York, NY 10014

Library of Congress Catalog Card Number: 95—71061

A full catalogue record for this book can be obtained from the British Library on request

Cover design by Rex Ray
Phototypeset in 10½pt Janson by Intype London Ltd
Printed in Finland by Werner Söderström Oy

'The five skinheads moved with the speed and grace of wolves descending on their prey. The kid didn't stand a chance! Johnny reached the bastard first, tensing the muscles in his hand before karate chopping the punk's neck. The youth shuddered and then his legs crumpled beneath him. By the time the bozo hit the deck, the gang had him surrounded and their boots were slamming hard against his prostrate body . . .'

One

JOHN HODGES GAZED vacantly at the doctor for the best part of a minute. Maria Walker shifted uncomfortably in her chair. The skinhead was young and ruggedly handsome. Professional ethics ruled out sexual liaisons with patients but the doctor felt like throwing caution to the wind. Maria needed some excitement in her life. After two years' co-habitation with a social worker who showed more interest in the affairs of the local Labour Party than a woman's need for genital satisfaction, Walker fancied a bit of rough.

'Speak up,' Maria chirped. 'What can I do for you?'

'Well, you see doctor,' John blurted, 'I think I'm a nutter!'

'You think that you're mad?' Walker repeated in disbelief.

'Yeah,' Hodges confessed. 'I'm a fuckin' loony!'

'What makes you think you're mentally disturbed?' Maria enquired.

'Whenever I go out,' Hodges elaborated, 'I think

people are following me. Sometimes I beat up suits just for looking at me. But the worst thing is jazz music, whenever I hear it I go fucking mental, can't control myself at all. If something isn't done about it, I might kill somebody. All this violence has got completely out of hand.'

'I see,' the doctor said blankly as she scribbled a note on a sheet of paper. 'And when do you think these problems began?'

'About ten years ago,' John hissed, 'when I was fourteen. Ever since then, me mates have called me Johnny Aggro. When I was a kid, my family lived in King's Cross. Then, for no reason at all, me mum decided she wanted to live in Ilford. Being a nipper, I had to go with her. I came to Poplar a couple of years ago. Thought it would do me good to get out of Essex. It helped a bit—but I only feel sane when I'm in the centre of town, down the West End, in Notting Hill, Camden or Islington.'

'So why don't you get a flat somewhere more central?' Maria demanded.

'Now there's the rub,' Hodges snarled. 'I'm on social, haven't got the dosh to bag a pad in the West End. The only way I'd get a place in the centre of town is if the social services referred me to a housing association as needing cheap accommodation way out West.'

Walker had met the skinhead's type before—and she could see that he was one hundred per cent sane. After all, like any enterprising young man, he wanted to get out of Poplar and was prepared to fake madness to do so. The doctor liked Hodges' attitude and decided to emulate her patient. It was high time she struck out and grabbed what she desired.

'Okay,' Maria said. 'I want you to drop your pants and trousers.'

John stood up, loosened his braces, then let his sta-prest slide to the floor. Moments later, his Union Jack boxer shorts were also around his ankles. Walker took the patient's balls in her hand and ordered him to cough. Hodges obligingly cleared his throat.

'My boyfriend's like that in bed,' Maria laughed. 'Two coughs and it's over!'

'You should find yourself a real man,' John observed.

'I think I have,' the doctor cackled as she squeezed his prick.

'Give me a blow job!' the skinhead instructed.

'I'm not gonna do anything now,' Walker chided. 'I've got other patients to see. I'll call on you at six-thirty this evening.'

'It's a date,' Hodges shot back. 'Have you got my address?'

'Of course I have, silly,' Maria giggled. 'It's in your file.'

Fitzgerald House towered above Chrisp Street Market like some monstrous megalith erected to commemorate the millions whose lives had been blighted by post-war planners. Johnny Aggro lived on the twenty-third floor, with only a thin wall separating his pad from the space occupied by two wannabe art stars, Don Pemberton and Penelope Applegate aka Aesthetics and Resistance.

'Make me a cup of tea Penny,' Don commanded.

'Make it yourself,' Applegate snapped.

'I've got a headache,' Pemberton complained,

'brought on by all the reggae music played by the skinhead next door. It's unhealthy, it's making me ill.'

'That prole went out at least an hour ago, the only music that's been on is my Miles Davis CD—and since I know you love jazz, there must be some other reason for you feeling out of sorts.'

'Make me a cup of tea,' Don pleaded. 'I'm ill.'

'You're not the only one who's sick,' Penny scolded. 'I'm suffering from PMT, a bad back and severe depression.'

'What have you got to be depressed about?' Pemberton demanded.

'The review we got in the last issue of *Art Scene* for a start!' Applegate bawled.

'I've as much right as you to be fuming over that!' Don protested. 'How do you think I feel about being branded a trendy hack? Now make me a cup of tea.'

'Make it yourself,' Penny seethed as she threw down a glossy catalogue and picked up a desk diary.

'Please make me a cup of tea,' Pemberton persisted.

'There's a Karen Eliot show tonight,' Applegate announced as she threw down the diary. 'We have to go, Eliot could do a lot for our career, if we can butter her up.'

'You're right,' Don concurred, 'Karen is the biggest thing to hit the British art scene since Gilbert and George!'

'I hear she's a right bloody raver,' Penny yelped. 'Don, if you could just worm your way into her knickers, then maybe she'd do things for us.'

'Someone told me Eliot's bisexual and heavily political,' Pemberton snarled. 'She'd probably think it was terribly patriarchal if I tried to seduce her. Penny, darling, it would make a lot more sense if you got to rub pussies with her.'

'Sex is disgusting!' Applegate tutted.

'Yes,' her boyfriend agreed. 'Sex is disgusting—but one of us has to make the ultimate sacrifice if we're to further our careers. Given Eliot's interest in sexual politics, you're the ideal candidate.'

'Don,' Penny purred as she stepped toward the kitchen, 'I'll make you a cup of tea, then we'll sit down and talk about this rationally.'

'No!' Pemberton howled as he leapt up from his seat. 'Let me make the tea.'

'I thought you were ill,' Applegate snorted.

'Let's be fair about this!' Don cried. 'I'll make the tea and you can bed Eliot.'

'I'm making the tea,' Penny wailed as her boyfriend pushed past her, grabbed the kettle and filled it with water.

Johnny Aggro covered the distance between Russell Square tube station and Coram Street in a couple of minutes. He punched out the numbers one zero one on the entry phone and split seconds later Karen Eliot was demanding to know who was at the door.

'It's John,' Hodges replied. 'The geezer you picked up at The Nursery last Saturday night.'

'Yeah, I remember, you told me I gave the best blow job you'd ever had.'

'It's true,' John laughed.

'All the boys tell me that,' Karen responded.

'Can I come up and see you?' Hodges persisted.

'If you must,' Eliot conceded.

John was a little confused by the maze of stairs

in the five-storey block but he eventually found his way to Eliot's flat. The pad fascinated him as much as the chick who rented it. Before he met Karen, Hodges hadn't known there was the remotest possibility of getting a place like this, right in the centre of town. Now he realised that with a bit of hard work, anything was possible.

'You dirty bastard,' Eliot sneered as her guest pecked her on the cheek, 'you've got a hard-on!'

'No I haven't!' Hodges protested.

'You have now!' Karen laughed as she unzipped John's flies and took out his plonker.

'Give me a blow job,' Hodges pleaded.

'Later,' Eliot decreed as she put the penis away and rezipped John's flies. 'First I wanna know why you've come to see me!'

'For a bit of the old genetic action,' the skinhead leered.

'Nah,' Karen railed. 'That ain't it. You've got bulges in all the right places, if all you wanted was nookie, you could get it virtually anywhere. There's something else.'

'Okay, okay,' Johnny concurred, 'I wanted to ask you about getting certified as a nutter. You told me that's what you done to get this place.'

'The way I did it,' Eliot explained, 'was to go to my GP and tell her I thought I was mad. She gave me an appointment with a specialist and once I'd convinced the shrink I was mental, I was registered as having special housing needs.'

'I went to my doctor this morning about being a headcase,' Hodges complained, 'but she didn't send me off to the local loony bin to have me head tested. All she done was arrange to come around and see me this evening, so that we could have a fuck.'

'That sounds somewhat unethical!' Karen laughed. 'What did you tell her before she propositioned you?'

'I said I was a nutter,' the skinhead explained, 'and the only thing that would cure me was a cheap flat in the West End.'

'That was pretty dumb of you,' Karen observed. 'Even an imbecile would have seen straight through your act. You made it bloody obvious you weren't really mad, that all you wanted was to be rehoused.'

'So how did you get yourself certified?' John demanded.

'I said I was suffering from compulsive behaviour patterns and that sometimes I thought I was a machine,' Eliot confided. 'My shrink thought I'd be better off living in the centre of town where it would be easier for me to socialise and make new friends. She arranged for me to move into this flat.'

'So what would you advise me to do now?' Hodges asked. 'Have I blown it with my doctor? Will I ever convince her that I'm mad?'

'Go home and fuck your GP,' Karen commanded. 'Then blackmail the bitch into getting you certified. Doctors aren't supposed to have sexual relations with their patients.'

'Do I have to go now?' the skinhead replied.

'Yeah,' Eliot instructed. 'I've got things to do. Here, write your number in my address book and I'll call you sometime.'

'You're weird,' John sighed as he scribbled his details. 'Before Saturday, I'd never been with a chick who called a taxi to take me away after I'd fucked her.'

'I've an account with the firm,' Karen spat. 'I might as well make use of it.'

Maria Walker glanced at her watch. She had another five patients to see before she could take her lunch break. The doctor was performing her work like an automaton. Maria had spent most of the morning thinking about the steamy sex session she'd have with Johnny Aggro before returning home. Once the skinhead had spunked up inside her, it would be a right laugh making her right-on boyfriend lick out the funky twat. Unfortunately, this pleasant train of thought was interrupted by a knock on the door.

'Come in,' Walker ordered.

'Hello doctor,' Donald Pemberton wheezed as he seated himself. 'I'm having a dreadful time, I've got the most awful depression.'

'How's your sex life?' Maria enquired.

'Great!' Pemberton replied. 'My girlfriend shares my sentiments about sex. We both think it's degrading, we have a purely spiritual relationship. I've no problems in that department. What's bothering me is something that afflicts all great artists, you see, I'm suffering from a deep spiritual sickness. I think it's got something to do with the plastic society in which we live! People no longer have time to appreciate the great depths of intellect to be found in works of genius. I suppose it's a problem encountered by all artists, the impossibility of communicating with the emotionally stunted masses—but being possessed of an extraordinary talent, I suffer much more on account of this than anyone else living today. I know . . .'

'Okay, okay,' Walker snapped. 'I get the picture.

I'll prescribe you valium. Give it a couple of weeks and you'll be feeling much better.'

'But you don't understand!' Donald wailed. 'I've touched the infinite, I've communed with the Godhead, the knowledge of the ages is mine to impart to anyone who'll listen attentively. And that's just the problem, no one will listen.'

'If you don't mind,' Maria replied tardily, 'I'm rather busy. Here's your prescription, now please go.'

'I'm a flaming genius!' Pemberton protested as he took the script the doctor held out for him. 'You can't treat me like this! In a few years' time, people will kiss the very ground I walk upon, they'll worship at the well of my creativity. I'm gonna be bigger than Warhol! I've got talent and the application! I'm a Renaissance man, compared to me, even the greatest living artists are spiritual pygmies! You can't just dismiss me as though I'm some flunky. I'm more than just another patient, I've already prefigured every new development within the visual arts for the next five hundred years!'

'I think you're exaggerating,' Walker giggled.

'How dare you suggest I'm a liar!' Donald thundered. 'You're a disgrace to the medical fraternity. I'm going to lodge a professional complaint against you. We'll see how funny you think I am once you're struck off the medical register. I'll not waste any more of my precious time on you!'

The doctor turned around and began writing in Pemberton's file. She ignored the slammed door as her patient stormed out of the room. Maria was glad to see the back of the bastard. Now there were only four more patients to see before lunch.

Flipper Fine Arts was situated in London's

Mayfair. The business had long been established as the world's leading avant-garde art gallery, with branches in Berlin, Paris and New York. The firm's annual turnover ran into several billion pounds and the profits made many a manufacturing business look like a Mickey Mouse operation. Amanda Debden-Philips had been exhibitions director at Flipper for a good few years, she'd an eye for talent and her lust for young cock enabled many a bronzed Adonis to secure themselves a place on the international art circuit.

Karen Eliot was the hottest thing to hit Flipper in a long time. Amanda knew that her lunch with the young star was of enormous significance to the gallery. Karen's contract with Flipper ran out when her latest show closed. The official opening was another six hours away and yet every piece on display had already been sold to punters who'd paid telephone numbers for the privilege of owning an Eliot. Debden-Philips understood that a number of galleries were making Karen very lucrative offers and knew she had to top what her rivals were bidding.

'It was a wild idea of yours coming to this fast food joint for a business lunch,' Amanda laughed. 'So what would you like?'

'Beanburger, fries, strawberry milkshake, apple pie and a coffee,' Eliot replied. 'I'll grab a seat while you queue up for the nosh.'

Karen suppressed a fit of the giggles as she parked her arse. Debden-Philips had wanted to take her to one of those posh restaurants where it was rumoured punters were even billed for the air they consumed. The exorbitant cost meant nothing when set against tax-deductible expenses. Amanda had been looking forward to a top-flight meal but meekly accepted the substitution of junk food when Karen insisted that they go to Burger King.

'The service isn't too bad,' Debden-Philips observed as she set a tray on the table, 'for a place where you have to stand in line to get your food. They've got the queues moving pretty fast.'

'They have to do that,' Eliot blasted back, 'to keep the profits up. Eating here is like working on an assembly line. That's what I like about this place, it appeals to the machine element in my psychological make-up.'

'Don't put yourself down!' Amanda cried as she lifted food from the tray and placed it in front of the artist. 'You're a very talented young woman. There's millions of people who'd give their right arm to possess your gifts.'

'I'm not putting myself down,' Karen explained as she bit into her burger. 'I'm just being a little too modest. Andy Warhol wanted to be a machine, whereas I've achieved his ambition. I make art the way someone else would produce plastic mouldings, that's the secret of my success!'

'Well then,' Amanda thundered as she lifted a coffee to her lips, 'let's drink to profits!'

'Yes,' Eliot roared as she raised her milkshake. 'Here's to all the filthy lucre we're gonna make. Art is dead, long live hype! Pretension is what made Britain great!'

'Does that mean you'll sign a new contract with Flipper?' Debden-Philips enquired.

'Yes,' Karen pouted. 'One identical to the deal that's just expired except I'm to get an extra ten per cent on all sales and you're to sign thirteen artists of my choice to the gallery. The latter point won't actually be written into the contract—but I'll go ape-shit if you don't stick to it.'

'You're asking for a hell of a lot,' Amanda croaked.

'Don't even think about haggling,' Eliot shot back, 'because the Europa Gallery have already agreed to an identical deal.'

'Okay, you win,' Debden-Philips acceded.

Their business concluded, the two wimmin ate in silence.

Johnny Aggro had time on his hands. The doctor wasn't due at his pad until early evening, which meant he'd hours in which to knock around the West End. Johnny strode down Carnaby Street, soaking up the admiring glances of tourists who'd come to see London's vibrant youth culture. Although a few cameras clicked, trippers who were happy to ask punks to pose for them left Johnny alone. There was a primitive violence about the youth, he wasn't approachable like the young degenerates who were accompanied by dogs tied to pieces of string. Only a pretty girl was capable of distracting his attention and a Japanese bird did just that when she came rushing up to him.

'Photo? Photo?' the teenager was chanting.

Johnny draped his arm over the chick's shoulder, while her sister took a picture. The girls swapped places. Hodges just grinned at the camera.

'Thanks you,' the second bird said as she threw her arms around the skinhead's neck and pecked at his cheek.

'Any chance of a blow job?' Johnny enquired.

'No understand,' the girl said as she beamed up at Hodges.

'Forget it!' Hodges hissed as he stomped off down the street.

The boot boy headed east and it wasn't long before he found himself in Rupert Street. A bird with ebony skin, pink hot pants and a white top caught Hodges' attention. He smiled at her and she smiled back.

'So, you're looking for business,' the chick laughed as Johnny approached her.

'I don't believe it,' the skinhead moaned, 'you're a hooker!'

'What's so surprising about that?' the street walker snapped. 'Have you got some hang-up about it?'

'No,' Hodges shot back, 'it's just that you're much better-looking than most babes who put a meter on their twat, I figured you were young, free and single!'

'I don't charge any more than the other girls!' the prostitute said as she took Johnny's arm.

'The problem is,' the skinhead sighed, 'I'm strapped for cash.'

'You could peddle your arse to some business-man and come back later,' the girl suggested.

'Never,' the boot boy bellowed as he walked away. 'I've got too much pride to do that!'

Like Johnny Aggro, Penny Applegate and Don Pemberton had deserted Fitzgerald House for Soho. Old Compton Street was their favoured location. Like many other young trendies, the wannabe art stars could often be found among the Pâtisserie Valerie clientele. At number 44, it was possible to make the art scene while downing tea and a selection of quality cakes. Penny and Don had just placed their order when Ramish Patel wandered in from the street. Recognising the couple, he went and sat with them.

'How's it going?' Ramish asked.

'Very well,' Applegate replied, 'we're negotiating to do a show in the toilets at the CIA.'

'The institute thinks it's a wonderful idea,' Pemberton added. 'They're just a bit worried about how they'd protect the exhibition, members of the public might object if closed circuit security cameras filmed them as they relieved themselves.'

'The CIA are doing a retrospective of all my films,' Patel announced. 'It'll be on next year. I want to premier my new movie during the season.'

'Is that the one that's about racism and the art establishment?' Penny wanted to know.

'Yeah,' Ramish confirmed. 'The working title is *White Lies*.'

'Super, super!' Don put in. 'Art will be critical or it will not be at all!'

'What?' Patel fizzed.

'It's a quote from the latest Aesthetics and Resistance manifesto, a tract entitled *Beyond the beautiful*,' Applegate explained. 'It'll be printed as an editorial in the next issue of *The Journal of Immaterial Art*.'

'I've been thinking about the way you work,' Ramish confessed, 'and while you've yet to sign up with a gallery, all the writing you've had published in the art press has certainly got your names around. You've inspired me to put pen to paper in a bid to make myself more famous!'

'Thanks!' Applegate and Pemberton chanted in unison. 'It's praise indeed to be complimented in this way by someone who's as big an art star as you . . .'

The conversation was momentarily interrupted as a waitress brought Aesthetics and Resistance their tea and then took Patel's order. Once the woman had departed, the three friends turned their thoughts once more to the art world.

'I'm going to the Karen Eliot opening tonight, then making a mad dash to the East End for the *Computer Conceptualists* bash at the Aldgate Gallery. Are you going to either?' Ramish wanted to know.

'Yeah,' Don retorted. 'We're going to the Eliot do at Flipper.'

'We haven't had an invite to the *Computer Conceptualists* party,' Penny complained. 'And they say it's the latest trend. We'll get in somehow but it's a bloody affront for the Aldgate to drop Aesthetics and Resistance from their mailing list. I think they were offended by the review we gave their *Young Contemporaries* show in *The Gallery Gazette*.'

'But that show was trash!' Patel shouted. 'It was totalitarian the way every work chosen had been placed in a vacuum-sealed frame. I thought it was sharp of you to pick up on the fact. The review was very amusing.'

And in this fashion, over endless cups of tea and a good few cakes, the three artists ranted and raved about the iniquities of the art world. It went without saying that all three should have been bigger than Warhol! Instead, Aesthetics and Resistance were marginalised even within the art world, while Ramish was unable to transform the acclaim he'd received from the cultural establishment into a multi-million pound career in the mainstream entertainments industry.

When he got back from the West End, Johnny Aggro found his gang watching a porno video in his pad. Hodges was not only the acknowledged leader of the Raiders, he was also the only member of the firm to live alone. It was therefore natural that his flat should double as a club house and that every member of the gang had been issued with a front door key. Johnny went through to the kitchen and took a can of Stella from the fridge, before sliding into his favourite armchair. Trevor Kay, known among the lads as TK, had just vacated the seat. Rebel and Slim moaned as Trevor squeezed on to the sofa. Samson smirked, he'd taken the second best armchair, figuring it wouldn't be long before Johnny came home.

'There's a tart coming over to visit me,' Johnny announced as he pulled the ring-top on his can of lager. 'You lot can stay if you behave yourselves but I'll go fucking mental if you mess up my scene with this bird.'

'Why can't we have a gang bang?' Slim demanded.

'Because she's a doctor!' Hodges shot back.

'What's that got to do with it?' Slim objected.

'Don't you read the wank mags we buy with club funds?' Johnny growled.

'No,' Slim hissed. 'I just look at the bloody pictures.'

'Why don't you go on a diet?' Rebel put in. 'Once you've lost a few pounds, you'll be able to pull birds like any normal bloke, instead of relying on line-ups and self-abuse.'

'Fuck you!' Slim swore as he whacked Rebel with the back of his hand.

'You fat bastard, you fat bastard!' the rest of the boys chanted in unison.

'Okay, okay,' Slim wailed. 'So I've got bulges in all the right places and a few more to boot. That still doesn't explain why this doctor chick won't pull a train.'

'According to last month's *Peek*,' Johnny explained, 'GPs have no imagination when it comes to screwing. When you get down to the sexual nitty-gritty, doctors haven't got beyond the idea of a man on top and the woman underneath.'

'So why don't we teach the bitch some new tricks, like serial promiscuity?' Slim suggested.

''Ave you just swallowed a sociology text book or what?' Rebel growled.

'Just shut up and watch the video!' Samson howled. 'This is the best bleedin' bit, the two nuns are about to take the donkey into the field and fuck it!'

'Jesus!' Slim exclaimed. 'That bird's going down on the fuckin' beast. What a bloody waste! I'd like to get my dick in her mouth!'

'You'd be lucky to get your cock up some pervert's arse!' TK taunted.

'Fuck you!' Slim cursed as he slapped TK's face.

'Shut up and watch the video!' Samson thundered.

The footage of an actress deep-throating a donkey eventually reduced the Raiders to silence. The boot boys watched open-mouthed as the bestial action heated up. Samson hadn't seen a sex video have such an effect on the gang since they'd first acquired a copy of *Piss Pot Party.*

The Karen Eliot opening at Flipper was scheduled to run from six until eight—but the gallery began to fill half an hour before the event officially kicked off, and within fifteen minutes it was difficult to move. There was a buzz associated with the name Karen Eliot. Without doubt, she was one of the brightest stars shining above the contemporary art scene—and the entire cultural establishment had turned out to pay homage to her genius.

'Wonderful work, wonderful,' Sir Charles Brewster was muttering.

'Yes truly amazing,' Ramish Patel agreed. 'The way Eliot has developed vindicates the Progressive Arts Project completely. I seem to recall you got a lot of flak when you first began backing her work with tax payers' money.'

'That's right,' Sir Charles confirmed. 'But once again it simply proves that PAP are qualified experts when it comes to arts funding.'

'Have you had a chance to look at the grant application I put your way?' Ramish enquired. 'It's to fund the next full-length film I hope to make.'

'Not yet,' Brewster apologised. 'But don't worry, I'll make sure every proposal you put in gets approved by the film panel. That's what friends are for.'

Aesthetics and Resistance had button-holed Emma Career of the Bow Studios and were ranting at her about why their output was the most important development within the visual arts for the past five hundred years.

'You see,' Don Pemberton was explaining, 'our work is all about contamination. Taking ready-made domestic objects and constructing arrangements of them in the privileged space of an art gallery brings together two alien realities. The result is a confrontation between two discourses, an encounter that subverts both of them. As Lyotard said in *The Post-Modern Condition . . .*'

'Look,' Penny Applegate interrupted as she pointed across the gallery. 'There's that bastard Jock Graham.'

'I saw the review he gave you in *Art Scene*,' Emma Career put in. 'It was rather nasty. You seem to know a lot about philosophy. It was very unfair of him to call your work and ideas half-baked.'

'I'm going to pour my drink over him,' Pemberton announced. 'That'll teach the bastard not to be rude about Aesthetics and Resistance!'

Don pushed his way through the crowd and eventually got to within two feet of the marxist arts hack. By flinging his arm forward, Pemberton succeeded in emptying the contents of his wine glass into Graham's face. The writer lunged at the artist—but before he reached him, the two men were pulled apart by bystanders. Karen Eliot missed the altercation, she was kept busy all evening socialising with millionaire art collectors and top-flight critics.

Dr Maria Walker had one thing on her mind as she took the lift to the twenty-third floor of Fitzgerald House—a steamy session with Johnny Aggro. Within seconds of the GP knocking on the front door, Hodges ushered her into his flat and led her straight through to the bedroom. It was furnished with a double bed, a fitted carpet and very little else. There wasn't a stitch of clothing in sight, built-in cupboards enabled the skinhead to keep the room free of clutter. Beyond a set of weights in one corner and an alarm clock on the floor, there were no signs of regular habitation.

'Very Spartan,' Maria commented. 'It's as anonymous as a hotel room!'

'That's the way I like things,' John roared. 'Hard and smart.'

'I prefer sex hard and fast,' Walker pouted.

'In that case,' Hodges said as he undressed, 'get your knickers off.'

Maria didn't waste any time getting naked and

within a matter of seconds, the doctor and her patient were groping each other on the bed.

'You're all wet!' Johnny observed as he slid his right hand between Walker's legs.

Hodges worked his middle finger into Maria's hole, then withdrew it and rubbed sex juice around the doctor's clit. Johnny had locked his lips against Walker's mouth and was greedily sucking on the tongue that had darted between his teeth. Genetic codes were being scrambled and unscrambled across the surface of Hodge's bulk, while narcotic endorphins were pumped through his brain.

Maria had left Poplar, left this world behind. Johnny rammed his love muscle into her black hole of a cunt. Walker was out on the mudflats of prehistory, where she imagined herself to be the first amphibian to crawl out of the sea and feel the warmth of the sun on her skin.

Johnny wanted to lose himself in the primitive rhythm of sex. But something was pulling him back to this world and the ecstasies of alienation. Slowly, Hodges' brain processed the sounds he was hearing. Some bastard was trying to kick in his front door!

Johnny withdrew his prick from Maria's cunt and split seconds later, the GP's fingers were working the hole that the boot boy had vacated. Hodges slipped into his sta-prest and loafers, then raced out of the bedroom. The skinhead wrenched open his front door and a youth clad in dungarees stumbled towards him. Johnny launched himself at the cunt and the two of them flew through the portal and into the hall. The kid landed on his back, Hodges was on top of him. The skinhead banged the youth's head against the floor—one, two, three times—dazing the bastard.

Another long-haired tosser was moving towards Johnny as Rebel, Slim, TK and Samson came rushing out of the flat. They chased the bastard down the stairs. Hodges stood up, stepped on his adversary's pony-tail and yanked the kid up. This caused the teenager to wail a great deal. Once Johnny had got the youth on his feet, he threw the bastard against a wall.

'Don't beat me up,' the boy pleaded as he slid to the floor. 'I knocked on the door and no one answered, I thought you were out.'

'No one turns over my drum!' Hodges snarled. 'You'd better remember that!'

'Don't kick me,' the youth begged as Johnny laid into him.

The thief's pleas did him no good. Hodges was hopping mad and determined to inflict grievous injury on the young criminal. The skinhead grinned malevolently as his loafers thudded against the prostrate body. It wasn't long before the bastard blacked out. Johnny stripped the kid, bundled his unconscious bulk into the lift and sent it down to the ground floor before going back into his flat. He went through the pockets of the dungarees and removed twenty quid, a knife, a packet of fags and a lighter, then attached the garment to his living room window. The dungarees would fly from the block as a trophy! Hodges was about to make his way back to the bedroom when his firm returned.

'The other bastard got away,' Slim panted, 'but we saw what you did to the cunt you caught, smart work!'

'Why the fuck didn't you answer the door, or at least do something once it was being kicked in?' Johnny demanded.

'We thought the sound was coming from next door,' Rebel replied lamely.

'Get back to your porno video,' Hodges snorted, 'I'm getting back to the real thing!'

Maria was still masturbating when Johnny returned to the bedroom. The skinhead kicked off his shoes, dropped his trousers and leapt on to the bed. He slipped inside the doctor like a cross channel ferry entering the docks after making its journey across the sea. There was nothing subtle about what happened next, there didn't need to be. Johnny simply beat out the primitive rhythm of sex while imagining that he was basking on the mudflats of prehistory.

'Fuck me, fuck me!' Walker moaned. 'I wanna feel you spurt inside me!'

Hodges pumped up the volume, he could feel love juice boiling inside his groin—split seconds later, liquid genetics were flooding Maria's creamy hole. The skinhead and the GP came together in an ego-negating simultaneous orgasm. They'd reached that peak from which man and woman can never jointly return. Almost instantly, Walker and Hodges were catapulted back to a world that is fractured at its very core by the ecstasies of alienation.

Two

JOHNNY AGGRO WATCHED as the numbers one zero one disappeared from the electronic display screen. He pressed the clear button, punched out the numbers, then pressed the call bell again. The skinhead stood by the entry phone awaiting a reply. When, after several minutes silence, the digits disappeared from the display screen for a second time, Hodges cursed. The bitch was probably still asleep. Johnny figured the best thing to do was find a caff, down a cuppa and come back later.

'Come at eight-thirty and don't be late, that's what the slag said on the phone!' Hodges blustered as he stepped down to the street.

'You're early!' Karen Eliot grumbled as she raced around the corner.

'Where have you been?' Johnny demanded.

'Buying chocolate croissants for our breakfast,' Karen replied as she unlocked the door. 'They'll only take a minute to heat up if I pop them in the microwave.'

Hodges followed Eliot up the stairs and into her

flat. He seated himself on the sofa, while Karen went through to the kitchen. Eliot returned a couple of minutes later with a laden tray.

'Do you want milk or cream in your coffee?' Karen asked.

'I always have tea for breakfast,' Johnny growled.

'In that case,' was Eliot's riposte, 'it's about bloody time you changed your habits. You're not having tea here, not with croissants anyway!'

'Oh, alright,' the skinhead yielded, 'I'll have cream.'

'I think I will too,' Karen said as she fixed the beverages.

The boot boy's mood improved as he chomped on the croissant his hostess had placed before him. He was enjoying swigs of his coffee too. It was strong and sweet, the way he liked it.

'This is nice, isn't it,' Eliot observed as she put down her mug.

'Makes a change from cornflakes,' Hodges admitted, 'but I don't get it, you didn't invite me round here just to have breakfast. What is it you want, a good fuckin'?'

'Don't imagine that you're the only walking dildo in my life,' Karen laughed. 'I don't have any problems in that department.'

'You middle-class birds are all the same,' Johnny sneered. 'You like a bit of rough.'

'But do you know why?' Eliot enquired.

'Yeah, coz posh blokes don't cut it between the sheets!'

'You're not very bright are you,' Karen replied as she patted the skinhead's leg. 'You probably think the middle classes can't fight either—and you'd be wrong about that too. Professional wimmin like getting their claws into teenage proles because rough trade actually finds it harder to establish a patriarchal domination over them than the seemingly more mild-mannered males of their own class.'

'Jesus,' Hodges swore, ''ave you swallowed a dictionary or something?'

'No,' Eliot reassured him. 'I'm just demonstrating that brute force isn't the only means by which an individual can attain a dominant position within any particular set of social relationships. In fact, brute force rarely results in pre-eminence for any extended period of time. What's needed is a combination of force and cunning.'

'You what?' the boot boy cried.

'Don't worry your pretty little head about it,' Karen said as she ran her fingers along the inside of John's left thigh. 'Instead, tell me how things went with the doctor last night.'

'We had a good screw.' Then after pausing for several seconds, Hodges blurted out, 'but in every other respect it was a bloody disaster.'

'Tell me about it.'

'Well, after we'd fucked, I asked Maria to certify me as a nutter,' the skinhead explained. 'She told me I was probably the sanest man she'd ever met and that I'd never make the grade as a loony. I said if she wouldn't certify me, I'd make an official complaint about her and she'd be struck off. The bitch just laughed and said I'd never make the charge stick.'

'I think she's right,' Eliot put in. 'If it comes to a group of middle-class professionals making an investigation into the case, I think they're far more likely to accept the word of a well-spoken GP than believe the accusations of a working-class herbert such as yourself.'

'But you told me I should fuck the bitch and then blackmail her into certifying me as mad!' John protested. 'At this rate, I'll never get a cheap flat in the West End! Why is all the best housing reserved for loonies? It isn't bloody fair! Anyway, what do you think I should do next?'

'Try and see the doctor again,' Karen suggested. 'If you have an affair with her, maybe she'll certify you as a favour.'

'Maria told me she was coming to see me again at six-thirty this evening!' Hodges squawked. 'Even if I can't blackmail her, she's a bit of alright in bed.'

'You'd better give her a quickie,' Eliot advised, 'I want you to come here at eight for a shagging.'

'But this is absurd!' the skinhead complained. 'What do you think I am, a bleedin' machine?'

'It doesn't matter what I think you are,' Karen ejaculated as she took John's arm and led him to the door. 'Just be here at eight if you want to exercise your fuck stick.'

Moments later, the boot boy found himself back on Coram Street. In his book, Eliot was a pretty weird chick. But what the hell, she'd a body that was made for loving and Hodges wanted what Karen had got. Maybe the bitch was a genuine fruit-cake and that was why the social services had set her up in the posh flat. It didn't make any difference to John. The skinhead had no doubts about this bird's ability to perform in bed and so he'd return at eight o'clock sharp!

Aesthetics and Resistance rented a large room in a studio complex off Carpenter's Road in Stratford. They didn't really need the space because they worked solely with arrangements of ready-made domestic objects. However, since all great artists have a studio, Aesthetics and Resistance had to have one too. The rent was cheap and in any case, as Donald Pemberton received an extremely generous allowance from his father, monetary considerations didn't even enter into the duo's calculations when they'd taken on the space. It was a place to hang out and meet other bohemians, people like Ross MacDonald and Joseph Campbell, who spent their days making plaster casts of rocks and then exhibiting the products of this fruitless labour in state-funded galleries.

'Yeah, man,' Donald Pemberton was remonstrating. 'You've gotta fight the system. The masses are just mindless zombies who sit around watching soaps on TV and getting pissed up on lager at the weekends. We artists are a spiritual élite, we're in touch with higher realities, which means that by rights we should be dictating the nation's cultural tastes!'

'You're right,' MacDonald agreed. 'If people spent time communing with our art, instead of blobbing out in front of second-rate videos, the world would be a much better place.'

'What's more,' Applegate shrieked. 'Although I'm prepared to embrace material poverty if that's the only way I can bring the New Wo/Man spiritual enlightenment through my work, it's not right that I'm given no financial reward for the enormous service I render the community. After all, without my art acting as a beacon to light the path of the élite that will eventually transvalue all values, civilisation would collapse and we'd be back in the dark ages! Every artist ought to be guaranteed a minimum wage at least as high as the take-home pay of a doctor or bank manager!'

'Society has reduced Ross and I to penury!' Campbell wailed. 'We've lost our home and now we're living in our studio!'

'Isn't that a breach of the lease?' Don enquired.

'Yes!' Joseph cried. 'But what else can we do? Men of genius should not be reduced to sleeping on the streets!'

'Let's drink,' Penny said as she broke open a bottle of vodka and poured the alcohol into four chipped mugs, 'to a world of the future where everyone recognises the spiritual worth of artists. Let's drink to a world where our genius is honoured above that of all other wo/men!'

'To the future!' the four friends thundered in unison as they raised their mugs of vodka.

'To success,' Pemberton added, 'and contracts with top-flight galleries!'

'To success,' his three comrades roared.

The artists gulped down their drinks. Ross picked up the vodka bottle and poured himself a second shot. Don threw his mug against the wall where it shattered and the shards crashed to the floor.

'How about that for a new art work?' Pemberton shouted. 'Its called *Domestic Arrangement 917—Family Argument*, it'll be in a museum before you bloody know it!'

'You're a flaming genius!' MacDonald howled as he slapped his friend on the back.

'I knew it would be worth renting this studio!' Applegate exclaimed. 'The atmosphere is one of pure inspiration. If we can create a few more works of this calibre, Aesthetics and Resistance will soon be signed up by Mayfair, making international acclaim a foregone conclusion!'

*

It wasn't difficult for Karen Eliot to locate the health centre. She walked through the reception area and into the corridor beyond, which branched in two directions. Eliot took the left fork and within seconds spotted a name-plate marked Dr Maria Walker. A conversation going on inside the room was clearly audible from the other side of the door.

'I can't see anything wrong,' the doctor was saying, 'but we'll get some blood tests done, your fatigue might be caused by a vitamin deficiency. However, there are some other possibilities too. Would you agree that the mind can affect the body?'

'Yes,' the patient replied.

'Then you'll admit that what you've got could be psychosomatic. We can't be sure in your case, not until we've done further tests at any rate—and even if your fatigue is psychosomatic, I'm not implying that the symptoms are any the less serious. However, what it does mean is that to treat you, we'll have to take a look at your life-style. So, I'd like to start by asking you what you're doing at the moment?'

'I'm taking a sociology Ph.D.,' the student confessed, 'in which I look at the relationships between GPs and their patients.'

'I see,' Walker hissed, completely taken aback by the way the patient had undercut her professional position. 'I presume you're familiar with most of the issues I was going to raise and would have told me if you were having any difficulties with your sex life or whatever. If you can make an appointment for a blood test at the reception desk on your way out, we'll see if anything turns up from that.'

'Thank you,' the patient said politely.

'Good day,' was the doctor's curt reply.

Karen slipped past the student as she stepped into the corridor. Walker looked up from the notes she was writing as Eliot pulled the door shut. A flash of anger crossed the doctor's face.

'Please leave!' Maria yelled. 'If you've made an appointment, you'll be called in good time!'

'I don't need an appointment,' was Karen's rejoinder. 'I've come about John Hodges.'

'Oh no,' Walker cried as she slumped in her chair. 'He can't be serious about making a professional complaint! He's not articulate enough to pull it off, don't tell me you're gonna help him!'

'Helping him make a complaint against you is the last thing on my mind!' Karen stated emphatically. 'I'm here because we're both sharing the same piece of rough and . . .'

'I'll leave him alone if that's what you want,' Maria interrupted. 'I've got a live-in boyfriend you know, I can survive without a piece of beefcake on the side.'

'You've got me completely wrong,' Eliot laughed. 'I'm not the jealous sort. I figured that if we were seeing the same bloke, we could turn it into a bit of fun.'

'I don't understand,' Walker said shaking her head.

'Let's look at this practically,' Karen suggested. 'I know you're seeing Johnny at six-thirty tonight, while I've insisted on seeing him at eight. I live in Bloomsbury, which means that he'll only have time for a half-hour session with you if he's gonna get to my place on time. What I want you to do is keep him in until at least seven-thirty, so that he'll be late. Johnny will be in a complete bloody stew after rushing to my flat—and imagine his confusion if he arrives at my pad and finds you there!'

'But how the hell am I gonna get to Bloomsbury before him?' the doctor demanded.

'Have you a car?'

'Yeah.'

'In that case, what's the problem?' Eliot asked. 'Johnny's on the dole, so the only way he can get about is by public transport. Even without a head start, you'd make it to the centre of town long before our clockwork skinhead.'

'What would you have said if I wasn't able to drive?' Maria wanted to know.

'That's easy,' was Karen's retort. 'I'd have told you to get a taxi!'

As the two wimmin plotted and planned, Walker realised she needed a friend like Eliot to brighten up her life. A GP's lot was pretty dull, about the only thing it had going for it was a forty-grand salary!

Johnny Aggro had spent the morning pissing about in Soho. He got a buzz from just walking round the area. Time seemed to pass faster in central London. The skinhead liked that, it gave him a sense of being at the cutting edge of a society which was hurling itself into the future. Hodges marched up Charing Cross Road, on the lookout for a chick to chat up.

'What do you think of the European parliament?' a militant asked as he stepped into Johnny's path.

'Not a lot,' the boot boy replied.

'In that case, perhaps you'd like to buy a copy of *Marxist Times*,' the tosser said as he held up the magazine. 'There's a special pull-out supplement on why British workers should oppose the European superstate.'

'I'm very interested in what you've got to say, but I'm illiterate,' Hodges lied. 'Do you think you could read some of it out loud to me?'

'You could buy a copy of the magazine and get one of your friends to read it,' the marxist suggested, fearing he'd end up wasting time on the skinhead when he could have been flogging party literature to an educated passer-by.

'It's not my fault if I'm thick,' Johnny exploded. 'Me mum and dad always worked in factories and I didn't get on with the teachers at school, I was hardly ever there. I grew up on a council estate, I've never had no one teach me nothing. Go on, read me a bit of the magazine, I'm very interested in your ideas. I bet you've been to university and all that, you'd read it much better than me mates, none of them would know how to pronounce the long words.'

'Oh, alright,' the militant granted. Then after turning over some pages he began: 'In its struggle to overthrow the capitalist system of commodities, of alien things, and replace these antagonistic relationships with a socialised totality where the products of human labour are no longer turned against the proletariat in its estrangement from the surplus value it creates, the working class faces . . .'

'Hold on a minute,' Hodges interrupted. 'I thought you was gonna tell me about why the European parliament is shit. I don't wanna know about all this working-class stuff, it's got nothing to do with me.'

'Look,' the marxist replied impatiently. 'I'll get to the European parliament in a minute. The article starts off by establishing the relationship between the proletariat and European politics. That ought to make the whole piece more interesting to you. It's written from a perspective you share with the party because you're working class!'

'If I'm working class,' Johnny spat, 'why am I on the dole? Why ain't I got a job?'

'That's just semantics!' the militant protested.

'Fuck you!' the skinhead screamed as he rammed his fist into the marxist's mouth. There was the satisfying crunch of splintering bone and the bastard staggered backwards spitting out gouts of blood and the occasional piece of broken tooth. Johnny was about to move in for the kill when he noticed two coppers running down the street.

'I'm so glad you're here,' Hodges told a WPC. 'This creature attempted to head-butt me after I told him I wouldn't listen to the lies he was spouting about our wonderful police force. Although I didn't start the trouble, once I was attacked, I had no choice but to defend myself. I'm so glad you've come because it's proved my point, there's always a bobby around to sort things out when he or she is needed.'

'Don't worry son,' the youthful WPC replied as her male colleague handcuffed the militant. 'We'll make sure this trouble-maker is prosecuted. Now, before I send you on your way, I'll have to take your details and a statement . . .'

Karen Eliot thought the Crest on Camden's Royal College Street was a dump. Nevertheless, Karen had arranged to meet Jock Graham in the pub because she knew the marxist art critic thought squalor was romantic. Eliot was less than impressed by the seedy drinking-hole—it was patronised by posh drop-outs who failed miserably in their attempts to fake membership credentials for some mythical underclass.

Karen came from the lower middle classes and was not ashamed of this fact. She'd always wanted to better herself and much preferred exotic theme pubs to those, such as the Crest, that exploited an upper-middle-class obsession with poverty. Eliot had come a long way since she'd flown the family nest—a semi in Hersham. She earned more money than her dad, had a pad in Bloomsbury and got to socialise with millionaires thanks to her status as an art star. Eliot felt she'd a right to look down upon the scum around her who despite having had all the advantages of a private education lacked essential social graces, such as regular bathing habits.

'So tell me,' Jock Graham was saying, 'why this ongoing fascination with Neoism?'

'Well,' Karen replied, 'aside from money and fame, my chief interest in relation to art concerns the process of historification . . .'

'Hold it,' Graham interrupted while simultaneously lifting his right hand, 'my tape has run out. I'll just turn it over. These Walkman Professionals are brilliant, you know. I can't imagine how journalists functioned before they were brought on to the market. Right, we're just about ready to go, so I'll ask you again, why this obsession with Neoism?'

'What you have to understand about Neoism,' Eliot explained, 'is its dialectical relationship to everything from futurism, dada and surrealism through to the lettristes, situationists and fluxus. It drew on this anti-institutional tradition, while simultaneously exposing the way in which such discourse still forms part of the nexus of serious culture. Neoism completed the project begun by those adhering to earlier manifestations of this tradition by reducing it to a single, limited focus. That is to say, the Neoists were simply interested in historifying themselves as an important art movement. By producing absolutely no works of any worth and concentrating exclusively upon publicity stunts, the Neoists exposed the mechanisms by which the culture industry seeks to endow objects, individuals and events with value.'

'I see!' Jock exclaimed. 'So that's why all you've ever done is produce portraits of the hundred or so individuals involved with what you call The Neoist Revolution. What you're driving at is the fact that the movement had no content other than the personalities of its adherents!'

'Precisely!' Karen whooped. 'And those personalities change as history is made and remade. That's why every time I do a show, it's simply a set of Neoist portraits done in whatever artistic style was flavour of the month when I produced them!'

'But don't you think that you've reached a dead end?' Graham demanded. 'Since you've now become flavour of the month yourself?'

'That's an essential part of the process!' Eliot announced gleefully. 'I'm already working on a new collection—and it consists of exact copies of my early work. The originals were sold for peanuts, these new versions will fetch enormous prices!'

'You're so subversive!' Jock cried. 'What you're doing brings out all the contradictions in an art system organised for profit!'

'Excuse me,' a long-haired tosser lisped as he leaned over from an adjoining table, 'but I couldn't help overhearing your conversation. I'm an artist too and I'm finding it completely impossible to get my work shown. Have you got any tips about what I should do?'

'Yeah,' Karen murmured. 'Get your hair cut and

have a bath, buy yourself some smart clothes. Once you've done that, you might find that people who run galleries are prepared to look at your work.'

'That's a bit extreme!' the boy whinged. 'My girlfriend says I'm very talented and that I shouldn't make any concessions to the system. She'd probably pack me in if I got my hair cut. Christ, I have enough problems with that chick as it is! The allowance I get from daddy barely stretches to buying the bitch drugs! Only last night she was threatening to get back together with an old flame who deals smack!'

'Fuck off, loser!' Eliot bellowed as she clouted the kid's ear.

Stepping out of the lift and on to the twenty-third floor of Fitzgerald House, Johnny Aggro could hear Martha Reeves' gutsy voice belting out Holland, Dozier, Holland's all-time classic 'No Place to Run'. This was Motown at its best, Hodges reflected as he opened his front door and the rush of sound almost lifted him off his feet. Martha and the Vandellas pissed over any other soul act to come out of Detroit. And there'd been stiff opposition back in the heady days of the mid-sixties!

The skinhead strolled through to his living room, where he found not only the entire membership of the Raiders—but also Maria Walker. The doctor was holding court, hardly a surprising turn of events considering that she was an attractive woman used to commanding the respect of the many working-class patients who belonged to her practice.

'Hello Johnny,' Maria greeted the skinhead. 'I got here a little early—and you're a little late! Not that it matters, your friends have been entertaining me. They tell me that you think GPs have no imagination when it comes to sex.'

'It ain't my opinion,' Hodges growled. 'It said so in the last issue of *Peek*.'

'Come over here and I'll show you that you're wrong,' the doctor replied as she hitched up her skirt.

'Jesus!' Slim exclaimed. 'Is this gonna turn into a gang bang or what?'

'It's not a bleedin' gang bang!' Johnny thundered as he hauled Slim up from the sofa and hurled him across the room. 'Now get out of my fuckin' flat before I really lose my temper! And the same goes for the rest of you, go on, get out!'

Once the Raiders had obeyed his orders and trooped out of the flat, Hodges turned his attention to Maria. The doctor was waiting for him with open arms. The skinhead loosened his braces and his sta-prest fell to the floor.

'That's it baby,' the doctor whispered as Hodges rubbed her clit with a finger. 'Get me well juiced up and then slip inside my cunt!'

'It won't be difficult!' the skinhead laughed. 'You're really wet!'

Maria grabbed Johnny's cock and guided it through the petalled gates of her mystery. Once inside, the skinhead beat out the primitive rhythm of sex.

'Naughty boy!' Walker chided as she slapped Hodges across the cheek. 'Do you expect me just to lie here while you do all the work? I want you to keep still so that I can drive you crazy by repeatedly contracting my cunt muscles.'

'Okay,' Johnny agreed.

'Can you feel it?' Maria demanded. 'Do you like the way I'm squeezing your prick?'

'Yeah,' Hodges grunted.

But the skinhead was actually craving more traditional forms of sexual action. He didn't like taking a passive role when it came to exploring his genetic kinks. Hodges wanted to feel his balls banging against Walker's body as his love pump worked her hole. Vaginal contractions were too subtle a buzz for the boot boy—who figured that with no other stimulation it would take him about a million years to cum. After five minutes of this, Johnny could stand it no longer. He got up, removed the Martha and the Vandellas CD from his deck, then programmed the machine to repeat-play his favourite track from *Tighten Up—Volumes One and Two*.

'It's you who lacks sexual imagination!' Maria taunted. 'That's why you don't get off on anything but banging away on top of me!'

'That's not true!' Hodges protested. 'I like blow jobs as well!'

Johnny jumped back on to the sofa and shoved his swollen member up the doctor's cunt. The skinhead pumped up the volume, moving his body in time to 'Return of Django'—a classic cut by the Upsetters. Repeat plays of the tune guaranteed Maria and he would have a really frenzied fuck.

It has been argued elsewhere that Old Compton Street is the centre of our world. Truth, as we know, is relative—it varies according to certain historical and geographical laws. A teenager living on the East Coast of the United States would probably rubbish London's claims to pre-eminence and view Rivington Street on the Lower East Side as the mysterious centre from which all life pulsates—while a member of the British power élite is likely to opt for Threadneedle Street in the City of London. However, for the young and hip living in South-East England, Soho would undoubtedly form the focal point from which their psychogeographical map of the world radiated to other urban centres. Penelope Applegate and Donald Pemberton shared this world view with their many peers—and so we should not be surprised to find them quaffing wine at 23 Old Compton Street.

'Look,' Penny said as she pointed across the Soho Brasserie. 'There's Stephen Smith and Ramish Patel.'

'Shall we go over?' Don asked.

'Yeah,' Penny replied. 'You can tell Steve about throwing your drink over Jock Graham last night. He's hated the bastard ever since his first one-man show got slagged in *Art Scene*.'

'Hello,' Ramish said, slapping Pemberton on the back and giving Applegate a wicked wink.

'Hi,' Don squeaked and then turned his attention to Smith.

'Stephen, why on earth weren't you at the Karen Eliot opening last night? We had a wonderful time.'

'I had to have dinner with mummy and daddy,' Smith whined. 'The old man made turning up for his birthday celebrations a condition of paying off my debts. The cad made an enormous issue of the whole thing, told me I'm irresponsible. He's such a bore, it was only thirty thousand—a mere drop in the ocean against what he's worth. My entire family are philistines, they simply don't appreciate artistic genius.'

'Hard luck old chap,' Pemberton commiserated. 'You really should have been at Flipper last night. I threw a glass of wine over that bastard Jock Graham, he was absolutely terrified! I don't think he'll ever give Aesthetics and Resistance another bad review.'

'If he does,' Applegate put in, 'Don's going to throw petrol over him and I'll set light to it.'

'Darlings!' Stephen exclaimed. 'If you ever do that, you're to let me know first, so that I can place a tyre around his neck.'

'Jock isn't that bad!' Patel protested. 'I know he's been a little hard on you but he likes my work, he's given virtually every film I've ever made a rave review.'

'That's no excuse,' Smith woofed, 'for his failure to recognise that I am the future of British art! Do you know what he called my paintings? He said they were bad pop art made thirty years too late! The man has no taste, it's a pure fluke that he likes your work.'

'And besides,' Don roared, 'although the bastard calls himself a revolutionary marxist, he's actually a fixture of the art establishment. It's our job as young geniuses to fight the system—and Graham is part of the coterie that we must overthrow. Most of the stuff he champions is rubbish, little more than sulphurous daubs!'

'I can see what you're driving at,' Ramish allowed. 'I just think that the views you're expressing are a little bit extreme.'

'Of course my ideas are extreme!' Pemberton thundered. 'I'm God's gift to mankind, so I'm not about to conform to the mediocre opinions of the submen! It's my task to blaze a trail so that the creative élite can adopt new modes of being. The rabble will either be put out of their misery or turned into slaves! There can be no half-measures if art is to save the world from its present slide into decadence and degeneracy!'

Johnny Aggro knew he wasn't going to make it

to Karen Eliot's pad by eight o'clock. It had taken longer than he'd expected to satisfy Maria Walker with the steamy session she'd demanded. Co-habitation with a sexually incompetent social worker had made the bitch fucking randy! After hustling the doctor out of his flat, Hodges ran around like a blue-arsed fly. After washing and jumping into a clean set of clothes, he grabbed his Walkman and sprinted to the DLR station.

Now that the skinhead was on the final leg of his journey, he was sitting on his backside enjoying a tape of the Ethiopians. Johnny's foot was beating time to 'Everything Crash', a classic cut about the Jamaican strikes of 1968. Since Prince Buster's song 'Taxation' dealt with the same subject, Johnny figured the virtually simultaneous strikes by firemen, policemen, water workers, telephone operators and others, must have had a big impact in the Caribbean. However, Hodges wasn't really interested in post-colonial politics, he just loved blue beat, ska and early reggae music.

When the tube pulled into Russell Square, Johnny leapt from the train and rushed to Coram Street. He punched out one zero one on the entry phone and Karen Eliot chided him for being late as she let him in. Hodges was out of breath by the time he'd run up the stairs to her flat.

'Typical,' Karen fumed. 'Bloody typical. Being unemployed has destroyed your ability to keep time. There's a friend of mine in the bedroom who's been getting very impatient waiting for you to arrive. She wants a shagging, go through and see to it.'

If the skinhead hadn't been slightly disorientated from rushing around, he'd have objected to being ordered about in this way. But Eliot had planned everything perfectly and he did as he'd been told.

'What the hell is going on?' Johnny erupted upon discovering Maria Walker lying on Karen's bed.

'We played a trick on you,' the doctor giggled. 'Now come here and have sex with me.'

The boot boy didn't need a second invitation. Maria wore her thirty-odd years very well and the sight of the doctor's naked body had given him a hard on. He stepped out of his DMs, dropped his sta-prest and leapt on to the bed. Walker had already juiced up and the skinhead's prick worked her hole like a piston inside a piece of well-oiled machinery.

'Give it to me, baby,' the doctor moaned. 'Shove your big stiff cock right up inside me!'

As she had her first orgasm, Maria saw a flash that she took to be an action replay of the first star exploding. Actually, it was Karen taking pictures with a Polaroid camera. Johnny didn't notice Eliot's presence either. He loved to hear middle-class birds talking dirty—and the doctor was pouring pure filth into his ears.

'Fuck me, you hunk, fuck me!' Walker rasped. 'I wanna feel your balls banging against my cunt!'

The boot boy pumped up the volume—and as he did so, DNA codes were scrambled and unscrambled across the muscular structure of his bulk. A genetic programme written several billion years ago had seized control of Johnny's brain.

'Stick it up me!' Maria bellowed. 'Harder!'

Hodges did as he was told. He could feel love juice boiling inside his groin, he was only a few strokes away from orgasm. The rhythm was perfect and there was a pleasant pressure beneath Johnny's forehead, as endorphins were pumped through his brain.

'I want it in my mouth!' the doctor bellowed as she wriggled beneath the boot boy.

Walker struggled free of the skinhead's embrace, then spun around and licked the tip of his cock. Maria worked the shaft with her hand and moaned crazily as the head bobbed about in her gob. The doctor was having multiple orgasms as she sucked and chewed on the plonker. Hodges was no longer in control of his body and liquid genetics spurted from the love pump. Walker swallowed a good part of this offering, while the rest dribbled down her chin.

'Bravo, Bravo!' Karen enthused as she put down her Polaroid camera. 'I got some great pictures. You can both have a look at them in a bit. But first, Maria, I want you to go and get yourself cleaned up, so that Johnny and I can have a few words in private.'

As the doctor got up from the bed and headed for the bathroom, Eliot sat down beside the skinhead. The boot boy's body glistened with sweat and Karen ran her fingers over the hairs on his chest.

'Jesus!' the skinhead exclaimed. 'That feels so nice I can hardly stand having it done to me!'

'Listen Johnny,' Karen said. 'I had a good reason for getting Maria to help me pull this trick on you. I wanted to demonstrate what can be done to a third party when two or more people plot in secret. You didn't know whether you were coming or going when you arrived—simply because I arranged for you to be held up in Poplar, having made it clear that I'd be pissed off if you were late getting here. What happened tonight was nothing, with sufficient organisation it's possible to exercise enormous influence—perhaps even to alter the course of history! I want to set up a secret society—but I need someone to approach potential members for me. I can't do it myself because I want to keep my identity concealed. I want you to front the operation for me. Will you do it?'

'I dunno,' Johnny hedged. 'I wouldn't know what to do.'

'You don't need to,' Karen shot back. 'I'll issue instructions to cover every situation you'll encounter. It'll be a laugh pulling fast ones on bastards who under normal circumstances wouldn't even give you the time of day!'

'Okay,' Hodges agreed.

'Good boy!' Eliot crowed before pressing her mouth against the skinhead's lips.

Three

JOHNNY AGGRO WAS listening to the *Dream with Max Romeo* album on Pama Records. Hodges wondered what had happened to the Palmer brothers, the brains behind this venture. All he knew about them was that they'd released dozens of classic rock steady and reggae cuts between 1967 and 1973. Johnny thought listening to cool music was the best way to start a Saturday morning. Although the skinhead was out of work, he still looked forward to the weekend because it meant going to football if the Hammers were playing at home, then donning his best gear and heading out for a night on the town.

'Wine Her Goosie' was blasting out of the hi fi when Rebel dropped in. TK arrived during 'Club Raid' and after 'You Can't Stop', the newcomer took the Max Romeo album off the deck and replaced it with the Temptations' *Puzzle People*. Although TK could groove to reggae, he much preferred soul and as far as he was concerned, *Puzzle People* was one of the finest records ever released on Motown. The Raiders were always arguing among themselves about whether skinhead reggae or sixties' soul was the ultimate form of dance music.

Slim and Samson finally showed as the Temptations were doing 'Message from a Black Man'. The gang lounged about the flat, slurping at the tea Rebel made for everyone. For the time being, the gang could relax. But once they'd laid their plans for the day, their lives would become a non-stop schedule of action and kicks.

'I'm sorry about last night,' Slim apologised to Johnny. 'I should have known better than suggesting a bit of posh pull a train. We'll have to pick up a scrubber before we do that!'

'Forget it,' Hodges said magnanimously. 'Maria took it in her stride! But you've gotta drop this idea of having a gang bang. We're skinheads, we've got too much pride to go in for that sort of thing, it's an activity for schoolboys and greasers! A skinhead should be able to satisfy a woman without any help from his mates. Hairies resort to line-ups as a means of keeping birds happy because they don't cut it between the sheets.'

'What about having an orgy instead?' Slim asked.

'If you get it together, I'll be happy to take part!' Johnny shot back.

'But you're the leader,' Slim moaned. 'You should organise an orgy for us!'

'I run this firm,' Hodges snapped, 'which means I work out what we're gonna do as a group. Sex is something you've gotta sort out for yourself, I'm not your bleedin' mother!'

'Anyway,' Rebel put in. 'What are we gonna do today?'

'I figured we should go up Finsbury Park,'

Johnny replied. 'There's a free pop concert, it should be a laugh.'

'You can't be serious!' TK lamented. 'I don't wanna go to the *Lark in the Park*, loadsa hairy bands and not one decent act! That grunge group Junk are headlining, I fuckin' hate them.'

'I wasn't suggesting we listen to the music,' Hodges explained. 'I was more interested in finding a few heads to bash! It'll be great, thousands of hairies shitting themselves because five skinheads turn up! We'll massacre the cunts!'

Sir Charles Brewster was waiting for Karen Eliot in the Monmouth Coffee Shop. Covent Garden was a convenient place to meet, Sir Charles had an afternoon appointment with a high-class hooker who worked out of Neal Street. The Progressive Arts Project supremo was nursing his second coffee by the time Eliot arrived.

'Hi,' Karen said as she sat down. 'Am I late?'

'No,' Brewster assured her after checking his watch. 'I was early and you're on time.'

'Have you had a chance to think about the stuff we discussed last week?' Eliot enquired.

'Yes,' Sir Charles replied, 'and I think what you were saying about creating a timetable for bringing the Neoist movement into mainstream art history makes a lot of sense. As you said, we need to build the thing up with some publications and small shows featuring individual Neoists before doing a big retrospective in about ten years' time. I can get the Progressive Arts Project behind this, so money won't be a problem. I also intend to buy up a lot of Neoist material myself, while it's still cheap, by reselling it after we've done the retrospective I'll make a small fortune!'

'There shouldn't be any problems in the profits department!' Karen laughed. 'Just look at the way Stewart Home used the situationists to advance his career and how the prices paid for post-war art jumped as a result! There are a lot of similarities between the Neoists and the situationists, right down to the fact that both movements got their work archived in museums so that art historians would find it easy to write up their activities once they discovered all the documentation was readily obtainable!'

'I know!' Brewster panted, rubbing his hands with glee. 'Neoism is tailor-made for historification. It tidies up the loose ends left by the previous generation of avant-garde artists by drawing on the legacies of both the situationists and fluxus. Neoism is an art critic's wet dream!'

'So after looking at the portfolio of work that I gave you,' Eliot lent forward before completing the sentence, 'which members of the movement are you going to push forward for individual attention before we organise the big retrospective?'

'I'm approaching Neoism with a view to marketing it internationally,' Sir Charles prattled, 'and I've plumped for Stiletto as the creative genius thrown up by the movement. The Germans will like that, he's one of their own. In his case, there's also the added bonus that he's already got a reputation on the commercial art circuit. I know he's more of a designer than a fine artist—but so what, he's made film and video, done all sorts of things really. We'll put the biggest push behind Stiletto. Then, to satisfy the underground, I guess we'll organise one-man retrospectives by Pete Horobin and Michael Tolson. That way you get a good balance—a British artist and an American, one classical temperament and one romantic. Yes, that'll do nicely!'

'What about the Canadians?' Karen demanded.

'Oh, I'd forgotten about them,' Brewster confessed. 'I could do with some more documentation of their work—but from what I've seen, I'd opt for Kiki Bonbon as the major figure within the Montreal group, he'll have to cover the French as well! There wasn't anybody in France itself, do you think Paris will accept a French-Canadian?'

'We'll have to do some research into that,' Eliot sighed. 'But what about the Italians?'

'Vittore Baroni,' Sir Charles shot back. 'He's our man in the Mediterranean.'

'I think the Dutch need a look-in too!' Karen enthused.

'Arthur Berkoff!' Brewster thundered. 'And I haven't forgotten about the feminist angle either! There's you, of course, and also Eugenie Vincent from the States. Vincent's work is brilliant. The critics will love the idea of this zany Neoist becoming a top model as part of an extended performance art-piece!'

'That's more than enough visual artists for our purposes,' Eliot bellowed. 'As long as you chuck in the film-maker Georg Ladanyi to cover Eastern Europe!'

'Sure,' the PAP supremo agreed. 'With Ladanyi in the bag, we can abandon the visual field.'

'Yes, we've had quite enough of the ocular, so let's move on to writers and theorists,' Eliot chirped. 'Was it difficult making a choice?'

'No, it was easy!' Sir Charles cried. 'I've gone for John Berndt from the States and Bob Jones here in London! We'll have to get some anarchist publisher to reprint their work, that way it'll gain maximum credibility by appearing to bubble up from the underground. Once things start moving, commercial firms can take up the slack and make the books available to a wider reading public.'

The wheels of the cultural industry were slowly grinding into gear. Thanks to Karen Eliot's tireless efforts, Neoism would soon be considered a vital part of the world's cultural heritage.

The *Lark in the Park* was largely patronised by the unwashed children of the upper middle classes. Some were students, others simply lived on an allowance from their family or inherited wealth, a few had jobs, although you'd never have guessed this from the state of their clothes. The Raiders were less than impressed by the hairy scum who frothed around the main stage and an assortment of beer tents.

'Jesus,' Rebel swore. 'We'd need to be tooled up with flame-throwers if we were serious about cleaning up this mess!'

'It's disgusting!' Samson chipped in. 'These cunts aren't human beings, they're vermin, they ought to be put down!'

'They smell vile,' TK complained. 'The government should bring back National Service for anyone under thirty who doesn't wash regularly. A regime of square-bashing and cold showers would soon sort these bastards out. They might not be normal now—but a bit of army discipline would soon knock some sense into 'em!'

'Look at that cunt over there,' Johnny Aggro said pointing at a youth who looked like he'd sniffed one too many bags of glue, ''ee's wearing a Perry with both the buttons undone.'

'That's an insult to the Skinhead Nation!' Slim observed.

'Fuck me!' Samson hooted. 'The bastard's sporting an FP and a pair of bondage strides, what a bleedin' combination!'

'Let's do 'im!' Hodges yelled.

The five skinheads moved with the speed and grace of wolves descending on their prey. The kid didn't stand a chance! Johnny reached the bastard first, tensing the muscles in his hand before karate chopping the punk's neck. The youth shuddered and then his legs crumpled beneath him. By the time the bozo hit the deck, the Raiders had the cunt surrounded—and their boots were slamming against his prostrate body. The kicking lasted no more than a minute—but in that time, the skinheads succeeded in giving the bastard a severe bruising as well as cracking several ribs.

'If this cunt is gonna wear his FP with the buttons undone, he doesn't deserve to own such a beautiful garment!' Slim announced as he pulled the sports top from the punk's body.

'Hey!' Rebel screamed. 'Give me the Perry! It won't fit a fat bastard like you!'

'I'm not fat,' Slim growled as he unbuttoned his shirt. 'I'm just well-built, and this FP ain't so small that I can't get it on!'

'Give Rebel the Perry!' Johnny barked. 'You'd look bloody ridiculous in that shirt—there's no way it'd stretch over your gut.'

'Oh, alright,' Slim consented. 'But keep your bloody hair on! It's only an FP—from the way you lot are going on, anyone would think it was a religious icon!'

'Let's get some beers in,' Johnny suggested as a

way of changing the subject and restoring the balance between the various members of his gang.

Karen Eliot had just delivered a short lecture entitled 'Neoism and the Avant-Garde of the 1980s' to an audience of art trendies who'd flocked to the CIA so that they could learn about a movement which had not as yet been given full credit for its enormous influence. Question after question was being thrown up from the floor. Neoism had suddenly assumed a fantastic importance in the lives of those who were present.

'What are the best archive sources for Neoist material?' an art historian was demanding.

'Here in London,' Eliot replied, 'you'll find basic materials are lodged with the Tate Gallery Library and the National Art Library. Between them, these two institutions hold most of the books and magazines you'll need to consult. To do really detailed research, you'll need to get in touch with individual members of the movement. As far as British Neoists are concerned, Pete Horobin and Bob Jones have the most extensive collections of material.'

'Could you elaborate,' a student put in, 'on why the eighties were a Neoist decade?'

'I explained that in the course of my lecture,' Karen prated. 'But I'll go through it again. What you've got to understand is that history is a mythological discipline—a gross simplification of the complex tangle of events it attempts to explain. If we look back to an earlier period—one that constitutes a kind of prehistory to Neoism—we can see how situationism has come to stand for what were actually a lot of very diverse aspects of the sixties underground. Punk rock is often described as being influenced by the situationists—obviously, a claim such as this is utter nonsense if all the person making it intends to convey by their use of the 'S' word is the theory of Debord and Vaneigem. However, if you subsume counter-cultural movements such as the motherfuckers, Dutch provos, yippies, diggers, white panthers etcetera, under the rubric of situationism, then there is a grain of truth in the claim that punk was influenced by the situationists. Have you understood what I've said so far?'

'Yes!' the student assured the speaker while simultaneously nodding his head.

'Okay,' Eliot said, 'so despite its anti-sixties rhetoric, punk was clearly a development of the darker aspects of the counter-culture. Punk is now defined as situationist because historians are unable to deal with the complexity of sixties youth movements. The eighties were equally diverse and complex—all sorts of tendencies developed autonomously of Neoism. But historians need to reduce cultural history to a few catch-all terms—and, as a result of this process, a number of movements that until now had nothing to do with Neoism are slowly becoming identified as Neoist.'

'I'd like to develop some of the ideas implicit in the discussion we've been having,' Penny Applegate shouted. 'I'm here with Don Pemberton and together we constitute the theoretically coherent art group Aesthetics and Resistance. Basically, what we've been talking about today is the way in which art movements are manufactured. The general thrust of the debate seems to be that Neoism was a major development of the futurist/dadaist/surrealist/situationist tradition because it focused our attention on the highly artificial process of cultural legitimation. What I'd like to suggest is that Aesthetics and Resistance have gone much further than the Neoists in their exploration of collaborative cultural work. Aesthetics and Resistance have reduced the art group to its bare minimum—just two individuals. By experimenting with the component parts of larger cultural movements, Aesthetics and Resistance have developed a really deep understanding of the creative process.'

'Yeah,' Pemberton bullshitted, 'Aesthetics and Resistance is a name you'll be hearing again and again and again—because Penny and I are the most important artists to hit this planet in about two million years! Penny is bloody smart and I'm the most creative individual in the entire history of the world!'

There were groans from various sections of the audience, many of whom were familiar with the methods Penny and Don used to draw attention to themselves. Karen Eliot couldn't be bothered proceeding with the debate—which Aesthetics and Resistance had more or less stopped in its tracks. It was announced that the lecture was over and most of those present retired to the CIA's plush bar, where many a glass of mineral water was consumed.

The Raiders were well tanked up, having spent most of the afternoon guzzling lager in a beer tent. The free concert was drawing to a close and as Junk began their set, the bar staff refused to serve the thirsty crew of skinheads with any more drinks. The beer tent would soon be dismantled and the *Lark in the Park* no more than an unpleasant memory for the people of North London.

Johnny Aggro led his crew to the front of the stage. They shoved their way past hairies who were idiot-dancing, stomped on couples snogging in the grass and verbally abused many of the scum who were in desperate need of a bath.

'Get your 'air cut, you slithering piece of shit!' Slim spat at a particularly obnoxious example of unwashed leather and denim.

'Don't oppress me with your fascist views man,' the hippie warbled. 'You should loosen up, relax, let everybody do their own thing!'

A punch on the nose sorted the hairy out. The bastard collapsed like a bellow that had been punctured by a pin, then proceeded to writhe in the dirt, clutching his bruised beak in a futile attempt to stem the torrent of blood that was pouring from it.

'Ha, ha, ha!' Slim laughed as he booted the cunt in the ribs.

'The next song is from the new album,' lead singer Sebastian Sidgwick announced. 'It's called *A Dialogue in Hell Between Rimbaud and John Dee*.'

'Let's do 'em!' Johnny Aggro shouted to his crew as the band strummed the opening bars of the number.

The Raiders leapt on to the stage and split seconds later Hodges grabbed a mike stand and slammed it into Sidgwick's face. The singer reeled backwards into the drum kit, blood pouring from his mouth. Rebel took care of the bass player, while TK laid out the guitarist. Samson beat off two roadies who tried to rescue the band. Slim grabbed a microphone and shoved it at Rebel's mouth. Each skinhead knew what was expected of him.

'What's he like, Slim?' Rebel asked as he ground the heel of his boot into the bass player's face.

''Ee's a real hard bastard!' Slim thundered into the still live mike.

'Aggro, Aggro, Aggro, here comes Johnny

Aggro, Johnny Aggro's gonna do ya in!' the two skinheads sang.

The tune was not to the assembled peaceniks' liking. But the bozos were too frightened to hiss in case this led to skinhead boots thudding into soft hippie groins. Most of the hairies had come specifically to hear Junk's grunge rock and did not like the fact that the Raiders had put an end to their favoured choice of entertainment.

'You fuckin' cowards!' Johnny screamed at the hippies after taking the microphone from Slim. 'There must be three thousand of you out there—but all it takes is the appearance of five skinheads like us and you're all shitting yourselves!'

This abuse raised a few of the neanderthals from their lethargy. Some bottles were thrown at the stage, one hit Rebel, shattering against his temple. However, the skinhead didn't do so much as take a step backwards. He just stood his ground and glowered at the hairies as blood poured down his face. The rest of the gang got behind one of the PA stacks and kicked at the speakers until they toppled over, breaking the leg of a hippie who hadn't moved fast enough to escape injury as the sound system fell. Seconds later, Johnny caught a glimpse of the old bill running towards the stage. He shouted instructions and the Raiders split, successfully evading Met clutches.

The Bonnie Cockney on Argyll Street was your typical West End death trap. Situated right by Oxford Circus tube station, the bar-cum-restaurant catered for the type of tourist who wanted to sit in a dimly lit cellar sipping over-priced cocktails. Had the Raiders ever visited the place, they'd have been disgusted to discover that beer was only to be consumed in halves—there wasn't a pint glass to be found on the premises! However, the bozos who hung around Aesthetics and Resistance didn't find this state of affairs in the least bit off-putting—which is why fifteen individuals who'd recently attended the Karen Eliot lecture on Neoism were now to be found ordering pitchers of beer and avocado dips in this particular establishment.

'Didn't I tell you the sun shines out of my arse?' Donald Pemberton hissed rhetorically. 'Did you see the look on the faces of the audience when I made my intervention? They were dazzled by the brilliance of my contribution to the debate! What I said was like dawn breaking over a new intellectual horizon! It's me, and me alone, who can light the way to a higher stage of civilisation!'

'But what about Neoism?' Stephen Smith demanded. 'Do you really think it's as important as Karen Eliot was suggesting? Eliot's such a big name on the art scene, there's no reason for her to drag up a minor episode from the early stages of her career and then hype it as though it was the greatest thing since Marinetti invented futurism—unless she fervently believes her own assertions. However, from the little I know about the Neoists, I'd say they don't deserve the praise that's beginning to be heaped upon them.'

'Of course Neoism is important!' Ross MacDonald chided. 'The CIA wouldn't organise a talk on the subject if the Neoists didn't constitute a seminal but as yet unrecognised avant-garde art group.'

'Aye,' Joseph Campbell put in. 'Ross is right! Besides, you've already admitted that you know very little about the Neoists. And since we're unfamiliar with the work done by most of those who constituted the group, we'll have to base our provisional judgments on the work of those Neoists who have gone on to achieve fame within the mainstream art world!'

'That's a completely ridiculous assertion!' Smith exclaimed. 'The only Neoists to enjoy successful gallery careers are Karen Eliot and Stiletto. While I'm prepared to admit that these two individuals are immensely talented, it's crazy to judge the group as a whole on the basis of their work.'

'Nonsense!' Campbell yodelled. 'Give it ten years and you'll find examples of work by every last member of the Neoist Network in the world's major museums!'

'Neoism,' Penelope Applegate chipped in, 'is only important in as far as it provides a link between the classical avant-garde of the twentieth century and the work of Aesthetics and Resistance. Don and I are creating a culture that will serve wo/man for the next ten thousand years!'

'That's right!' Pemberton droned. 'Penny is bloody smart and I'm a flaming genius!'

Rebel was glad that the firm had sent him back to Fitzgerald House to get himself cleaned up. He didn't feel like a night of booze and dancing after being bashed on the bonce by a flying beer bottle. The lads had insisted that he keep out of his mum's way until his head healed up a bit. His old dear would have thrown a fit if she'd seen what her son looked like after the Raiders' escapade in Finsbury Park! There was blood all over the skinhead's Sherman and his face was a right fucking mess. Rebel slapped a copy of *Hand Clappin', Foot Stompin', Funky Butt—Live* on to Johnny's record deck before stripping to the waist and striding through to the bathroom.

The sound blasting from the hi fi speakers lifted the boot boy's spirits. Rebel had stood his ground as the bottles cascaded down upon the Raiders. Even if he was missing out on a Saturday night piss up and the chance to tap-off with a tart, he'd only have to endure five working days before it was the weekend again! The dose of Genomania miraculously packed into the micro-grooves of the Ram Jam Band's first album was doing a lot more for the skinhead than the warm water with which he was washing his cuts and bruises!

Rebel loved the frantic stax-style riffing, the manic singing and lack of pauses between songs. As far as the boot boy was concerned, the trendies could rant and rave about Geno Washington and the Ram Jam Band being crude until they were blue in the face. He'd always prefer brash, no-nonsense, stomping soul to the tasteful jazz selections and élitist wank favoured by the purists. So what if song choices such as 'Ride Your Pony', 'Up Tight' and 'Road Runner' were obvious favourites among the rent-a-mob set? At least the material was stronger than that found on your average Miles Davis album!

This train of thought was interrupted by a loud knocking at the door. Rebel was inclined to ignore the summons but it crossed his mind that the jazz freaks from next door might have come around to complain about the noise. As Rebel strode through the flat, he was fervently hoping that fate was about to offer him a golden opportunity to give the trendies from flat 223 a bloody good hiding.

'Hello Rebel,' Dr Maria Walker chirped as the

skinhead opened the door. 'What on earth have you done to your face?'

'We had a bit of a ruck down Finsbury Park,' the boot boy replied as he led the doctor through to the living room. 'Five of us took on three thousand hippies. We won, of course, but I got hit by a bottle. However, I stood my ground, these colours don't run!'

'Do you feel alright?' Maria enquired. 'Do you think the bottle did you any serious damage?'

'I'm a bit worried about my Ben Sherman,' Rebel confessed.

'What's that?' Walker demanded. 'I'm not au fait with cockney rhyming slang.'

'I'm not using rhyming slang,' the skinhead laughed. 'A Ben Sherman is a button-down shirt, the best money can buy! I got a lot of blood on me Benny and I suspect it might leave a permanent stain on the white sections of the check.'

'Can't you just go out and buy another shirt?' the doctor asked.

'No!' the boot boy admonished. 'It's an original Sherman from the sixties, the company stopped making shirts with that check years ago. Of course, you can get imitations down Carnaby Street—but they're no good at all! They don't have the crosshatching on the pocket and pleat, the sleeves are too baggy and don't have enough buttons on them. In other words, the copies are poxy. Shirts like mine don't grow on trees, they're bloody hard to find! It's not exactly compensation—but I did liberate a Perry from some geezer who was wearing it with the buttons undone.'

'What's a Perry?' Maria wanted to know.

'A sports top,' Rebel informed her.

'Look,' the doctor put in. 'Is Johnny around?'

'No,' the skinhead crooned. 'He's down the West End with the rest of the Raiders having a Saturday night piss up!'

'Then he's no bleedin' use to me!' Walker cursed. 'I want a fucking—do you think you could stand in for your friend?'

'Sure!' the boot boy grinned.

Maria pulled off her dress and wriggled out of some lacy black knickers. The doctor pushed Rebel on to his knees and shoved her cunt in his face. The boot boy didn't need to be told what to do next—he simply got licking! It wasn't long before Walker juiced up. Rebel was running his tongue around the doctor's clit and simultaneously working two fingers in and out of her hole. Maria moaned crazily as million-year-old genetic responses seized control of her bulk. She'd left Poplar, left this world behind—and was basking on the mudflats of prehistory.

Rebel pulled the doctor down on to the carpet, he unzipped his Levis and split seconds later the jeans were around his ankles. DNA codes were scrambled and unscrambled across the surface of the boot boy's bulk. The skinhead's love pole was battering into the crepe-tissue of Walker's cunt. It was warm and wet down there, with an ocean of sex juice frothing around Rebel's genetic pump.

'Fuck me!' the doctor exhorted. 'Harder, fuck me harder and faster, fuck me you fucker!'

Rebel loved to hear middle-class birds talk dirty and the words Maria screeched into his ear encouraged the boot boy to pump up the volume. The doctor grabbed the skinhead's balls with her hands, yanking them in time to the primitive rhythm her sexual partner was beating out. Rebel let rip with a great scream of pleasure and pain. He could feel love juice boiling inside his groin.

'I want you right up inside me!' Walker cajoled. 'I want your prick and your balls inside my cunt. I wanna feel your spunk spurting inside me. Oh God, I want it up my cunt and I want it in my mouth! Fuck me! Fuck me!'

Maria and Rebel came together in an ego-negating simultaneous orgasm. They'd reached that peak from which man and woman could never jointly return. Although they descended the steep cliffs of desire as atomised individuals, they did so knowing that for a few fleeting moments during their union, two bodies had fused and functioned as a single organism.

The Raiders were standing by the bar, sipping lagers, when Karen Eliot strolled into the Nursery. 'Goodbye, Nothin' To Say' by Nosmo King was blasting from the sound system. Karen pulled Johnny Aggro out on to the dance floor, leaving the rest of the firm to look after his drink. The two of them looked good together as they stomped in time to the Northern Soul classic. They stayed on out on the floor for 'Right Back Where We Started From' by Maxine Nightingale, 'Love on a Mountain Top' by Robert Knight and 'I Lost My Heart to a Starship Trooper' by Sarah Brightman. Karen needed a drink by the time the DJ slowed things down with 'The First, the Last, My Everything' by Barry White.

'What do you want?' Johnny enquired.

'I'll get them,' Eliot deliberated. 'You can't afford it, you're on the dole!'

'Okay,' Hodges acquiesced after downing the

remains of the lager he'd abandoned in favour of the dance floor. 'I guess it's pints all round.'

The other Raiders nodded their heads in agreement.

'Four pints of lager plus a Pernod and black please,' Karen said to the barmaid.

'What do you reckon about our chances of getting off with those two black chicks?' Slim asked TK as he pointed across the room.

'They're gorgeous and so alone!' TK sighed. 'Neither of them would look twice at a fat slob like you, I think I'll chance my luck with Samson.'

'Yeah,' the third skinhead put in. 'You leave this to me and TK. Watch a couple of experts in action, if you pay attention you'll learn a fair bit about pulling birds.'

The two skins thanked Eliot for the drinks she handed them and then marched across the room. A few minutes later, Samson was back at the bar investing hard cash in two very expensive cocktails.

'I think we're in luck!' the boot boy crowed after winking at his overweight mate.

Slim didn't understand the conversation Johnny Aggro was having with Karen Eliot. It was all about conspiracies, secret societies and manipulating the behaviour of third parties. The boot boy's attention wandered and somehow he found himself talking to a skinny bloke dressed in lycra cycling gear.

'Do you come here often?' the geezer asked.

'Every Saturday,' Slim assured him. 'Why do you wanna know?'

'I've just moved to London and I'm looking for places where I can make some new friends.'

Johnny Aggro and Karen Eliot were back on the

dance floor shaking their thang to 'Love Train' by the O'Jays. 'It's in His Kiss' by Linda Lewis kept their hips swinging and Curtis Mayfield's 'Superfly' had them in ecstasy! The club was beginning to fill as Karen and Johnny retired to the bar to get fresh drinks. The rounds were cheaper than earlier in the evening because TK and Samson were dancing with the black girls, while the cycling enthusiast was supplying Slim with drinks.

'I wanna get moving with this secret society business,' Eliot informed Hodges. 'There's a *Midnight Happening* at the Crypt in Bloomsbury Way tonight, if we go along we should pick up our first recruit. I'll tell you exactly what to do and say. It's . . .'

'But,' Johnny interjected, 'the DJ told me she'll be playing a solid hour of early reggae between twelve and one. If we go to the *Midnight Happening* I'm gonna miss it!'

'Don't be a prick!' Karen enjoined. 'She'll be doing another reggae hour next week! We've got to get moving with this secret society of ours—you'll love it, exercising power over a bunch of wanky artists!'

'Oh, alright,' Hodges whined.

Emma Career and Linda Forthwright had just been to see a stage version of the Bay City Rollers mid-seventies' hit 'Shang-A-Lang'. The dialogue consisted solely of repeated phrases from the teeny-bopper anthem—it was amazing the nuances an avant-garde theatre company could give to a set of banal song lyrics! Feeling spiritually renewed, the two arts administrators decided to grab some liquid refreshment at the Bonnie Cockney before speeding off to the alcohol-free zone of the Bloomsbury Crypt for the *Midnight Happening*.

'Fancy running into you here!' Linda Forthwright exclaimed.

'Hello.'

'Hi.'

'Alright?'

'Hello.'

'How's it going?'

Stephen Smith, Penny Applegate, Joseph Campbell, Don Pemberton and Ross MacDonald repeated these greetings as Emma Career plonked two cocktails on the table.

'Hi gang,' Emma chimed. 'I could see you had half-full pitchers of lager so I figured it wasn't worth asking if any of you wanted a drink.'

'You look stunning, darling,' Pemberton drooled at Career as he pondered the possibilities of her offering Aesthetics and Resistance a show at the Bow Studios.

'You don't look too bad yourself!' Emma rejoined. 'Are you all ready for the big fight?'

'What fight?' Don demanded.

'Haven't you heard?' Career asked in dismay. 'Jock Graham has got together a gang of his cronies from Glasgow and he's intending to take you on outside the Crypt when you turn up for the *Midnight Happening*.'

'I could have that coward any day of the week,' Pemberton shot back. 'You saw how I pulped him at the Karen Eliot opening! I'd be more than happy to take on Graham and his gang single-handed—but unfortunately, I have a terrible headache and I'm going to have to miss the *Midnight Happening*. In fact, Penny and I are going to go home right now!'

Karen Eliot and Johnny Aggro walked to the Crypt. The rising star of the international art circuit gave the skinhead a pep talk as they made their way to the *Midnight Happening*. With the exception of Don and Penny, the crowd who'd gathered in the Bonnie Cockney caught a cab. The taxi was Linda's idea—but she made everyone else chip in for the short ride.

'Unfortunately,' Stephen Smith announced to the assembled crowd, 'Don Pemberton is unwell and so Aesthetics and Resistance aren't here to perform their piece.'

'Cowards, cowards!' Jock Graham and his gang chanted.

'So what we're gonna do instead, is kick off with one of my visual poems,' Stephen chirped.

Smith then proceeded to run the short distance between two walls of the Crypt. The piece was supposed to continue until the audience got so pissed off with it that they physically assaulted the performer. Unfortunately, the ability of your average trendy to put up with pretentious shit is virtually limitless—and so Stephen had to call a halt to the 'poem' after ten minutes because he was out of breath.

The next artiste stood on top of a table which he proceeded to saw in half. While the crowd cheered, Johnny Aggro snorted in disgust. He felt like punching out the cunts who were inflicting this garbage on a gullible public. But he had his orders from Karen Eliot—and he mustn't draw attention to himself. The skinhead followed Stephen Smith to the rear of the club. The bozo sat down with his back against one of the brick walls of the Crypt. He was alone.

'My name is Hiram,' Hodges blathered into the artist's ear. 'I am a representative of The Zodiac. If you want to be signed up by a major gallery, go and stand in the middle of Cork Street at ten o'clock tomorrow morning. Don't breathe a word about this to anybody. The Zodiac is a secret society, we can transform you into an international art star—but in exchange you'll have to obey whatever instructions I pass your way. Sleep on this proposition. If you're in Mayfair tomorrow morning it will mean that you've bound yourself to my masters. I have no more to say.'

'Can't you tell me what it's all about?' Smith asked.

Johnny Aggro ignored the question, he was already making his way out of the Crypt. He had a set of keys for Eliot's pad. His instructions were to get undressed and into bed. Karen had assured the boot boy that she'd be home by two o'clock at the very latest. It was important they leave the happening separately. No one on the art circuit should know they were an item! While Eliot was at the Crypt, she had professional duties to perform—pressing the flesh of critics, administrators and other dignitaries. Handshakes, kisses and cheesy grins were an essential part of every artist's PR routine!

Four

KAREN ELIOT CHECKED her bedside clock. It was six-thirty in the morning. Karen decided to let Johnny Aggro enjoy another half-hour's kip before rousing him from his slumbers. After a soak and a thorough towelling down, Karen got back into bed. She woke Johnny by fingering his balls.

'What time is it?' the boot boy mumbled.

'Seven,' his hostess replied.

'It's too bloody early for sex,' Hodges murmured. 'It's Sunday morning for Chrissakes!'

'Come on!' Eliot exclaimed as she tugged at the skinhead's morning glory. 'I wanna play around with you. You're unemployed and can sleep in any day of the week! There won't be time later on, we've got a lot to do today!'

'I'm tired,' Johnny complained. 'You should have let me screw you last night, I prefer having it away in the evening.'

'You don't have to fuck me, lover!' Karen giggled

as she sat on the skinhead's face. 'All I said was that I wanted to play around—now get licking!'

Hodges could see he'd get no peace unless he complied with Eliot's request and so he ran his tongue over her cunt. Karen placed the middle finger of her right hand on her clit and began to rub it gently. Johnny was lapping enthusiastically at the beaver. Eliot threw back her head and moaned crazily.

'How does it taste?' Karen demanded.

'Of soap,' Johnny replied. 'You must have had a bath before waking me up.'

'Is that okay?' Eliot wanted to know.

'Yeah,' Hodges lisped, 'I don't like my pussy too strong.'

After this brief conversation, Johnny got his tongue back into the snatch. The skinhead didn't do anything particularly inventive, there wasn't much room to manoeuvre because of the way Karen had him pinned down. He just worked her hole with his tongue. After thirty minutes' cunt-licking, Hodges wriggled free and flipped Karen on to her stomach. It was time to work a different crack—the girl's arsehole.

'That tickles!' Karen giggled as Johnny ran his tongue along her bum.

Hodges applied a bit more pressure and Eliot got into what he was doing. The rim was clean and tasted of bath oil, just like Karen's cunt. Johnny wasn't a shit freak and was more than happy about this state of affairs. In fact, he never gave a girl this sort of treatment unless he knew she was clean. Hodges pulled the cheeks of Karen's arse apart, so that he could work the depths of this hole. His partner squealed with delight. A few minutes later, Johnny stopped licking and hauled himself up Eliot's back—he wanted to take her dog style.

'No!' Eliot said firmly. 'I told you, I just wanted to play around, I don't want a fucking!'

Hodges let out a snort of disgust and then fell back against the bed. Karen spun around and took his cock in her right hand, wrapping her fingers and thumb around it, then worked the member in a steady rhythm. As Johnny's groans of pleasure became more strident, Eliot pumped up the volume. Hodges could feel love juice boiling inside his groin. Split seconds later, spunk was spurting from the genetic pump and splattering across the skinhead's stomach and chest.

The chicks TK and Samson picked up at the Nursery shared a flat in Brixton. The boys hadn't slept much—but they'd had a lot of fun! Now the skinheads were making their way back home. It was a tedious Sunday morning tube journey with a change at Victoria and then the long ride on the District Line to Bromley-By-Bow.

'What was yours like?' TK asked nudging his mate.

'A right bloody raver!' Samson exclaimed. 'She had me doing things that couldn't be imagined by a life-long student of the Kama Sutra!'

'Mine was hot too!' TK crowed.

'I reckon the whole of Brixton must have been kept awake by your bird, I've never heard such a screamer!' Samson barked.

'Bet you wish you'd had my lay!' TK bragged.

'Leave it out,' Samson murmured. 'I'm not falling for that one, you've pulled it on me before. Why don't you come straight out with it and boast you're so hot between the sheets that you'd have had my bird bawling her head off if you'd been given the chance?'

The boot boys' interest in this conversation waned when a bonehead got on at the Embankment. He was wearing a pair of DMs that reached his knees, a tatty pair of jeans and a cardigan over a torn Lonsdale sweatshirt. The kid was simply a shaven-headed punk. It was most unfortunate that the general public didn't realise that the Raiders were a breed apart from this creep. Without saying a word to each other, TK and Samson got up and walked over to the cunt.

'Alright mate?' TK spat. 'How long you been a skinhead?'

''Bout five years!' the geezer demurred.

'If you're not new to the scene,' Samson fulminated, 'why's the bottom button on your cardigan done up?'

'What d'ya mean?' the bonehead demanded.

'Skinheads leave the bottom button on their cardigans undone, you fuckin' moron!' Samson bellowed as he rammed his fist into the youth's flabby stomach.

'You ain't a skinhead!' TK remonstrated as he brought his boot thudding against the kid's bollocks. 'You're just taking the piss!'

The bonehead was doubled over, Samson clasped his hands together and brought them smashing against the creep's neck. Split seconds later, the bozo was sprawled on the deck. TK kicked the cunt a few times—but soon tired of the game because his adversary passed out after a couple of blows to the head. The two Raiders then stripped the bonehead. It wasn't long before the kid was clad in no more than a pair of piss-stained briefs and white sports socks.

Samson and TK strolled through to the next carriage, which was as empty as the one they'd just left. They opened a window and dumped the unwanted boots, jeans and sweatshirt on to the track. Samson tried on the cardigan, it wasn't a bad fit. He figured that once his mum had given it a wash, the garment would be as good as new.

'Here you are,' TK told Samson as he handed him the bonehead's red braces. 'You keep the gear, I found twenty quid in that dickhead's jeans, it'll do as my share of the booty.'

'That ain't fair!' Samson whined. 'I'd rather have the cash.'

'The cardigan wouldn't fit me!' TK snapped. 'They cost forty quid and that one's hardly been worn! I reckon you've got the best part of the bargain.'

'Oh, alright!' Samson agreed sullenly.

Karen Eliot was making coffee and toasting muffins in the kitchen. Johnny Aggro swung his legs over the edge of her double bed and padded across the inch-deep carpet to a bookcase. Hodges scanned the shelves for something to read. There were a lot of philosophical works and a generous selection of political texts. These ranged from Paul Mattick's *Anti-Bolshevik Communism* and numerous books by Marx, through to *The Foundations of British Patriotism* by Esme Wingfield-Stratford and *Aristodemocracy* by Sir Charles Waldenstein. One shelf was devoted to conspiracy theory, running from John Robinson's *Proofs of a Conspiracy* of 1798 via Nesta Webster through to more recent works such as *The Unseen Hand* by A. Ralph Epperson. Other items in Eliot's collection included such unlikely titles as *Out of Step: Events in the Two Lives of an Anti-Jewish Camel-Doctor* by Arnold Spencer Leese M.R.C.V.S. and *Confessions of a Capitalist* by Ernest J. P. Benn. What finally caught Johnny's eye was a novel by K. L. Callan entitled *We Don't Pose*. The skinhead opened the book, then snapped it shut again as Karen Eliot marched into the room. She deposited a tray laden with breakfast goodies on a bedside table, handed Hodges a coffee, then climbed back into bed.

'This is nice,' Karen sighed. 'Breakfast in bed with a real live bloke! I haven't done this for a long time!'

'That's because you usually send your conquests home in a taxi once they've satisfied your sexual lusts!' Hodges shot back. 'Mind you, I reckon you only let me stay overnight because you wanted to make sure I was here early enough to receive my orders for today. You're completely obsessed with organising a secret society!'

'We'll get on to that a bit later,' Karen replied—and then quickly changing the subject added, 'What were you reading?'

'Something called *We Don't Pose*, it's a novel about a skinhead,' Johnny hissed as he reached down and picked the book off the floor. 'I didn't get it at all, the bit I glanced at was some sorta cross between a sex scene and a socialist newspaper.'

'K. L. Callan is one of my favourite writers,' Eliot chirped. 'He's a bit of a mysterious figure, no one really knows very much about him, but he's written theoretical books as well as fiction. Callan juxtaposes high and low brow styles of writing in an attempt to negate world culture in its entirety. He wants to wipe humanist platitudes from the face of the earth, so that new cultures can roll off the production line of contemporary life!'

'What you're saying is way beyond me,' Hodges confessed. 'I guess *We Don't Pose* just ain't my kinda book.'

'There's stuff in here you'd like,' Karen insisted as she took the book from Johnny and picked a passage. 'Listen to this: "the skinhead had once known a schizophrenic who taunted people by asking them to pour scalding coffee over his head. A psychiatrist who was earning fifty pounds an hour to cure the bozo's problems had made no progress with the case—but Blake set the spoilt brat to rights within the space of a few seconds. When the teenage loony asked Terry to pour a cappuccino over his bonce, the boot boy obliged. The schizophrenic never bothered Blake again . . ." '

'Yeah, that's good,' Hodges laughed. 'I like the attitude! The world's problems could be sorted out within the space of a few weeks if only the do-gooders would take off their kid-gloves and deal with evil the way any self-respecting skin sorts out his opponents!'

Stephen Smith could feel butterflies fluttering in his stomach as he positioned himself in the middle of the street. Smith rolled up one of his trouser legs and placed a blindfold around his eyes. Stephen was desperate to make it in the art world and he fervently hoped that this submissive gesture would please The Zodiac. Of course, it was possible that the character who'd approached Smith at the *Midnight Happening* was a practical joker and there was no secret society prepared to transform him into an art star in exchange for his unquestioning obedience to some unknown cause. If that was the case, he'd chalk the whole thing up to experience. But Stephen desperately wanted to believe that Hiram was a genuine emissary from the thirteen financiers who were rumoured to don robes once a month and then sit together in a dimly lit room somewhere in the City, making decisions about the fate of the world.

'Hello Stephen,' Amanda Debden-Philips raved. 'I'm so glad you could make it. I've got a contract for you to sign in the office. Is this some sort of performance you're doing to celebrate the fact that you're about to join Flipper Fine Art?'

'You could say that,' Smith gushed as he undid his blindfold. 'Do you know Hiram or anyone else who belongs to The Zodiac?'

'I'm afraid I don't know what you're talking about,' Amanda sighed as she unlocked the door to her gallery.

'Mum's the word, eh?' Stephen laughed. 'Well don't worry, I can keep a secret too, you know. Have you got any instructions for me?'

'All I want you to do,' Debden-Philips replied as she led the artist through to her office, 'is glance through the contract I've prepared and then sign two copies for me.'

'Sure,' Smith agreed. 'But are there any secret handshakes or other signs that you want to teach me?'

'No,' Amanda said firmly as she sat down at her desk and handed the artist the two contracts.

Stephen perused the document he'd been instructed to read. Debden-Philips shuffled some papers. She wondered what on earth Karen Eliot was planning. It was obvious that Smith had been fed some particularly crazy line in bullshit. Amanda decided that it was pointless speculating on this subject. Her job was to keep Eliot at Flipper and if this entailed contracting a few second-rate artists to the gallery to keep their star act happy, then so be it. Stephen signed the papers and pushed them across the desk.

'You get to keep one of them,' Debden-Philips explained as she held out the artist's copy of the contract.

'Cheers!' Smith cried as he snatched the document, folded it and then placed the precious sheets of paper in a pocket. 'What happens next?'

'I'll visit you in your studio tomorrow,' Amanda elaborated. 'I'll take away all the pieces of work I like and bring them back to the gallery. That way, I'll have material to sell to Flipper's customers. We'll put at least one thing into every group show we have, in about six months' time we'll arrange a one-man exhibition. It's all very straightforward.'

'I see,' Stephen crowed, 'becoming an art star is that simple! Are you sure you don't want to teach me a set of passwords or send me out on a dangerous mission?'

'Don't be silly!' Debden-Philips snorted. 'This is an art gallery—not a front for a secret intelligence network!'

'Right!' Smith exclaimed while simultaneously tapping his nose with an index finger.

Karen Eliot had been through all the angles with Johnny Aggro before sending him off to Stephen Smith's pad. Given that it was Sunday morning, it seemed likely the artist would return home after signing up with Flipper Fine Art. All the skinhead had to do was break into Smith's flat and once the painter showed up, issue him with his instructions from 'The Zodiac'.

'Wanna buy some grass, man?' a hippie asked Hodges as the boot boy strode into the courtyard giving access to the various blocks that made up Gray's Inn Buildings.

Johnny shoved the troglodyte back against a conveniently placed wall and smashed his right fist against the bastard's jaw. Hodges felt terrific as his knuckles bounced off the hairy's nose and mouth. There was nothing like a bit of savagery to restore the balance within the boot boy's atavistically inclined system. In his blind rage, Johnny hit the hippie again and again—until the cunt's face was as red and raw as mincemeat. The pusher's head bobbed about, smashing back against brickwork and then flopping forward for a fraction of a second until Hodges got in the next punch. The peacenik would have slid to the ground if Johnny had not been holding him upright. Like a prize-fighter gone berserk, Hodges proceeded with the attack, slamming right hooks against the jaw of an opponent he'd already pulped beyond submission and into a black-out. Finally, the skinhead eased up, kicking the drop-out in the bollocks as the bozo's unconscious bulk crumpled in upon itself.

Split seconds later, Johnny had removed two dozen £5 bags of grass, twelve blotters and £30 in cash from the dealer's pockets. Hodges didn't object to drug-taking. The boot boy simply felt insulted whenever some bastard assumed he was stupid enough to buy bags of crap from a stranger. Johnny had regular connections who he could trust not to rip him off when he wanted to get out of his head—and besides, he much preferred speed to weed. Hodges pulled down the neanderthal's filthy jeans. As he'd suspected, the bastard was wearing a money belt. Having bagged another £300 in notes, Johnny left the hairy where he belonged—in the gutter!

Stephen Smith lived on the top floor. There was a mat outside the artist's front door—and Hodges found a key beneath it. The skinhead let himself into the flat. The floorboards in the living room were painted grey. The pad was sparsely furnished with a black three-piece suite and little else. The bedroom floor was covered with a black carpet, a futon was rolled up against one wall with a duvet draped over it. Hodges looked inside a wardrobe and found nothing more exciting than jackets, trousers and shirts. It was the same story when the boot boy went through a chest of drawers. Likewise, the kitchen lacked a fridge, while crockery was kept to an absolute minimum. There was a table at one end of the narrow room and above this a shelf of books. Hodges scanned these but the titles didn't mean anything to him—*The Post-Modern Condition*, *A Beginner's Guide to Post-Structuralist Literary Theory*, *The Foucault Reader* etcetera. There was nothing the boot boy wanted to read, it was all high brow stuff, there wasn't a single novel!

Johnny took a key from a hook and stalked out of the flat. He tried the lock of an unnumbered door. As he'd suspected, it opened into a bathroom and toilet suite. Hodges checked out a laundry-basket; beneath a couple of neatly folded sheets, he found a stack of wank mags. The skinhead carried a pile of these back into the flat. He'd keep himself amused with back issues of *Big Boobs* and *Fifty Plus*.

Penny Applegate had cleaned the kitchen, hoovered and dusted the living room, wiped down every light switch in the flat and was now making breakfast. Once the coffee had percolated and the toast was buttered, she carried the food through to Donald Pemberton who was still lying in bed.

'Wake up Don,' Penny said shaking her boyfriend gently. 'I've bought you some coffee.'

'I'm a flaming genius,' Pembertom mumbled. 'I should be allowed to sleep all day.'

'We're meeting the gang for lunch, remember?' Applegate persisted. 'You'll have to get up soon.'

'But I'm a flaming genius!' Pemberton repeated

as he turned over. 'The public expect me to stay in bed until at least two in the afternoon. They'd be fucked off if they knew I was behaving like a suit.'

'I've done the housework,' Penny said changing the subject. 'How about giving me the money I need to get those new clothes?'

'I'll have to check your cleaning is up to scratch first,' Pemberton stated emphatically. 'Are you sure you've done everything?'

'Yeah,' Applegate babbled.

'Including the toilet?' Pemberton demanded.

'You never said anything about the bog,' Penny whined.

'You're not getting those new clothes until you've done the john!' Don snapped. 'And don't argue with me about it, I'm brilliant and I should be left in peace. However, you might as well hand me my coffee since I'm now fully awake thanks to your endless pestering.'

'Hey!' Applegate jabbered, thinking she'd better change the subject again or she'd never get those new clothes. 'I've had an idea! This Neoism thing seems as if it's about to break, so we ought to ride the trend by doing an Aesthetics and Resistance show entitled the *New Neoism*!'

'Brilliant!' Pemberton cried. 'Why do I always have my best ideas just before I fall asleep or as I'm waking up? I suppose it's because I'm so naturally talented!'

'Any chance of getting the money for my new clothes?' Penny enquired.

'Don't bother me with that!' Don bellowed. 'Jesus, I've just invented the *New Neoism* and you're trying to panhandle me for a bit of spare change! Forget about your new clothes, otherwise you might go down in history as the berk who interrupted me during a creative outpouring, thereby depriving the world of who knows how many priceless cultural treasures! God, I know just how Coleridge must have felt when that tradesman came to settle the bill!'

'Would you like some toast?' Applegate asked, attempting to change the subject yet again.

'Yes,' Pemberton nodded. Then after nibbling at the slice added, 'That's much better, I should be pampered, not nagged.'

Johnny Aggro leafed diffidently through Stephen Smith's wank mags. It wasn't that Hodges was lacking in the libido department, he just didn't share the artist's tastes in skirt—and in particular a fixation with huge breasts! At first, Johnny had stared in disbelief at the knockers on display—they were abnormal, freaks of nature! But pretty soon, the spectacle began to bore him. Hodges went for slim girls in high heels, leather miniskirts and purple lip gloss. He simply wasn't turned on by the idea of making it with a chick who had fifty-inch tits. Apart from anything else, Johnny figured the womun's mammories would get in the way while he was doing the business.

'Hi, you took your bloody time,' the skinhead raged at Smith when the artist finally showed up.

'I didn't know you were gonna be here waiting for me!' the bozo blurted.

'You left the key under the mat!' Hodges fumed. 'You must have known I was coming!'

'Where did you find those magazines?' Stephen demanded as Johnny threw a copy of *Big Boobs* on to the floor.

'In the laundry-basket,' the boot boy replied. 'Since you don't have a TV, I needed something to read and this was the best entertainment I could come up with.'

'It's research material,' Smith lied. 'I'm doing a series of landscapes based on the contours of wimmin's breasts.'

'Yeah, sure,' Hodges laughed lazily. 'Anyway, where do you keep the rest of your gear?'

'I've a studio in Stratford,' Stephen divulged, 'and I rent another flat in Islington where I store a lot of my possessions. Anyway, how could you tell I had stuff apart from what's here?'

'That's bloody obvious,' Johnny spat. 'This pad is just a minimalist showcase for your arty lifestyle. Being devoid of the junk everyone accumulates, the whole place comes across as a complete fake. If any of your crowd are taken in by this drum, then they're complete morons! Besides, it doesn't matter any more because you've got a contract now and I've come here to talk to you about it!'

'Yeah,' Smith whooped. 'I've got a legal document in my pocket that says I'm one of the élite band of painters represented by Flipper Fine Art. I can't wait to tell my friends! A lot of people are gonna be gutted that I've joined the art establishment while they're still waiting to have a crack at the big time!'

'In that case,' Hodges sneered, 'you won't have any difficulty in carrying out the rest of your orders from The Zodiac! You've got to find a bunch of artists desperate for a gallery contract and form them into a Lodge. The fact that you're now a part of Flipper Fine Art demonstrates that my masters can deliver the goods. Everyone else in your Lodge will have to prove their ability to serve the great cause that I represent before strings are pulled and they land in situations as potentially lucrative as the one you're in now!'

'Okay, Hiram,' Stephen cried. 'I get the picture, I can do it for you and The Zodiac!'

'Right,' Johnny snarled. 'We need to recruit another twelve people into your Lodge. I'm gonna allow you to pick ten of them, the other two work together as Aesthetics and Resistance. It's up to you how these individuals are approached, just make sure they're told nothing about The Zodiac. Your Lodge is to be called The Semiotic Liberation Front. This is the only name you'll mention to its members. You might learn a little about The Zodiac later—but only if you prove yourself worthy of such knowledge. Your Lodge must study Neoism and do everything it can to promote the movement. Also, my masters want you to begin a campaign of vandalising statues and sculptures. I want you to start work on these projects immediately. Once The Zodiac is satisfied with your progress, you'll be issued with instructions about your initiation into higher mysteries.'

Johnny Aggro did more than carry out Karen Eliot's instructions. He'd added a few extra twists and turns of his own. Although Eliot considered herself to be in charge of this caper, the skinhead was smart enough to realise that while she remained in the background, it was he who actually controlled the operation. Hodges could therefore see no reason why this particular scam shouldn't be used to his own advantage. Karen wouldn't even know what he'd done until it was too late for her to do anything about it! To use a metaphor, Eliot was the major shareholder who 'owned' The Zodiac Corporation—but it was Johnny, acting in a managerial capacity, who held the real power in his hands!

*

Karen Eliot and Dr Maria Walker met for a lunch-time drink at the Prospect of Whitby. Situated as it was on the banks of the Thames at Wapping Wall, in times past the pub had been frequented by pirates. Lurid tales were told about the sea and its notorious underclass—chiefly by guides from the local history association, since nowadays smugglers ply their trade through Gatwick and Heathrow. Rather fittingly, many a tourist haunted the Prospect, giving it an international flavour which sometimes approximated that of the London airports.

'So tell me,' Maria begged Karen, 'what's really happening on the contemporary art scene?'

'Nothing very much at the moment,' Eliot revealed. 'Most of what's getting coverage lacks substance. If you read the art press, you'll see a lot of hype about new trends but none of the artists being reviewed are gonna change the direction of our visual culture. However, there's a steadily growing revival of interest in an eighties' art movement called Neoism. The Neoists developed the avant-garde tradition that stretches from futurism and dada, through surrealism to the situationists and fluxus. The Neoists were very innovative—and because they were ahead of their time, most people are only just beginning to realise the importance of the group. It'll take ten years before the average artistic hack catches on to what Neoism was about—and when this happens, the consequences will be revolutionary. In the meantime, it's down to a few individuals—like me—to draw inspiration from the legacy of Neoism and do what we can to propagate the cultural advances made by the movement.'

'Wow!' Walker exclaimed. 'The Neoists sound absolutely amazing—do tell me more about them!'

'I suppose it's easiest to start at the beginning,' Karen stated knowledgeably. 'Neoism was founded in 1977 by a group of artists centred around Al Ackerman, David Zack and Maris Kundzin in Portland, Oregon. Initially, the movement was known simply as ISM and No Ism. However, by 1979, the virus had spread to Montreal in Canada and ISM was transformed into Neoism. In 1982, Neoism crossed the Atlantic and important events were held all over Europe and North America.'

'I still don't understand exactly what Neoism is or was,' Maria sighed. 'I really want to know all about the movement, so that I can impress my medical friends with a detailed knowledge of contemporary art.'

'Making sense of Neoism,' Eliot pontificated, 'is like trying to hold water in your hand. Neoism eludes all formalistic attempts at classification, its meaning slips from your grasp whenever you attempt to pin it down. Like all avant-garde art, Neoism is ambiguous. Perhaps what the Neoists created is not art at all but a critique of world culture in its entirety! Neoism is like a river that just keeps flowing, flowing, flowing. It is the alpha and omega of Western Civilisation—and because Neoism marks the very boundaries within which the artist is forced to function, it will not be comprehensible to wo/mankind for many a year to come. To understand Neoism, we must raise the lamp and drop the idiot. It may be a hundred years before the achievements of each individual Neoist is fully appreciated!'

'Amazing!' Walker cried. 'But what on earth do you mean by raising the lamp and dropping the idiot?'

'The lamp,' Eliot explained, 'is the light of knowledge, the idiot is the reptilian brain that is unleashed by sex, an acid trip, fear and many other things.

Neoism was a form of techno-atavism! Since there's a lot of symbolism connected to the movement, I don't want you to get confused by hearing too much at once. Let's forget about Neoism for the time being and get something more to drink instead. Then we can chat about Johnny Aggro's performance in bed. After that, we'll go back to my place, I've got a lot of Neoist material and it'll be far easier to explain the movement to you once you've seen some of this.'

'I'll get the drinks!' Maria insisted as she stood up. 'Talking to you is so interesting. I'm fucking sick of mindless conversations with medical bores or trying to work out what's wrong with some lumpen patient who can only talk in monosyllables!'

The London art world is a tiny microcosm of our alienated society—and gossip travels around this pathetic 'scene' at something approaching the speed of light. The life of artists, critics and administrators consists of endlessly jumping on and off bandwagons. One week abstraction is in, the next everybody's decided to drink Bulgarian wine. Within hours of a degree show being hung, an art student from the 'right' college might find their paintings worth telephone numbers—a few months later, the market is glutted and nothing short of suicide will reverse a sudden collapse in the value of the young star's output.

Karen Eliot was one of the few contemporary artists to survive the swings of fashion and establish herself as a fixture on the international gallery circuit. Once word got around that an aspiring art critic had clocked this cultural giant enjoying a tête-à-tête with Amanda Debden-Philips in the Oxford Street Burger King, every cunt who wanted to maximise their cultural capital could be found pigging-out at this junk-food paradise. It's therefore not surprising that Stephen Smith, Aesthetics and Resistance, Ramish Patel, Ross MacDonald, Joseph Campbell and the group of young hopefuls who flocked around them should choose to hold one of their regular Sunday lunch-time get-togethers at this high-kitsch venue.

'My visual works are dazzling!' Don Pemberton bellowed as he banged his fist against a plastic table. 'And I say pretension is what made this country Great!'

'Listen,' Ramish Patel babbled as he rose from his seat. 'I'd love to debate you on the question of imperialism—but I have an important meeting at the CIA, so I'm afraid I'll have to go.'

'Bye Ramish.'

'Don't forget to send me an invite to the CIA opening!'

'See you next week.'

'Remember to show that critic the slides I gave you!'

'Take care.'

Ramish smiled at his many friends, waved and was gone. Stephen Smith breathed a sigh of relief, Patel was a good bloke but he wouldn't be interested in what Stephen was about to propose—the formation of a secret society Lodge to ensure that everyone present was signed up by a major gallery. Ramish had a well-established career, he didn't need any help from The Zodiac!

'As I was saying,' Pemberton boomed, 'I am the greatest living artist in the world and Britain needs men like me if its culture isn't to degenerate into a mish-mash of pop clichés!'

'Forget that,' Smith thundered. 'I've just been

signed up by Flipper Fine Art and everyone here can get a contract with a major gallery if they'll just listen to what I say.'

'But I'm a flaming genius!' Don protested. 'I say . . .'

'Shut up!' everyone present chanted in unison. 'We want to hear Stephen out!'

'I don't believe he's got a deal with Flipper!' Pemberton snarled.

Smith unfolded a copy of his contract and it was passed from hand to hand as if it was one of the Dead Sea Scrolls or the stone tablets that Moses brought down from the mountain. There was the occasional awed comment as wannabe art stars got to touch the sheaf of papers that Amanda Debden-Smith had validated with her signature.

'Wow!'

'Amazing!'

'Stone the crows!'

The last comment came from Donald who was distraught because his obvious talents had been passed over by the folks at Flipper while schmucks such as Smith were signed up. Stephen carefully folded the contract and put it back in his pocket. The atmosphere was electric, everyone was waiting for Smith to speak. He made the most of this situation, using a pause to great rhetorical effect. After staring out his friends for the best part of a minute, Flipper's latest find broke the silence.

'I was approached by a man called Hiram, who told me that if I successfully completed various tasks I'd been assigned by his masters, I was to be rewarded with a gallery contract. I agreed and before long I'd been signed up by Flipper. Now that I've been initiated into the mysteries of the organisation Hiram represents, his masters want me to form a new Lodge of the Semiotic Liberation Front by recruiting twelve of my trusted friends to this ancient and noble fraternity. Everyone who joins up and successfully completes a probationary period will be signed up by a major gallery. This is a chance for each and every one of you to make it big in the art world, all you have to do is swear blind obedience to my masters . . .'

'Count me in!'

'Me too!'

'I'll do anything the SLF wants. Christ, I'd rip the entrails out of a baby and eat them if it was guaranteed to get me a gallery contract!'

'I'd murder my entire family!'

'I'm with the SLF!'

'Me too!'

Without further ado, it was agreed that everyone present would join Stephen Smith's newly formed Semiotic Liberation Front Lodge and that from now on, the leader of their cell would be known by the code name Spartacus. Oaths of secrecy were exchanged, along with dark mutterings about a direct line of descent from the Bavarian Illuminati. Plans were laid for research into Neoism and the wanton destruction of sculptures. The Minervals were eager to please their unknown masters—they would get cracking right away!

Five

HEARING HIS NEIGHBOURS leave their flat at eight-thirty in the morning raised Johnny Aggro's spirits. It was good to know that Applegate and Pemberton were ensnared in the trap he had laid for them. As he ate breakfast, Hodges listened to his *I Am the Ruler* CD, a selection of material recorded by Derrick Morgan during the ska and rocksteady eras. Next he slapped 'Moon Hop' and 'Derrick Topa Pop' on to his deck—these reggae hits were among the best tracks Morgan cut during his long career. The session was brought to a close with the rude boy anthem 'Tougher Than Tough'. Johnny briefly wondered why Jamaican music had taken such a downhill slide in the quality department after 1972, then pushed the thought from his mind. The boot boy had money in his pocket, lifted from the Gray's Inn pusher, and was eager to spend it!

The tube ride into town was uneventful. An American teenager offered him a fiver to pose for a photograph, a proposition the skinhead turned down, instead he suggested the girl meet him at the Spice Of

Life at seven that evening. She agreed, hoping to get a few snaps later in the day. Johnny got off the train at Oxford Circus. As he was striding out of the station, some berk selling the *Marxist Times* stepped into his path.

'What do you think of the European parliament?' the militant demanded.

'That it's just semantics!' Hodges shot back.

'What?' the marxist moron gasped.

'It's just semantics,' Johnny repeated. 'That's the reply your organisation's programmed you to give me if I put forward an argument you're unable to counter—which means virtually anything I happen to say.'

'That's not true!' the leftist protested. 'The party is full of original thinkers. We might be highly disciplined but we're certainly not programmed.'

'In that case,' Hodges sneered, 'why do you all say the same things?'

'Well,' the red cretin spluttered. 'We all read the *Marxist Times* and then develop our own thoughts from the views put forward by the most advanced proletarian thinkers. When the cadre picks up handy phrases from party literature, I guess it's just a kind of shorthand.'

'Snap outta it!' Johnny snarled. 'Are you a fuckin' robot or what? Christ, your lot are worse than the bleedin' moonies!'

'But that's just semantics!' the retard cried triumphantly.

Hodges could feel anger surging through his body as a DM slammed into the marxist's bollocks. The militant was lifted a few inches off the ground and then collapsed like a bellow that had been punctured by a pin. Johnny enjoyed this spectacle, he had a feeling for violence and the thud of a boot in someone else's groin did something for his soul. A few vicious kicks to the ribs finished the job, the leftist was an unconscious heap on a floor that should have been cleaned three weeks ago.

'Well done, son,' a passing businessman congratulated Hodges—and then after handing him a card added, 'I like to see young men put the boot in on tossers. It reminds me of the glorious time I had in the army. If you're ever in need of a job, give me a ring, I could put your talents to good use!'

Spartacus, as Stephen Smith now styled himself, had assumed full control of the newly formed Semiotic Liberation Front Lodge. He was determined to demonstrate his trustworthiness to his masters and thereby prove that he deserved initiation into the inner mysteries of The Zodiac. As Grand Dragon of the Lodge, Smith had issued Joseph Campbell and Ross MacDonald with orders to examine all the Neoist material held by the British Library. Penelope Applegate and Donald Pemberton were making a nuisance of themselves at the Tate Gallery, while Spartacus was hard at work in the National Art Library. The rest of the Lodge had been instructed to spend the day visiting art galleries, bookshops, public libraries and colleges, where they were to ask for material relating to Neoism. Even if this failed to turn up any useful information, it would give the impression that Neoism was a growth area within the culture industry.

Having taken notes on a number of magazines, Stephen was examining a book published by the Kryptic Press of Würzburg entitled *The Neoist Network's First European Training Camp*. Spartacus flicked through the tome admiring the black and white photographs. Some of the pictures had been coloured in by a previous reader—who'd also added beards and moustaches to a few faces. Smith tutted when he observed this, not realising that these modifications had been made by a Neoist who'd intended them to illustrate his theories on the relationship between fame and easily recognisable visual characteristics. Spartacus scribbled a few words in a notepad—'Pete Horobin (British), Stiletto (German), Peter Below (German).' Being hard at work, Smith didn't notice the librarian who'd approached him. Spartacus nearly jumped out of his skin when the woman addressed him:

'Excuse me, sir.'

'Y . . . y . . . yes?' Stephen stammered.

'I'm sorry to bother you,' the librarian apologised, 'but a rather important art critic has just come in and he wants to consult the material you're looking at. Obviously, you can only look at one thing at a time—and so I was wondering if you'd mind sharing our Neoist collection with this eminent gentleman.'

'Who is he?' Smith demanded.

'Jock Graham,' came the reply.

'My God!' Spartacus gagged as he pressed a hand against his forehead. 'Britain's most famous left-wing art critic and he wants to look at the same books as me! Tell Mr Graham to come right over, he's more than welcome to share your Neoist literature with me!'

After shaking hands and exchanging a few words, Jock and Stephen settled down to their studies. Graham recognised Smith, he'd seen him at numerous art openings—although as far as Jock could recall, he'd never spoken to the young man, who he took to be an unsuccessful artist. Stephen's mind was working double time, he knew that getting on friendly terms with a top-flight art critic would greatly aid his career. Spartacus figured that the best plan was to wait until Graham looked like he was about to go for lunch, and than tag along. The critic would have to speak to him, since he'd bagged the Neoist materials first and it was an act of generosity to agree to share them with the older man.

Johnny Aggro bought a lambswool cardigan in Sherry's and then headed for Rupert Street. With the money he'd lifted from the Gray's Inn pusher, Hodges could afford a session with the hooker he'd been too broke to hire the previous week. The thought of ripping off the tart's pink hot pants and ramming his cock up her dripping wet cunt made the skinhead wish his sta-prest weren't quite so tight! Johnny's lust for the street walker was even more intense than Thomas De Quincey's desire for a reunion with Little Annie—although the boot boy knew nothing about nineteenth-century literature, he'd have appreciated the comparison if a knowledgeable writer had taken the trouble of explaining it to him.

By strutting up and down Rupert Street, Hodges soon ascertained there was no sign of the harlot. It might have been too early for her to be at work—or perhaps she was performing for another trick. Johnny turned right on to Shaftesbury Avenue and headed down to the Dilly.

'Excuse me,' a pretty girl chirped as she stepped in front of the skinhead, 'but could you tell me what you think of the European Parliament?'

'Why did you get involved with this rubbish?' Johnny demanded as he pointed at the copies of *Marxist Times* the bird clutched against her chest. 'You're the second person who's asked me that question today. It's always the same bloody sales pitch, with each topical catch-phrase lasting a whole month. Your lot have been mouthing these platitudes for years, without any results whatsoever. You sound like a bleedin' robot, haven't you got a mind of your own? I mean, why do you bother?'

'I joined the party when I was at university,' the militant replied, 'because I wanted to get involved in the working-class struggle and fight oppression!'

'But can't you see,' the boot boy clamoured, 'the party and your student friends aren't fightin' oppression, they're just pissin' in the bloomin' wind. It's all a load of wank, innit, this communist revolution shit. I mean, how many people are there in your cell who didn't go to university?'

'None,' the chick confessed, 'and sometimes that worries me.'

'Don't fret about it,' Hodges shot back. 'Use your loaf and draw the obvious conclusion that what you've been doing is a waste of time. Why not just cut your losses and jack it in?'

'You make it sound easy,' the girl grumbled. 'But I can't just walk away from the party!'

'Yes you can,' Johnny insisted.

'How?' the militant whined.

'We'll find a quiet pub and I'll buy you a drink,' Hodges coaxed.

'But I'm supposed to be flogging copies of the *Marxist Times*!' the girl protested.

'Give me the magazines,' Johnny instructed.

The militant did as she was told, mindless obedience having been drilled into her by party leaders who were always droning on about discipline. Hodges took the publications and dumped them in the nearest litter bin.

'You see,' the skinhead assured the ex-militant,

'it was much easier walking away from that party bollocks than you thought.'

'Yeah,' the girl laughed. 'By the way, my name's Atima, Atima Sheazan.'

'I'm Johnny,' Hodges told her. 'Me mates call me Johnny Aggro. Now we're introduced, let's get that drink!'

Penny Applegate and Don Pemberton's efforts to read up on the Neoist movement got off to a bad start. They'd not realised that admission to the Tate Gallery Library was a privilege, not a right enjoyed by the general public. Before they received permission to proceed with their research, the deadly duo needed academic credentials, references and an appointment made days in advance. Remonstrations with a woman on the enquiry desk led to frayed tempers—and a threat that if Aesthetics and Resistance didn't leave her in peace, she'd have them thrown out of the Tate!

Applegate and Pemberton calmed themselves by communing with the great works of art housed in what was, when all is said and done, a temple to the aesthetic values of secular humanism. The Voice that screamed at Donald day in and day out, had on occasion whispered to all those whose talents were represented by items on display in the Tate. Every great artist found 'himself' touched—at least during creative peaks—by the same force that had moulded Pemberton from the very moment of his birth. If God is dead, 'His' ideological replacement is a Muse who works in equally mysterious ways.

Having squared the circle that is generally accepted as a conceptual model of serious culture, Penny and Don retired to the café in the Tate's basement, where they were enjoying a brew. There would be many more opportunities to demonstrate their acquisition of cultural capital and so, for the time being, Aesthetics and Resistance took a break from their mania for worshipping blobs of paint.

'It's not fair,' Pemberton moaned. 'I'm an artistic genius but the morons who run this place refuse to recognise the fact and won't let me into the library!'

'It's more serious than that!' Applegate exclaimed. 'If we don't succeed in finding out everything we can about Neoism and then propagating the movement, Hiram and his masters may consider us unworthy of a gallery contract!'

'What are we going to do?' Donald whined.

'I know!' Penny chirped, suddenly cheering up as she was struck by a flash of inspiration. 'We'll phone up Ramish, he knows the chief librarian here, I'm sure he can sort things out so that we can get in without references or an appointment.'

'Yes, yes!' Pemberton cried. 'What a brilliant idea of mine. Have you got some change, Penny? You must go and phone our friend. It's lucky I've got my wits about me and know how to make the most of our contacts!'

'What's the number?' Applegate asked.

'How should I know!' Donald snapped. 'Haven't you got your filofax with you?'

'No, I left it at home,' Penny lamented.

'Bollocks!' Pemberton swore. 'At this rate we're gonna waste a whole day.'

'Things aren't quite that bad,' Applegate retorted. 'I can phone up directory enquiries.'

'In that case,' Donald demanded, 'why the hell

are you pissing about? There's not a second to waste, I want you to get straight on the blower!'

'Can't I finish my tea?' Penny whimpered.

'No!' Pemberton bellowed. 'Our careers are at stake, you've gotta get your act together!'

Johnny Aggro had walked Atima Sheazan through Soho and across Oxford Street. They were seated downstairs at Bradley's—a Spanish bar on Hanway Street. Now they'd pints in their hands, the conversation flowed even more freely than during their brief stroll.

'It's such a relief to talk to someone about the party,' Atima confessed. 'I've had doubts about being a communist militant for a long time.'

'Haven't you got any mates who'd jabber to you about it?' Hodges asked in disbelief.

'But that was my whole problem,' Sheazan explained. 'Once I'd joined the party, I lost all my old friends. They thought I was a bore, always talking about politics and trying to sell them copies of *Marxist Times*. I'm not in touch with anyone I knew before I became a card-carrying communist—and even if I was, they wouldn't want to hear anything about the party. They all got bloody sick of it.'

'But what did you do with your spare time?' Johnny demanded. 'You can't have spent it all hanging out with those marxist morons!'

'You really don't have a clue what communist organisations are like!' Atima laughed. 'I didn't have any spare time. I had orders to follow—paper sales start at six every morning and go on until seven or eight at night. After that, all members are expected to attend meetings and seminars on political issues.'

'But what did you do when you wanted sex?'

Hodges enquired. 'I hope a chick with a body like yours wasn't reduced to wanking—that would be a tragic waste!'

'I was always too tired to wank!' Sheazan blushed. 'I'd fall into bed at one or two in the morning, after late-night sessions during which the party's policies were drilled into me. All the central London paper sellers would be gathered together and we'd go through a call and response routine based on topical political issues. I guess I've been brainwashed. Anyway, to get back to sex, I had more partners than I wanted or needed. I was very popular with the party leaders but since most of them were married, I mainly gave them blow jobs in the toilets during breaks at our meetings. Pretty sexist, huh? That's what really got me wondering about the party, their line on sexual equality doesn't bear any relation to their practice. Also, I had orders to sleep with anyone who seemed like they were interested in putting their name on a membership application form. I guess most of the male cadre were lured into joining through sex!'

'Imagine what it would be like if your leaders ever gained power!' Johnny exploded.

'It's a nightmare just thinking about it,' Atima cried. 'I guess most of the population would be put in camps. The elderly and disabled would be killed off, the party leaders sincerely believe that those who do not work, should not eat.'

'What have you been doing for money since you joined up with those scum?' Hodges enquired.

'I've been claiming welfare,' Sheazan explained, 'but I had to give half the money I got to the party, it was very hard surviving on what was left!'

Jock Graham was typing furiously on a battery-operated word processor. Neoism was the most exciting art movement he'd come across in years—and it was virtually unknown! The art critic was determined to write the standard work on the subject as the crowning achievement of his career. Graham had reached the first rank of his profession long ago—but the tome he intended to compose would place him on a par with the immortals, men such as Winckelmann and Ruskin, who'd altered the course of cultural history!

Spartacus also found himself drawn into the Neoist saga. He was fascinated by the endless bickering that went on between the assorted individuals who made up the group. It was incredible, as soon as one of the Neoists gained some success with a film or a book, all the others would denounce their former comrade as a show business sell-out. After a while, relations would be patched up and it then became another Neoist's turn to have a mountain of verbal abuse heaped upon them by the rest of the movement.

Smith scrawled down some of the messages sent to Bob Jones after his first novel was published—'You are like one of those stalinists who shit in wooden boxes; Try suicide, otherwise the public will forget your pathetic attempt at literature within the space of a week; You're a talentless prick, it's only by stealing ideas from all your friends that you've made the big time; I hope you drop dead after reading this epistle, so that I can have the pleasure of spitting on your grave.' Not only had virtually every Neoist sat down and written Jones an abusive letter, the group had actually gone to the trouble of publishing their hate mail as a pamphlet! Literary types within the British Isles generally considered this sort of thing a speciality of French intellectuals—but the text Spartacus was thumbing through proved that the surrealists and situationists weren't the only avant-garde groups to indulge in collective attempts at character assassination.

Jock Graham found it difficult to tear himself away from his research, although the art critic knew he'd work more efficiently if he took a half-hour break and ate a decent lunch. It was an act of will on Graham's part to shut down his portable computer. Eating seems like a trivial diversion to an art historian who's just spent a couple of hours immersed in exciting data about Neoism!

'Can I come with you if you're going for lunch?' Spartacus asked the older man.

'Sure,' Jock replied. 'I hope you don't object to the café here in the museum.'

'Not at all,' Smith gushed. 'The food is very good and the company will be even better. It's so exciting reading up about Neoism and now I've even got an expert with whom I can discuss this unknown art movement!'

'What is it you do?' Graham asked suspiciously, worried that this upstart was attempting to muscle in on his territory.

'I'm a painter,' Spartacus explained as the two men made their way to the restaurant. 'I've just signed up with Flipper Fine Art and I find Neoism very inspiring.'

'You're obviously an intelligent young man.' The art historian was relieved to discover that Smith's interest in the Neoists was perfectly innocent. 'I think Neoism is going to be enormous in a few years. In fact, I'm researching a book on the subject because the public needs to be enlightened about all the radical art activity that went on during the eighties. A lot of people think the period is typified by figurative wank and inflated prices—but that simply isn't true!'

Johnny Aggro was hanging out with Atima Sheazan in her Warren Street flat. The place was a dump—plaster was falling from the wall and the floor looked like it hadn't been cleaned in six months. They'd just swallowed a couple of the blotters the skinhead had liberated from the Holborn pusher.

'You've got what I've always wanted,' Hodges sighed. 'A W1 address, but this place ain't so great, I prefer my pad in Poplar. I thought all the housing in central London was supposed to be plush!'

'This flat is in a good location and the rent's cheap,' Atima replied. 'If the place didn't need renovating it would cost a bomb. Most of the other tenants are hookers, I think their clients expect to be taken somewhere seedy. It's funny coming home at night and running into these overweight businessmen on the stairs!'

'Hey,' Johnny asked, changing the subject. 'Have you got any fruit juice or sugar cubes?'

'No,' Sheazan said as she simultaneously shook her head. 'What on earth do you want with those things anyway?'

'One of the effects of taking acid,' the skinhead explained, 'is a constriction of the veins, so you need to increase the amount of glucose in your blood because of the slower rate of circulation. If there's not enough sugar in your system, the brain feels starved and that's what causes a bad trip!'

'That sounds like a load of old hippie shit!' Atima laughed.

'No, it's true!' Johnny protested. 'This doctor from Holland called Bart Hughes did a load of research into it. I'd better go out and get some orange juice before the acid starts taking effect.'

Hodges ran down the uncarpeted stairs and a minute later found himself out on the street. He went into the nearest grocery store and bought a carton of fruit juice and a packet of sugar cubes. Things seemed to be slowing down, it was as if Johnny was part of a super-eight movie that was being played at the wrong speed. Once he was back on the street, the skinhead popped a couple of sugar cubes into his mouth and rested against a plate-glass window. He'd feel better in a minute.

'Excuse me,' a bird in a leather jacket asked Johnny. 'Can you tell me how to get to Goodge Street?'

'Yeah,' the boot boy cackled. 'Turn left at the end of the universe and carry straight on till morning.'

'Very funny.'

The voice was coming at Hodges in great rolling waves. The skinhead figured it was best to get off the street and after what seemed like many hours wandering, he found himself back at Atima's flat. Sheazan was naked, she was sitting with her back against a wall. The ex-militant had a disposable razor in her right hand.

'You've shaved off your pubes!' Johnny exclaimed.

'I thought I might as well do something while I was waiting for you to come home,' Atima's voice was dripping like honey down the boot boy's throat. 'It's symbolic, now that I've left the party, I want to be born again!'

'Did I tell you I was a virgin?' Hodges figured he must be communicating telepathically because as far as he could work out, his mouth wasn't moving.

'I don't believe you!' Sheazan chided.

'It's true!' the skinhead protested. 'I've never had sex with you, have I?'

'I guess you're right,' Atima conceded.

Johnny was on his hands and knees, his tongue was snaking around Sheazan's shaved beaver. He could taste soap and blood. Hodges closed his eyes. When he opened them, his head was inside the girl's cunt. He licked at the pink ridges of flesh, after a while the skinhead blacked out. Later on, he found himself licking Atima's clit.

'You've cut yourself,' the boot boy observed, although he wasn't sure what the words meant.

'No I haven't,' Sheazan's voice was very far away. 'It's my period.'

What the hell, the skinhead figured the blood was nutritious and so it didn't really matter why he was lapping it up. Johnny just wanted to keep licking because the way Atima was moaning told him that she was more than halfway to paradise. The boot boy wanted to send the girl spinning through unknown aeons of outer space. The smell of rock music wafted up from under the floorboards and there was the thump thump thump of burnt toast coming from another flat. Hodges thought that Sheazan's swollen clit was going to explode in his mouth. He was working two fingers in and out of the girl's hole and she was shuddering in ecstasy.

Johnny's cock was twelve feet of pure manhood. Slithering, as if by a will of its own, through the four dimensions of time and space. Somehow, the love muscle found its way into Atima's mouth where it was licked, tickled and swallowed whole. The boot boy was rasping obscenities as love juice boiled through his groin. Sheazan kept working the tool as liquid genetics were pumped through it and down into her throat. As Hodges collapsed in a heap on the floor, he could see rats scuttling about in a basement that appeared to be located four or five hundred feet beneath him.

Aesthetics and Resistance enjoyed the time they spent in the Tate Gallery Library. Neoism was an inspiring subject and there was a great deal the wannabe art stars hoped to learn about it. Donald Pemberton considered it essential that he establish the exact date upon which the movement was founded. Tracing the demise of Neoism to December 7th 1986 was easy—but the movement's origins proved obscure. The word was first used in its modern sense during the summer of 1979 by a group in Montreal, Canada. The individuals responsible for this innovation included Kiki Bonbon, Lion Lazer, Napoleon Moffatt and Frater Neo. However, key concepts employed by these French Canadians were originated in the mid-seventies by mail artists David Zack, Al Ackerman and Maris Kundzin. Indeed, by 1978, the mail art cabal were using the term ISM to describe their activities. It appeared that the name adopted by the movement in its mature phase was coined by Frater Neo, who'd combined his own moniker with the descriptive term selected by Zack and company a year or so earlier. This state of affairs meant that the founding of Neoism could be placed virtually anywhere between March 1976 and May 1979.

'You'll have to pack up now, it's closing-time,' a librarian announced to the six individuals who'd been granted permission to study at the Tate that day.

'Damn,' Pemberton swore as he slammed a book shut, 'this stuff is so good I could spend all night reading it.'

'I'm afraid,' the woman said with a smile, 'it'll just have to wait until tomorrow.'

'Oh well,' Penny Applegate chipped in. 'I suppose that means I'll get a bit of sleep.'

'It's amazing the fascination our collection of Neoist material holds over the imagination of postgraduate students and art historians,' the librarian pontificated. 'Neoism is now the most popular subject among the scholars who use our facilities. Until recently, our most sought-after item was a collection of Mark Rothko letters—but not any more!'

'How did you come to possess such a remarkable collection of Neoist publications?' Applegate enquired.

'Various members of the movement brought in the material,' the librarian explained, 'and our buyer immediately recognised its importance. When Pete Horobin was living in London in 1984, he sold us an enormous number of goodies.'

'Did you get to meet him?' Penny cried in envy—she knew that Horobin had been a recluse for a good many years now and it was highly unlikely she'd ever speak to the great man.

'Of course not,' the librarian chided. 'I'm not old enough to have been working here in 1984! Now run along you two, I want to close up!'

Pemberton and Applegate did as they were told. Even if the library had stayed open all night, they'd have been unable to make much use of its facilities because they were meeting the other members of the Semiotic Liberation Front outside Mile End tube station at seven. From there, the gang would make its way up Grove Road to the Bow Studios where a major exhibition of contemporary sculpture was on display. The SLF had held a bull session on the attack the previous afternoon, so there was no need for any further discussion about this action. Spartacus had made sure that each Candidate for the Order knew exactly what was expected of them! Afterwards, they'd compare notes about their researches into Neoism.

Samson was hanging out in Johnny Aggro's flat listening to the *Do the Funky Chicken* album by Rufus Thomas—an old Stax classic that had long been a firm favourite with the membership of the Raiders. The skinhead was grooving to 'Turn Your Damper Down' and vaguely wondering what had happened to the rest of the gang when someone knocked on the front door. The boot boy fervently hoped Johnny's neighbours had come to complain about the noise because this would give him an excuse to punch them out—but the caller turned out to be Hodges' bit of posh.

'Hi!' Dr Maria Walker chirped.

'Hi!' Samson echoed.

'Is Johnny about?'

'No, but come in anyway.'

Maria accepted the offer and squeezed Samson's right buttock as she followed the skinhead down the hall. Walker wanted a good fucking and if Hodges wasn't at home, she was quite happy to make do with his friend.

'Hey,' the doctor cried as Samson was about to enter the living room. 'I don't want to muck about with small talk, let's just hit the sack!'

'You want me to screw you?' the skinhead asked in disbelief. He wasn't used to birds coming on this strong.

'Sure,' Maria replied, 'I want you to fuck my brains out! Do you think you're up to it?'

'I'll poke you so hard you won't be able to sit down for a week!' Samson snapped.

'Good!' Walker clucked as she stomped into the bedroom.

The skinhead followed the doctor through the door and split seconds later, they were both stripping. Samson had bulges in all the right places—and Maria thought he looked even better in the nude than when he was geared up in a pair of tightly cut sta-prest. After Walker stepped out of her black knickers, the skinhead threw her on to the bed. Samson had intended to jump on top of the doctor—but she was too fast for him and had rolled across the mattress before he was able to pin her down.

The boot boy liked rough sex and Maria was anything but submissive. It took a good ten minutes of wrestling and another five given over to cunt-licking before Samson got to sink his sausage in Walker's tunnel of love. There was nothing subtle about what the two of them were doing, there didn't need to be, this was sex at its primitive best.

'You send me, girl!' the skinhead rumbled.

'Fuck me!' the doctor bellowed.

'Your cunt is a black hole,' Samson rasped. 'It's like quicksand, dragging me under, sucking me in!'

'That feels so good!' Walker moaned.

'I can't stand it!' the boot boy spluttered. 'It feels so good, I wanna fuck forever, I'm about to cum!'

'Not yet, you bastard!' Maria chortled as she jabbed viciously at the skinhead's groin.

Samson's scream became a gurgle. Walker kept his body moving. It was like turning down the flame on a gas ring—the love juice that had been on the verge of boiling out of the boot boy's plonker was now simmering just below the crucial temperature. Samson and Maria were beating out the timeless rhythm of the swamps, squeezing flesh, running their hands over the innumerable tactile surfaces each possessed. The doctor was determined that the skinhead should not enjoy the psychic delights of sexual release until she'd taken him way beyond the limits of physical excess.

Spartacus led the Semiotic Liberation Front into the Bow Studios. Smith had stolen a set of keys from an artist-friend who worked in the building and so the operation was easily accomplished. On display were two dozen life-sized figures carved from solid blocks of wood. They represented the life's work of a recluse who'd turned to art after being jilted by the woman he'd hoped to marry. Each initiate was handed a saw and ordered to hack away at a sculpture.

'I can't do this!' Eugene De Freud whined. 'I can't wantonly destroy art. A man's put his whole life into these works!'

'What are you?' Don Pemberton demanded. 'A man or a bloody mouse? I feel no compunction about hacking up second-rate work. Besides, we'll never get signed up by top-flight galleries if we disobey the orders we've received from Hiram's masters!'

'Don's right!' Penny Applegate put in. 'Anyway, the guy who made this work died last year—and we can't allow the traditions of the dead generations to dominate the lives of the living!'

'What's more,' Spartacus hissed, 'we're not gonna destroy the work, we're simply improving it. Think about Asger Jorn and what he was doing with his Institute For Creative Vandalism or those detourned oil paintings. Like Asger, we're adding an air of mystery to a set of very conservative works. This is poetry in the true sense of the word, we're carrying on the great traditions of the surrealists, situationists and Neoists!'

'Okay, okay,' De Freud snapped. 'You've convinced me! So let's stop chattering and get creative!'

Without further ado, the Semiotic Liberation Front set to work. Spartacus decapitated a sculpture of an old man, Applegate sawed the arms off a young woman and Pemberton mutilated the genitals of a naked athlete. Ross MacDonald and Joseph Campbell were spray-painting two male figures a lurid shade of pink, while De Freud amputated a leg belonging to a milkmaid.

As limbs piled up on the floor, other members of the SLF organised them into aesthetically pleasing arrangements. After some time had passed, Spartacus was satisfied with the improvements he'd made to various sculptures and so he picked up a can of spray-paint and left the following message on a wall:

'*Our Flaming Star is the Torch of Reason. Those who possess this knowledge are indeed ILLUMINATI. Hiram, who was slain for the REDEMPTION OF SLAVES, has risen again. The Nine Masters are the Founders of the Order. Ours is a Royal Art, inasmuch as it teaches us to walk without trammels, and to govern ourselves. THE SEMIOTIC LIBERATION FRONT is the man or womun sitting next to you, they have a gun in their pocket and anger in their heart. You can't kill an idea. We are getting closer—Communiqué 1, SLF.*' As Smith underlined the last three letters of this message with a flourish, the gallery was still a hive of purposeful activity and any unbiased observer would have found it hard to believe that they were witnessing a guerrilla raid on the Bow Studios—since the scene so closely resembled a group of artists enthusiastically preparing work for an exhibition.

Six

JOHNNY AGGRO FELT rough. Had he been a pulp hack, the skinhead would have used some cliché about the bottom of a parrot's cage to describe his condition. The instant coffee Atima Sheazan had made was sloshing around Johnny's guts like bilge-water in a sinking ship. The boot boy's head was throbbing and the constant ringing on the front door bell wasn't doing him much good either.

'Fuck off!' Sheazan thundered out of the window at the caller—who was standing four storeys beneath her.

'You're backsliding,' some marxist moron billowed, 'you weren't at the meeting last night, your paper sales are down, you're not pulling your weight, come down here this minute and explain yourself.'

'Drop dead!' Atima barked before slamming the window shut.

The communist cunt had his finger jammed on the door bell. Hodges could see there was only one way to sort out the situation, and so he made his way down to the street. The skinhead whipped open the front door and hauled the red wanker into the hallway. Johnny threw the bastard against a wall and then slammed his fist against a weak chin. The boot boy liked the way the militant's head snapped back and cracked against the whitewashed plaster. In fact, the skinhead liked the sensation so much that he repeatedly smashed his knuckles into the marxist's face.

'You slithering piece of shit!' Hodges snarled as he slammed a steel toe-capped boot into his opponent's groin. 'You're bleedin' all over me button-down and sta-prest!'

'Pppplllleeeeaaaazzzzeeee!' the scumbag gurgled as he slid to the floor.

This request for mercy did the red bastard no good whatsoever. Johnny felt great as his boot crunched against ribs and landed with deadly effect at other weak points on what was an already broken body. The skinhead wanted to stomp the communist cretin into the ground. Political fundamentalism thrived in the concrete jungles of Europe and America, and this particularly vile manifestation of social atavism was most prevalent among the offspring of the idle rich. Those infected with this disease were semi-savage and understood but one thing—FORCE! Johnny wanted the skinhead movement to sort out this menace—because once you put teeth back into all the old bulldogs who'd once donned boots, sta-prest and a button-down shirt, then school kids would have a youth culture they could look up to and respect.

'Stop! Stop!' Atima hollered as she pulled at the boot boy's sleeve. 'You've beaten Michael unconscious. The party will have my guts for garters if you kill the poor sod!'

'Listen baby,' Hodges panted as he caught his

breath. 'If they touch one hair on your beautiful head I'll do the lot of 'em!'

'But what are you gonna do with Michael?' Sheazan demanded.

'Put him out with the trash,' Johnny snorted. 'That's where garbage belongs.'

'Don't you think we ought to call an ambulance?' Atima countered.

'Nah,' Hodges replied as he dragged the unconscious militant into the street. 'We'll just dump 'im 'ere, next to the bin bags. Hopefully the council's rubbish collectors will take the bastard away.'

Jock Graham stared unseeingly at the ceiling of the National Art Library. He'd been hit by the intangible sensation that crawls out of every professional researcher's guts when they're about to discover something BIG. The art historian wasn't certain just what it was he'd stumbled upon—but pieces of the jigsaw were beginning to fit into place. Bob Jones was the key to this enigma, Graham was sure of that. There was something maddeningly familiar about the Neoist theoretician's prose style. Jock instinctively knew that solving this mystery would give a massive boost to the historical standing of the eighties' avant-garde.

'Are you alright?' Stephen Smith asked from the other side of a study table. 'I hope this doesn't sound rude, but you look like you're about to throw a fit.'

'Let's get outta here!' Graham barked. 'I need someone to talk to. Come on laddie, let's retire to the Flower Pot and get a few drinks down our throats.'

'Sure, anything you say Mr Graham,' Spartacus whispered submissively, hoping he hadn't antagonised this important art critic when it looked as if the great aesthetician was about to offer his hand in man to man friendship.

As the two men walked to the pub, Jock mumbled incoherently about Neoism being a flaming comet that would burn, and burn, and burn. According to the art critic, the movement had risen above the event horizon of contemporary cultural history and the illumination it now spread would transform world culture in its entirety. Once Smith had got a brandy down his companion's throat, the aesthetician began to make a bit more sense.

'Have you noticed how Neoism confronts us with all the fundamental problems connected to the process of historification?' Graham demanded.

'I can't say I have,' Spartacus confessed, 'but if you elaborate a little, I'm sure I'll see your point,'

'Let's try phrasing the question in a slightly different manner,' the art historian pontificated. 'What exactly do you think Neoism is?'

'A major avant-garde art movement,' Smith shot back. 'The biggest thing to happen culturally in the eighties, an important development of the tradition that encompasses futurism, dadaism, surrealism, situationism and fluxus.'

'Ah,' Graham sighed. 'You don't get it at all, do you! Neoism in itself is of no consequence.'

'But on the way over here you were rambling on about it being a comet that would burn, and burn, and burn!' Spartacus protested.

'Yes, yes,' Jock snapped impatiently, 'but you've missed my point completely. Why is the average art critic interested in lettrisme?'

'Well,' Smith hedged, 'it isn't of much interest

in itself. I guess most people have only heard about it as a precursor to situationism.'

'Precisely!' Graham blared. 'And that's my point about Neoism, it's what various individuals who were once members of the group went on to do at a later date that makes the movement important. If Bob Jones hadn't gone on to act as a central figure in the Plagiarist and Art Strike movements, Neoism would be of no interest whatsoever. It's only by the utterly false subsumption of Plagiarism and the Art Strike under the rubric of Neoism that we can make the latter movement appear as a substantial development of the avant-garde tradition. My God! If Bob Jones hadn't gone on to write a notorious text under the name K. L . . . Bleedin' hellfire, that's it! That's what's been gnawing at my guts. You'll have to excuse me, Stephen, I've some important records to check.'

Ross MacDonald, Joseph Campbell and Eugene De Freud had blagged their way on to the set of an upmarket chat show called *Upper Crust*, a live lunch-time production with a TV audience largely carved out of As, Bs, C1s and their dependants. The three Lodge members sat impatiently through the prattle of Jeremy Rolf's first guest, a certain Lady Greta Bollingersands-Greensborough. This upper-class imbecile spent twenty minutes enthusing about the needlework she'd just commissioned to replace worn upholstery on her family's priceless collection of Chippendale furniture.

'My next guest,' Rolf announced, 'should need no introduction to those of you who keep up with developments in contemporary culture. He's Sir Charles Brewster, head of the Progressive Arts Project. Together, we're going to talk about the major new exhibition of surrealist paintings that opens in London this week. Sir Charles, could you kick off by explaining how this new exhibition at the Lyle Galleries differs from previous presentations of surrealist work.'

'What we're witnessing with this exhibition is a new approach to the group, that's why it's called *Understanding the Surrealist Dream*. What the curators have done, is take the Freudian ideas that provided the theoretical backbone of the group's work, and used them to explore the content of the paintings on display.'

The three Lodge members were nudging each other, it was time to make their intervention—if they didn't act soon, it would be too late. As the conspirators leapt up from their seats, the producer of this live TV show instructed one of his cameramen to zoom in on the young upstarts.

'But isn't this a rather obvious approach to surrealism?' Rolf countered. 'I mean someone must have thought of doing it before, if not in England, in . . .'

'Enough of that old rubbish!' Eugene De Freud pealed. 'We don't want to talk about surrealism, let's discuss Neoism instead!'

'You scoundrels, behave yourselves!' a Chelsea pensioner spat as he launched himself at De Freud.

The pensioner didn't get anywhere near his target, he tripped over a woman's legs and landed flat on his face. The old codger hit the ground with a dull thud and failed to get up again because he was concussed.

'Is the old boy alright?' someone asked.

'Forget about that bozo,' Joseph Campbell snarled. 'It's his own fault if he's hurt! Let's talk about the Neoist Cultural Conspiracy—it's the biggest thing to hit this planet since Johann Valentin Andreae started the Rosicrucian furore with his *Fama Fraternitatis*,

Confessio Fraternitatis and *Chemical Wedding of Christian Rosencreutz*!'

'But I've got Sir Charles Brewster up here as my guest!' Rolf protested. 'And he was specifically booked to talk about this surrealist exhibition.'

'Jeremy, Jeremy,' Sir Charles coaxed, 'let's not be too rigid about things. I know these lads rather rudely interrupted us—but youth must have its fling! These boys will no doubt acquire better manners as they mature, in the meantime, why don't we show a bit of indulgence towards their enthusiasm for Neoism and talk about this exciting and virtually unknown avant-garde movement?'

'We can't possibly do that!' Rolf popped. 'Unless we talk about this surrealist show, I can kiss goodbye to my payola from the exhibition's sponsors!'

The talk show host clapped a hand over his mouth; in the heat of the moment he'd gone too far. Now, instead of missing out on a two-week foreign holiday, he was about to witness the demise of his career. There was bound to be a scandal over this abuse of media privilege.

'Guards!' Sir Charles trumpeted at some security men who were closing in on the brothers from the Semiotic Liberation Front. 'Leave those youngsters alone. Jeremy looks too pale to carry on with the show. I want you to clear a path so that the three guys who are standing up can get across to the stage. Then we'll be able to engage in an intimate chat about Neoism without having to shout at each other.'

The Progressive Arts Project supremo had a way with words and his instructions were instantly obeyed. Rolf scuttled off the stage as the Lodge members seated themselves in three well-upholstered chairs.

'Great, great,' the producer was mumbling to himself. 'This is gonna get *Upper Crust* a load of press coverage, the ratings will soar!'

'Thank you Sir Charles,' Ross MacDonald said as he held out his hand. 'I'm also speaking for my two friends when I say we consider it a great honour that you should allow us up here to talk about Neoism.'

'No, no,' Brewster insisted, 'the honour is all mine. We can't allow graft in the art world, it should be a repository of great spiritual values. You've done us all a favour by exposing a sinister plot to manipulate the public. Now, for the benefit of our viewers, could you kick off by giving a brief definition of Neoism.'

'Well,' MacDonald paused for dramatic effect. 'Neoism was a cultural movement influenced by futurism, dada, fluxus and punk, that emerged from the mail art movement in the late seventies . . .'

After waiting an hour for Michael Douglas-Hunt to make a triumphant return to the *Marxist Times* HQ with a suitably chastised Atima Sheazan in tow, the grey eminence who ran the operation sent out a gang of five heavies to locate his errant follower.

'I hope Sheazan is assigned a sexual punishment for her transgressions,' the first heavy croaked to his comrades as they marched down Warren Street. 'I'd like to lead the gang bang as she's fucked by every man in our unit, then at the end of the session, go down on the bitch and lick all the spunk out of her cunt.'

'I'd like to shove my cock down Atima's throat,' the second heavy snarled. 'That girl should be punished for the way she looks, just the mention of her name gets my juices going.'

'Here we are,' the third heavy announced. 'This

is where she lives. Are we gonna ring on the bell or shall we kick down the door?'

'Try the buzzer,' the fourth heavy put in, 'if we don't get an answer within thirty seconds, we'll be completely justified in resorting to more primitive methods.'

Johnny Aggro stuck his head out of the window split seconds after the fifth heavy pressed the bell connected to Atima's top floor flat. The skinhead wasn't intimidated by the gang of communist cretins gathered in the street. He knew exactly how to deal with this type of scum.

'What d'ya want?' the boot boy demanded.

'Atima,' the first heavy replied. 'We want her to come down here immediately.'

'She's in the bath,' Hodges proclaimed. 'And she ain't getting out till she's finished washing.'

'If she doesn't get out of the tub this instant,' the second heavy barked, 'I'll come up and drag her out.'

Johnny didn't bother with a verbal response, he simply leapt out of the window. Heavies one and two crumpled like paper men as the soles of Hodges' size ten DMs smashed into their thick skulls. The boot boy was as lithe as a cat and landed on his feet after crushing his first two opponents with this aerial assault. The third heavy's teeth were rammed down his throat by a powerful punch. Heavy four was convinced that advancing on Hodges from behind made the skinhead an easy target. The marxist moron wasn't prepared for the elbow that pummelled backward into his guts or the heel that came crashing down on his right foot. Heavy five stepped back into the road hoping to give himself the time and space in which to launch a successful counter-attack. Unfortunately, the Green Cross Code hadn't been drummed into this bozo's head as effectively as Maoist propaganda—and the cretin was run down by a passing car.

Two policemen arrived at the scene as Johnny was demonstrating to heavy number four that the average human head isn't nearly as tough as a brick wall. Heavy number three was puking his guts, one and two were unconscious, while number five was dead.

'Hello, hello, hello,' one of the cops said as he tapped Johnny on the shoulder. 'What's going on here then?'

'Thank God you've arrived officer!' Hodges thundered. 'I was set upon by this gang of communist thugs. I don't know how much longer I could have held them off. You've probably saved my life!'

'Think nothing of it,' the PC replied. 'It's all in the line of duty. However, I'll have to take a statement from you once we've arrested your assailants.'

'He just stepped out into the road without looking,' the motorist was gibbering. 'He had his back to the road and he just stepped out. I slammed on the brakes but I was right on top of him. It's a nightmare, a nightmare.'

'Can I do anything to help?' Johnny asked as the cops handcuffed the red hoodlums.

'We've got everything under control,' one of the PCs assured the boot boy. 'Detaining suspects is best left to the professionals. However, as a concerned citizen, you could get involved with your local Neighbourhood Watch scheme. If you did that and helped lobby parliament for higher police pay, you'd certainly be doing your bit for law and order.'

'What a marvellous idea!' Hodges exclaimed. 'I've always supported the police and here's an eminently practical way of expressing my feelings on this matter.'

*

Karen Eliot hadn't been expecting any visitors and she'd ignored the first few rings on her doorbell. However, the persistence of this unexpected caller had ruined her enjoyment of a long hot bath and the top-flight artist figured she might as well find out who wanted to see her so desperately.

'Who is it?' Karen demanded as she secured a man's dressing-gown around her svelte figure.

'Jock Graham,' replied the disembodied voice at the other end of the entry phone.

'Come up, then,' Eliot replied as she pressed the button that opened the door.

Three minutes later, the marxist art critic was lounging in Karen's living room with a coffee perched on his knee.

'I've been doing some research,' Jock announced, 'and I've discovered that K. L. Callan and Bob Jones are the same person. I've checked the relevant birth records. Jones was born illegitimately and then adopted. His birth mother registered him with the authorities as Kevin Llewellyn Callan. After the adoption, his name was legally changed to Bob Jones. There can be no doubt about the fact that Jones is the Callan who wrote *Marx, Christ and Satan United In Struggle*.'

'If you're right,' Karen retorted, 'why has Jones never claimed authorship of that notorious work? It certainly wouldn't harm his outlaw reputation to be identified with the book.'

'I accept,' Graham lisped, 'that if the public were to know the truth, this wouldn't hurt Jones—but it would destroy the aura of mystery surrounding the text.'

'Anyway,' Eliot interjected. 'Why are you telling me this? Why not confront Bob about it instead?'

'I'll get on his case later!' Jock cried. 'I came

here first because I was doing some research down the road and I wanted to talk to you about the symbolism of a Neoist work entitled *The Alchemical Toilet*.'

'What about it?' Karen sparred.

'Well,' Graham snapped, 'if you spell Eliot backwards and then stick a "T" on the end, you get the word toilet!'

'And just what is the significance of the "T"?' Karen cackled.

'I was getting on to that,' the art critic persisted. 'The "T" has various esoteric meanings, among other things it stands for transformation—an alchemical transformation, spiritual changes as well as material ones. The way a capital "T" branches at the top represents the left and right hand paths to enlightenment in the Gnostic tradition, the ways of abstinence and indulgence. The "T" is also a truncated cross, a symbol representing St George, the Templars and the Rosicrucians.'

'It's also commonly used to represent Christ,' Eliot observed.

'Yes, yes,' Jock snorted. 'In *The Alchemical Toilet*, you are depicted as Keter Elyon, the supreme crown. In the Cabalist tradition this is a synonym for God. Keter Elyon represents God in all his guises, whether as Christ, the Father or the Holy Ghost. Furthermore, Karen is the Danish form of Katherine, meaning pure. Eliot is a diminution of Elias, which can be traced back to the Hebrew JAWE meaning God.'

'But,' Karen giggled, 'I'm the wrong gender to be the messiah!'

'Not in the Gnostic tradition,' the art critic explained. 'That's why the "T" has been added to the reversed version of your name, it's all about transformation. The references in *The Alchemical Toilet* to a second marriage between the Thames and the Rhine are the key to this mystery. As well as referring us back to the marriage of Elizabeth Stuart and the Elector Palatine which provided the inspiration for the first Rosicrucian movement, it tells anyone who understands the symbolism that this time the roles will be reversed according to Cabalist law. Stiletto represents both Germany and the femail principle, you only have to look as far as a womun's shoes to see the significance of "his"—or perhaps I should say "her"—name.'

'But this is crazy!' Karen insisted. '*The Alchemical Toilet* hardly ranks among Neoism's great achievements. Graf Haufen knew it wasn't up to scratch after completing it—which is why he issued the work under the *nom de plume* Monty Cantsin.'

'*The Alchemical Toilet* isn't second-rate!' Graham bellowed. 'It's the work of an evil genius. Haufen adopted the name "Can't Sin" because it provides a further reference to the Gnostic tradition within which the Neoists were working.'

'The public hardly needed reminding of the movement's connections to the occult,' Eliot countered, 'when the word Neoism was lifted from the writings of Aleister Crowley. Besides, the name Monty Cantsin was invented by David Zack, and Maris Kundzin was the first person to use it.'

'Look,' Jock decided to try the direct approach. 'I know you're the head of a secret society that traces its origins back through Freemasonry and the Rosicrucians to the Knights' Templar. The Templars weren't really suppressed by the Vatican in 1307, they survived as an underground stream—or sewer, if you like—in the history of Europe. This partly accounts for the title of *The Alchemical Toilet*. After a faked suppression, the Templars became the secret arm of the Guelph or Papal party. Although not of the same antiquity, the Rosicrucians were the Chibelline equivalent of the Templars. The founding of the Grand Lodge in 1717 marks the point at which the Templar Order fell under the control of Chibelline agents. From this date on, Masonry was used as a cover for the covert intelligence operations of the Chibelline or Empire faction. Neoism is simply a new Rosicrucian dawn, disguised in the form of an art movement! In its own way, the avant-garde is as important to the conspiracy as older institutions such as Gresham College, the Invisible College, that acts as the secret power co-ordinating the activities of both the Royal Society and institutionalised religion, on behalf of the Mercers' and Drapers' Guilds!'

'Preposterous!' Karen snorted.

'I knew you'd say that!' Graham exclaimed in triumph. 'Only someone deeply implicated in the Chibelline plot to destroy civilisation would dismiss my research in such a summary fashion! This proves that you are the evil genius controlling the forces of the conspiracy! Comrade Stalin was right to attack rootless cosmopolitan elements. Where he went wrong was in refusing to recognise that the British Crown and its allies in the City of London were the hidden hand directing the Zionist bankers!'

TK was hanging out in Johnny Aggro's flat. He didn't know when the rest of the gang would show up and so he'd decided to give *Piss Pot Party* yet another viewing. The on-screen action got the young skinhead well steamed up. As four studs pissed over a blonde actress, TK undid his flies and took out his cock. While the camera tracked across a locker room to where a brunette was pissing in a body-builder's mouth, the boot boy began to beat his meat.

'Don't let me interrupt you,' Maria Walker announced as she walked into the room.

'Who let you in?' TK demanded as he unsuccessfully attempted to zip himself up.

'Nobody,' the doctor replied. 'The door was on the latch. And do be careful, you could suffer a serious injury if your prick gets caught in your fly. In fact, I think I ought to take a look at your manhood, just in case you've hurt it.'

Walker got down on her knees, and once the swollen love muscle was in her hand, inspected it. The skinhead moaned crazily, what the doctor was doing felt really good.

'You're okay,' Maria observed. 'In a minute or two I'm gonna swallow your length but you'd better not cum in my mouth, you're to hold back so that you can give my cunt a thrashing!'

Walker ran her tongue along TK's genetic pump. The boot boy grunted in appreciation. The doctor's head jerked crazily as she licked her way up and down the length. Then, holding the base of the tool in her right hand, she took the tip of the organ into her mouth. Maria's head bobbed like a buoy in a storm-tossed sea as the prick disappeared into her orifice. TK's plonker slid into Walker's throat and the skinhead let out a great bellow of pleasure. If the boot boy had gone with the tidal flow of his desires, he'd have shot his wad there and then. Years of sexual discipline enabled him to hold on to his love juice. DNA codes were scrambled and unscrambled across two bodies that appeared to have merged and become one. Million-year-old genetic impulses were fighting for control of these human bulks. TK was howling for sexual release.

Maria hitched up her skirt and tugged a pair of lace panties down her legs. The doctor's twat was dripping wet. The skinhead wanted to lap up this sexual dew but Walker made him plunge his manhood into her black hole of a cunt. There was nothing subtle about what the two of them did next, there didn't need to be, they simply pumped up the volume. The boot boy was a piston and Maria provided him with lubrication. As a sexual athlete, the skinhead had no use for humanistic platitudes about love—instead, his personality had been abandoned to the superior programming of the DNA. TK and the doctor were not individuals, they were ciphers, the two digits required to set a binary system in motion.

'You're a machine, an android, a robot!' Maria roared as her partner worked her up towards orgasm.

'Overload, overload!' TK yowled as love juice boiled inside his groin.

'There's loads of it!' Walker stormed as she felt the skinhead cum inside her. 'It feels so good, all that cum, it feels like you're pissing up my cunt!'

The boot boy looked across at the TV screen. What he saw was yet another golden shower. He reflected that the repetitious nature of porno videos was deeply reassuring. Endless bump and grind routines gave shape to a world where everything solid melts into air.

Donald Pemberton and Penelope Applegate were strolling through Soho. Having put in a hard day at the Tate researching Neoism, they were on their way to Pâtisserie Valerie for tea and cakes. Don was musing on his standing as a genius. It vexed the young artist that while he was undoubtedly the single greatest personage alive, it would take a year or so before the man in the street recognised him as occupying a place above Nelson and Thomas à Becket in the pantheon of national heroes.

'Watch out!' Applegate clamoured as she pulled Pemberton back from the road. 'You nearly got yourself run down, you should look before stepping out from the curb!'

'Dear me, dear me,' the artist mumbled. 'I must take greater care of myself. If I was to die young, it would deprive humanity of the marvellous fruits that are still maturing in my imagination.'

'Hey look at that!' Penny exclaimed as she dragged Donald into the doorway of an empty shop. 'There's a set of keys in the door lock, I wonder if we can get inside?'

'Who cares!' Pemberton snapped. 'Let's get to Valerie's, I'm half-starved and my throat's parched.'

'But if we can get into the shop,' Applegate protested, 'we'd have a central London venue for the *New Neoism*!'

'What a great idea of mine!' Don observed as he turned the key. 'And look, I've opened the door! Wow, our own gallery in Old Compton Street! The chaps back at the Stratford studios will be green with envy!'

Aesthetics and Resistance took a wander around the building. At the back there was a cramped kitchen and toilet, a staircase took the deadly duo down to a basement that had once been used for storing goods.

'Perfect, perfect, ouch!' Pemberton yelped as he walked into a brick wall.

'Do be careful, darling,' Penelope warned a little too late. 'It's rather dark down here and you could easily hurt yourself.'

'I know, I fucking know!' Donald snarled. 'I'm a man of genius, so stop treating me like a cretin!'

'Sweetness,' Applegate demurred, 'why don't we call our gallery Akademgorod? If the first exhibition is to be the *New Neoism*, then it would be most fitting to name the venue after the movement's promised land.'

'That's it, that's bloody it, I'll call the gallery Akademgorod!' Pemberton thundered. 'What a great name for a squatted space!'

'Whatever you say, sugar,' Penny concurred.

'Aaaarrrrggggghhhh!' Don screeched as he tripped over a crate and fell flat on his face. 'Help me! Help me! Call a doctor, call an ambulance, call the police! I think I'm dying. I'm in agony, fucking agony!'

'You don't sound like you're dying,' Applegate ventured.

'Don't contradict me, slut!' Pemberton bellowed. 'Call a photographer and notify the press. I want a state funeral in Westminster Abbey and make sure the service is covered on live TV. I'm to be buried in my black beret and leather jacket.'

'Let me help you up, oooohhhh, you're heavy!' Penelope coaxed as she examined her boyfriend in the dim light that filtered down from the cellar's open door. 'Nothing more than a few bruises and a tiny cut on your right hand.'

Johnny Aggro was banging away at Atima Sheazan. The boot boy had a feeling for sex and the way this chick writhed beneath his naked body was something to behold. The join between Sheazan's legs was given over to a sucking pit of a cunt—and as the bird thrust her pelvis upwards, Hodges' love muscle penetrated fresh swathes of formless chaos.

'Oh baby, that feels so good!' Sheazan moaned. 'I want you to fuck me forever!'

'You dirty bitch,' Hodges hissed. 'You fuck so good that my guts will be shot through my prick when I cum!'

'Fuck me, baby, fuck me!' Sheazan bellowed. 'I don't want you to slacken the pace, I want you to flood my insides with your cum. Baby, baby, baby, thrust your cock right into me! Deeper, deeper! Fuck me, you fucker, FUCK ME! THAT FEELS SO FUCKING GOOD! SHOVE IT UP ME, SHOVE IT RIGHT UP ME! OH MY FUCKING GOD! OH, I CAN FEEL IT, IT'S LIKE A FUCKING EXPLOSION! THERE'S LOADS OF IT! I CAN FEEL YOUR SPUNK DRIBBLING OUT OF MY CUNT AND ON TO THE BED. OH, IT FEELS FUCKING LOVELY!'

Hodges rolled over and let his head sink against a pillow. He felt beautiful. Atima had opened up new vistas of sexual pleasure, sights that beckoned him towards Unknown Kaddath. Johnny wanted to fall into one of those satisfying post-coital sleeps—but some bastard had jammed their finger against the buzzer to Sheazan's flat.

'You stay where you are,' Atima told the skinhead. 'Get a bit of kip and let me sort this out.'

'No way,' the boot boy replied as he got up and pulled on his sta-prest. 'It's probably some cunt from the *Marxist Times* and I'm not gonna let them touch one hair on your beautiful head.'

'I can take care of myself!' Sheazan protested.

'That may be true,' Johnny countered, 'but it doesn't prevent me from doing the cunt who's come round to hassle you!'

In the end, both Atima and the skinhead raced

down the stairs. Some bozo was attempting to break into the building by kicking down the front door. Johnny worked the handle and the marxist moron fell flat on his back as the sole of his boot failed to connect with anything more than thin air. Hodges booted the cunt in the ribs, then smashed a heel into the bastard's face. Atima raced out into the street and was moving like a whirlwind among a score of her former comrades. Sheazan fought like a fury, breaking noses and teeth with her fists, then rupturing groins and guts with well-aimed kicks and savage elbow thrusts.

'You can really fight girl!' the boot boy shouted admiringly as he threw a communist cretin against a brick wall. 'I certainly don't fancy taking you on, you're fucking tough!'

Atima smiled, she appreciated this praise. Simultaneously, her fist cracked into an opponent's mouth, breaking two front teeth. The toothless Maoist stumbled back into the road and was knocked down by a passing cyclist. Sheazan's boot caught another of her former comrades in the bollocks. The cunt mewed like a mauled cat as his feet momentarily left the ground, then he fell back on his arse.

The odds in this battle had been decisively turned. Although the communists still held the numerical advantage, beneath their discredited ideology these bozos were yellow cowards who preferred hiding behind their university degrees and privileged backgrounds to engaging in a fair fight. Atima and Johnny had the reds on the run. The five Maoists who hadn't been floored were treated to boots up the arse as they bolted for safety.

'Tell your lousy leader that Atima's seen sense and quit his poxy organisation,' Johnny catcalled at the activists as they disappeared down the escalators at Warren Street tube station.

'I think we've seen the last of the *Marxist Times* crew,' Sheazan informed Hodges as they made their way back to her flat.

Seven

JOHNNY AGGRO WAS greeting a new day with Desmond Dekker's all-time classic album *You Can Get It If You Really Want* blasting from his hi fi. The disk had been well-played but back in 1970 Trojan still made their records with a sufficient thickness of vinyl for the platters to last a lifetime if they were looked after and didn't suffer any mishaps at the drunken parties where they were dancing favourites. The title track was one of two killer cuts on the LP written by Jimmy Cliff, the other being 'That's the Way Life Goes', the rest of the songs were original Dekker compositions. Hodges was grooving to 'Peace on the Land' when the phone rang.

'Hello!' the skinhead barked after picking up the receiver.

'Johnny baby, it's Atima,' a voice at the other end of the line announced. 'Are you okay?'

'Yeah,' Hodges assured her.

'Have you missed me?' Sheazan demanded.

'Sure,' Johnny replied, since this was obviously

what the bird wanted to hear. Actually, the boot boy didn't see how he could be missing Atima, since he'd only met her for the first time a couple of days ago.

'I think I did the right thing last night, sending you home and then phoning up my family to say I'd like to see them again,' Sheazan said in a soft voice. 'As I'd hoped, dad came straight over in his car, we packed up all my gear and I've moved back to Finchley. This reconciliation is working out alright.'

'Good,' Hodges put in.

'It all seems so strange,' Atima sighed, 'giving up the party and being back with the folks. Listen, I've got to stay in for dinner tonight—but could you meet me afterwards, what about nine o'clock at Camden tube?'

'That sounds alright,' Johnny affirmed.

'Good,' Sheazan purred. 'I'll see you at nine. I've got to go now, my mum's calling me. I love you, bye.'

'Ciao.' Johnny wasn't much given to using foreign expressions but this was one that he happened to like.

Hodges flipped over his Desmond Dekker platter. 'Pickney Gal' was the first track on the second side. The boot boy was speculating on how the partnership between the reggae singer and his brilliant producer would have developed if Leslie Kong hadn't died of a heart attack in 1971. The two men had been working together for the best part of a decade and had Kong lived another five years, it seemed likely Dekker would have been bigger than Elvis, the Beatles, Dylan or the Stones. Any objective observer could see that DD had more talent in his little finger than these rock acts displayed over the course of two dozen releases. The skinhead was tapping his foot to 'Polka Dot' when the phone rang again.

'Alright?' the boot boy boomed.

'Johnny, it's Karen. Where the fuck have you been? I must have rung you a dozen times yesterday!'

'I was out with a chick,' Hodges said indifferently.

'Is that supposed to impress me?'

'No, it's just a statement of fact.'

'Okay, okay. But get your arse over here, I want to have a chat with you about how our little caper with this secret society is progressing.'

'Sure thing boss,' Hodges yapped before hanging up.

Aesthetics and Resistance were having to swallow their pride and hide the resentment they felt towards Stephen Smith. As head of the Lodge, Spartacus had taken it upon himself to direct the artistic work of his brethren and dictate the shape of their *New Neoism* exhibition. Don Pemberton had wanted to rename their squatted shop Akademgorod. Smith made him hand-paint the words Thumbprint Gallery in crude lettering on the exterior of the building. Penny Applegate suggested cleaning and repainting the front space but Spartacus insisted that leaving it as it was lent the place an air of authenticity.

'It's beautiful, just beautiful!' the Grand Dragon exclaimed. 'Now, let's go and find some heavily fly-posted fencing and bag ourselves some art!'

'What on earth are you talking about?' Eugene De Freud demanded. 'I thought this was an opportunity to expose the public to our latest works? There won't be room for my canvases if we fill the place with rubbish scavenged from the streets.'

'Well that's just tough, ain't it!' Stephen snapped.

'The *New Neoism* should be a riot of avant-garde influences. Weathered posters provide an excellent reference to both Nouveau Realisme and Auto-Destructive Art. Besides, I've already decided we're having paper works not canvases on the walls!'

'In that case,' Freud whined, 'I'm going home!'

'Go ahead then,' Spartacus spewed, 'but if you piss off, I'm kicking you out of our Lodge and you can kiss goodbye to any hope of a gallery career!'

'You can't do that!' Eugene wailed. 'It's unethical, it's undemocratic, it's not fair!'

'I'm in charge of this Lodge!' Smith barked. 'I'm your chief and you've gotta knuckle under to the discipline I impose upon you. The very strength of the Semiotic Liberation Front lies in the fact that it is organised on a rigidly hierarchical basis. The élite is necessarily an organised minority whose control structure enables them to dominate the disorganised mass. You're to do what I say and we'll have no more gripes premised on decadent notions of equality!'

'Okay, boss!' Freud spluttered.

'That's better,' the Grand Dragon mewed. 'Now I want you out on the streets of Soho and I don't wanna see your face until you've got enough art to fill this gallery.'

Having dismissed the Minerval, Spartacus took tins of red, yellow, blue and black paint from a carrier. He assigned Penny, Don, Ross MacDonald and Joseph Campbell a colour each. Smith stood out in the street while his Lodge members created an instant action painting across the floor, walls and ceiling of the gallery. This was an excellent background against which to overhang ripped and torn posters.

'Get yourselves cleaned up!' Spartacus instructed

his paint-splattered co-workers. 'I'm off to find some malfunctioning electronic gear. We need a score of obsolete word processors that can be infected with a deadly computer virus. I could do with a few camcorders as well, fuck knows where I'll get any for free. I might have to send you all on a nicking spree. Anyway, I want you to hang on here while I check out places that might donate us unwanted gadgetry.'

'Yes, boss,' the Lodge members chanted in unison.

Karen handed Johnny Aggro a coffee and then sat down beside him.

'So how's it going with Smith?' the art star demanded.

'Great!' Johnny enthused. 'He's got a Lodge together and they've done a few actions.'

'I'd gathered that,' Eliot spouted. 'Word is out on the art scene that there's a surge of interest in Neoism. The research our Minervals have undertaken into the eighties' avant-garde has had a snowball effect and now hundreds of students are at it as well. I also heard about the attack on the Bow Studios, it's caused a furore among culture vultures.'

'In that case,' Hodges mumbled, 'I dunno why you had me come round, you know what's gone down.'

'What I want,' Karen said as she placed her hand on the skinhead's knee, 'is a first-hand account of life in the Lodge.'

'I can't give you that!' Johnny protested. 'I'm not a member, my only contact with the group is through Stephen Smith. As far as I can make out, Smith has set himself up as the leader and is dicking everybody else about.'

'I want you to attend a Lodge meeting,' the art star instructed as she unzipped the boot boy's fly, 'and then report back to me on everything you see.'

'But I might be recognised!' Hodges yelled.

'There's not much chance of that,' Karen assured him as his cock swelled in her hand. 'You don't know anyone in the art world. But if you're worried about being identified, you could always wear a mask as a security measure.'

'I hadn't thought of that!' the skinhead roared.

Eliot didn't give a verbal reply, she just worked Johnny's meat with her hand. Hodges slumped back on the couch, he liked being wanked off by good-looking birds. In many ways, it was better than fucking because a bloke didn't have to put in any effort. However, not liking to think of himself as passive, the boot boy pawed Karen's tits.

'You're a randy bastard,' the art star sneered as she dropped the meat she'd been working with her hand.

'Don't stop!' the skinhead squawked. 'I'm about to cum.'

'Tough on you!' Eliot laughed.

Johnny grabbed his meat and began working it himself. Karen got up, went across to a cupboard and took out her camcorder. By the time she had it running, Hodges had spunked up. The most exciting shot she got was one of the boot boy zipping up his flies.

'Hey,' Karen giggled. 'Don't you wanna perform for me? Are you camera shy or something? I'll put on some music and you can strip to it.'

'Nah!' Johnny erupted. 'That ain't my scene! What do you think I am, a bleedin' hunk of meat without any feelings of my own?'

*

Jock Graham had been doing intensive research. Having made a mental note of some of the books he'd clocked in Karen Eliot's flat, the art critic had subsequently checked out works like Still's *New World Order: Ancient Plan of Secret Societies* and Wurmbrand's *Marx: Prophet of Darkness*. As a consequence, Graham now realised that supporting the communist cause had been a terrible mistake on his part. Both the League of the Just and the Communist International had been fronts for the Illuminati! Neoism was another arm of the conspiracy and had to be smashed to prevent Satanic wreckers from destroying civilisation. Graham drew strength from his newly discovered faith in the Christian religion and thus fortified, set out on a mission to save the world from evil conspirators.

'Do you believe in Jesus?' Jock blubbered.

'You what?' Amanda Debden-Philips snorted in disbelief.

'Have you let Christ into your heart?' Graham demanded.

'Have you gone mad?' Amanda cried. 'Or have you taken up performance art because you're sick of being a critic?'

'Neither!' the fundamentalist snarled. 'I've simply found God, the true path, the way and the light.'

'I'm sure that must be . . .' Debden-Philips hesitated for a moment while she tried to think of the right turn of phrase, 'that must be very satisfying for you.'

'It's not a matter of personal satisfaction!' Jock snivelled. 'By turning to Jesus, I've saved my soul from eternal damnation! Having experienced God's grace, I now want to repay his love for me as an erring son. I want to save others from the mistakes I made, prevent them falling into the hands of communists who are fronting for Satan!'

'Well, I suppose it'll give you something to do on a Sunday,' Amanda observed. 'However, you've still got to earn a living. Have you written your review of our Karen Eliot show yet? I hope the interview you did with her went well.'

'I'm not giving that evil womun any further publicity!' Graham snapped. 'Along with various other members of the Neoist movement such as Bob Jones, she's a key figure in the conspiracy to destroy the Christian faith.'

'Come on!' Debden-Philips laughed. 'This is nonsense! We're both doing very nicely out of Karen, she's earning the gallery pots of money and you've made more than a few bob writing about her work.'

'You've got to drop Eliot!' the art critic babbled. 'If you continue to promote her now that I've given you this warning, then you're gonna suffer all the agonies of hell, burning forever amidst the fires of underworld!'

'You can't be well,' Amanda replied calmly. 'Should I get you a drink or would you rather I called an ambulance? Perhaps you'd just like to lie down for a little while? I've a camp bed, you could stretch out in my office.'

'There's nothing wrong with me!' Jock whooped. 'In fact, I've never felt better. You can't imagine how good it feels to have let Christ into my heart! I'm giving you a final warning, dump Eliot or God will make you regret it!'

'You're crazy!' Debden-Philips raged. 'Flipper Fine Art has invested a lot of money in promoting Karen's career, we're not going to drop her now that she's become a hot property and we're getting our pay-off!'

'You'll regret this!' Graham screeched as he stormed out of the gallery.

Slim was hanging out in Johnny Aggro's flat. He'd slipped a copy of the Fat Boys' *Big and Beautiful* into the CD player. While many skinheads refused to listen to any dance music made after the mid-seventies, the Raiders had more eclectic tastes and were fond of hip-hop, house and rap.

Slim had once read a review of the Fat Boys praising them for simultaneously offering a celebration and a critique of consumer society. The writer, Bob Jones, had suggested the group had a lot in common with punk bands such as X-Ray Spex. He'd also devoted several paragraphs to explaining that the Fat Boys' version of 'Wipe Out' was the realisation of punk. The argument ran that since they'd completely trashed the original song, the Fat Boys had symbolically 'wiped out' the sixties far more successfully than bands such as the Sex Pistols or the Clash. Slim didn't really have any opinions about the Bob Jones piece, he just liked the Fat Boys' music.

'Jesus fuck, open the door!' Maria Walker was screaming. 'I've only got an hour, I'm on my lunch break.'

'Been knocking for long?' Slim enquired as he let the doctor into the flat.

'A couple of minutes,' Walker replied as she sat down. 'You obviously couldn't hear me because of the music.'

Slim waddled across to the hi fi and adjusted the volume. Then he plonked himself down beside Maria.

There was plenty of room on the sofa but the skinhead squashed up against the doctor.

'Is Johnny about?' Walker asked.

'Nah,' the boot boy whispered. 'There ain't no one about but sweet little me.'

'Is Johnny likely to come back in the next hour?' Maria persisted.

'I doubt it,' Slim said as he placed his right hand on the doctor's knee.

'Stop pawing me, I'm not a bloody sex object!' Walker hissed as she grabbed the skinhead's wrist and yanked it upwards.

'Oh, come on!' Slim pleaded. 'Don't be such a bloody prude, I know you've fucked all the other fellas, so you might as well have sex with me.'

'I think you're repulsive!' Maria sneered as she stood up.

'You sound just like the dominatrix in one of the S/M films we've got,' the boot boy cooed. 'Why don't you tie me up! Once you've done that, you could sit on my face and make me eat your perfumed cunt.'

'Strip!' the doctor instructed.

Slim did as he was told. He didn't mind being humiliated. It was so long since he'd had a screw that the boot boy was prepared to submit to anything if it meant getting his end away. Maria found several belts in Johnny's wardrobe and used them to tie Slim to a radiator. Once she'd done this, the doctor left.

'Hey, you can't just leave me here!' the skinhead yelled after Walker. 'Untie me you bitch! I don't want my mates to find me strapped up and naked! It's a bloody embarrassment. It'll make me look like a complete cunt!'

Maria didn't reply, she simply slammed the front door and then stepped into the lift. For a few minutes,

Slim managed to convince himself that the doctor was simply teasing him. At any moment, she'd come back into the living room and fuck his brains out. However, he soon realised that this was a forlorn hope and resigned himself to being trussed up like a turkey until Johnny or another member of the Raiders came to the flat.

Johnny Aggro dialled Stephen Smith's number and an answerphone message told him that the Lodge leader was busy hanging a show entitled the *New Neoism* at the Thumbprint Gallery on Old Compton Street. The skinhead thought this was rather strange, because he often grabbed a snack in the Café Espana but had never noticed an art space in this part of Soho. Hodges made his way out of Leicester Square tube station and up to Cambridge Circus. Two minutes later, he'd found the building squatted by the Semiotic Liberation Front, it was virtually opposite his favourite caff. The boot boy had donned a Mickey Mouse mask before strolling down Old Compton Street and so he was able to march boldly into the gallery.

'Spartacus,' Johnny gibed, 'I'm calling a Lodge meeting, I want everyone in the back room!'

'Yes master,' Stephen Smith acquiesced.

'I am Hiram,' Hodges announced to his startled disciples as they followed him through to the kitchen, 'and I can transform base creatures such as yourselves into famous artists, if you'll just do my bidding!'

'We hail you as a representative of the Great Horned God!' the Lodge members chanted in unison.

'In the name of our Earth Mother Hecate, I command all femail cult members to shed their clothes!' As he issued this edict, Johnny made the sign of the five-pointed star rising in the East. The skinhead was a great fan of Vincent Price and had learnt how to do this from watching old horror films.

'That's not fair,' Penny Applegate whined. 'I'm the only girl in the Lodge, why should I get naked when you guys are still fully dressed?'

'Slut!' the skinhead scoffed as he slapped the chick's cheek 'You'll do as I say or else you'll be expelled from the Lodge and I'll see to it that you never get a single break in the art world!'

Applegate figured she'd better do as she was told. Like many a wannabe star, Penny believed in prostituting herself for art. As his girlfriend stripped, Donald Pemberton blushed with embarrassment. He didn't like what was going on but dared not intervene in case doing so blew his chances of making it big on the cultural circuit.

'Suck my dick,' Hodges gasped as he placed his hands on Applegate's shoulders and forced the bird on to her knees.

The skinhead was really enjoying himself. Penny wasn't the type of chick he usually fancied but Hodges was able to get off on the power he was exercising over this pathetic tart. Johnny groaned as the harlot unzipped his flies and sucked his prick into her mouth. Pleasant dreams flooded the boot boy's consciousness. This bird had a backside that was made for spanking and he fully intended to transform it from milky white into a bright red blush. In fact, once the skinhead began administering the drubbing, he wouldn't let up until Applegate's arse burnt the hand of anyone who touched it.

Pemberton felt sick as he watched his girlfriend swallow Hiram's cum. Penny had sworn to him that she hated sex and yet it looked like the bitch had enjoyed going down on their SLF chief! Don felt even worse when Johnny ordered Stephen Smith to take Applegate from behind, while Eugene De Freud stuck his dick down her throat.

'There's nothing like a touch of physical intimacy to reinforce group loyalty,' Hodges announced. 'Once everyone has fucked this floozy, we'll get down to Lodge business!'

Amanda Debden-Philips was feeling harassed. Jock Graham's sudden conversion to a rogue breed of Christian fundamentalism had shaken the arts administrator. On top of this, everyone of consequence was suddenly talking about Neoism and Debden-Philips had a very poor grasp of the subject. Amanda was considered an expert on the avant-garde and she'd look very foolish indeed if her ignorance of the Neoist Network was exposed. As a short cut to bluffing her way through the mine-field of the eighties' art underground, Debden-Philips set about picking Karen Eliot's brain over a late lunch in the Oxford Street Burger King.

'Well darling,' Amanda cooed as she placed a heavily laden self-service tray on the table. 'What I want to know is the date on which Neoism began.'

'I think there's a fundamental flaw in your question,' Karen hooted. 'Neoism was a development within the discourse of the avant-garde, as such it has shifting parameters and there's no way you can fix its point of origin.'

'But when was the term Neoism first used?' Debden-Philips demanded.

'In what context?' Eliot replied.

'In an art context!' Amanda sputtered. 'I've heard that the word was taken from the writings of some occultist but I'm not interested in that rubbish. All I care about is contemporary culture!'

'A tentative version of Neoism was cobbled together by Al Ackerman, Dave Zack and Maris Kundzin at the Portland Academy from 1977 onwards,' Karen bombasted. 'At that time, the terms ISM and No Ism were used to describe the movement. The word Neoism was first used to describe the group we're talking about in May 1979 in Montreal. As with dada, there's a great deal of argument as to who actually named the movement. Of course, the French-Canadians completely transformed Zack and Ackerman's conception of what the group was about. Then Bob Jones came along in the mid-eighties and re-invented Neoism, creating the movement as we know it today.'

'Okay, okay!' Debden-Philips squeaked. 'I'm an expert on the classical avant-garde and I don't wanna be bored with details. All I need to know is the essence of what went on. You seem to be telling me that the term Neoism was first used in an art context in May 1979.'

'No, no!' Eliot spouted. 'The whole story is much more complicated than that. What we now know as the Neoist Network had its origins in Portland in 1977, but the group didn't hit upon this name until May 1979. The first person to use the term Neoism in an art context was Hervé Fischer. He did so during the course of a performance in the Petite Salle at the Pompidou Centre on 15 February 1979. There's a brief description of the event in Hans Belting's book *The End of the History of Art*. Subsequently, various members of the Neoist Network attempted to conceal the fact that Fischer was using the term before Kiki Bonbon and his friends hit upon the idea of adopting it for their movement. And so, by the mid-eighties, one of the less intelligent individuals who'd been active in the Neoist Network was claiming that the group dated from a performance at Vehicule Art on 14 February 1979.'

'Are you telling me that this idiot claimed to have used the term Neoism in an art context one day before Hervé Fischer?' Amanda demanded.

'Yes,' Karen affirmed.

'That's ridiculous!' Debden-Philips cried.

'I know,' Eliot agreed.

'But this doesn't help me at all!' Amanda screeched. 'It simply makes it look like Neoism lacks a fixed point of origin!'

'I've already said as much to you!' Karen exclaimed.

'That's all very well for the critics and intellectuals,' Debden-Philips lashed back, 'but businessmen who buy paintings want hard facts with which they can impress their friends.'

'In that case,' Eliot responded magnanimously, 'simply inform the bozos that Neoism was founded on 24 March 1977.'

'But that isn't true!' Amanda protested. 'It's a fiction!'

'Truth is a fiction!' Karen barked. 'People who want hard facts will have to make do with fabrications!'

'I guess you're right,' Debden-Philips conceded.

'To use a cliché,' Karen giggled, 'in the beginning was The Word and The Word was a Lie!'

Ross MacDonald had his prick buried in Penelope Applegate's mouth, while Joseph Campbell was giving the art tart's twat a good thrashing. Donald Pemberton watched in horror as the entire Lodge got their jollies by filling his girlfriend's orifices with their spunk.

Hiram was grinning insanely behind his Mickey Mouse mask, he greatly enjoyed being in a position of power.

'Keep at it boys,' the Semiotic Liberation Front chief instructed his minions. 'I'm going out but I won't be long. I want to find you're still at it when I come back!'

'Yes, boss!' the male members of the Lodge chanted in unison.

When the skinhead returned five minutes later, he had four American youths with him. They'd parted with fifty quid each to take part in a gang bang. The tourists had never visited England before and so didn't think it odd that the pimp who'd offered them a good time was wearing a Mickey Mouse mask.

Ross and Joe shot their loads and vacated their positions. The new arrivals dropped their pants and stood around the table on which Penny lay spread-eagled. She took a prick in each hand and shook them vigorously. Applegate swallowed the plonker that was thrust at her mouth, while the floozy's buttered-bun accommodated the fourth love muscle. After two minutes in these positions, the boys moved clockwise around the table. The kids who'd been getting the oral and vaginal action were kept on the boil with hand jobs, while their buddies made the most of the tart's proffered orifices.

'I'm gonna cum!' the yank working Penny's love hole hollered.

'Get on with it, motherfucker!' the youth stationed at three o'clock retorted. 'Coz I want some of what you're gettin'.'

It wasn't long before this wish was granted. The bloke positioned at six o'clock felt love juice boil up through his groin and then explode out into the purple passages of unbridled womunhood. This slacker then abandoned his privileged position at the number of the beast. The kid who'd been stationed with the trinity replaced him, and was soon savouring the pleasures to be had from Satanic worship between dripping walls of flesh.

'Hey, sucker,' Hiram hissed in Don's ear. 'You're the only geezer here who hasn't had the bitch! Wouldn't you like a bit of what she's got?'

'You must be joking!' Pemberton winced. 'Sex is disgusting. Since I wouldn't fuck a prostitute, I've no intention of screwing my girlfriend!'

'Ooohhh, you're lovely!' the yank stationed at six o'clock thundered as he spunked up.

The youth at nine o'clock resumed his original position. The hand job he'd been getting had taken him to the edge of ecstasy and split seconds after battering his way back into Penny's twat, he spilt a great wad of his love juice. The kid getting the oral action was in two minds about what to do next, he was on the verge of orgasm and although the yank fancied plumbing the hooker's hole, there wasn't really time to do this. The boy felt as if his intestines were exploding out through his prick as liquid genetics filled the English babe's hot little mouth.

'Go down on her!' Hiram jeered at Don as the four tourists made a hasty exit.

'I can't do that!' Pemberton protested. 'It's disgusting just contemplating such a vile act!'

'Come on baby,' Applegate coaxed. 'Lick me out!'

'No!' Don screamed.

'Do it or I'll throw you out of the Lodge and

then you'll never make the grade as a famous artist!' Hiram snapped.

As Pemberton worked his tongue around his girlfriend's pussy, all he could think about was the prick that had just been up her twat. The salty taste of semen made him want to throw up. Only an overwhelming desire for cultural recognition enabled this pathetic straight to keep his lunch in his stomach.

Rebel had given his cousin Susan Jones a set of keys to Johnny Aggro's flat. The sixteen-year-old wanted to watch an amateur video two of her friends had made after they'd been picked up in a West End bar by a chat show host. Since Susan was still at school, her parents would have thrown a fit if they'd caught their daughter watching it on the VCR at home.

'Hey, help me, untie me!' Slim shouted as he heard someone coming in through the front door.

'Jesus fuck!' Jones exclaimed as she walked into the living room. 'What the hell are you doing tied up?'

'I'll tell you once I'm dressed,' the skinhead coaxed.

'You dirty bugger,' Susan giggled. 'You're getting an erection!'

'Just untie me!' the boot boy entreated.

'No way!' Jones tittered. 'You'll have to be nice to me before I do that!'

'Please,' Slim mumbled.

The schoolgirl didn't reply. Instead, she picked up the phone and made a local call. The damn thing seemed to ring forever—but eventually another school-girl came on the line.

'Sarah, it's Susan, I'm at Johnny Aggro's flat.

Come over here with Cath and your dad's camcorder. Don't worry about why, just get your arse in gear!'

'What's going on?' the skinhead demanded.

'We're gonna have some fun!' Jones replied as she pushed her friend's home porn movie into the VCR.

'Blimey!' Slim exclaimed as the monitor flickered darkly. 'That's the geezer off the telly. The girl he's fucking is young enough to be his daughter!'

'What do you think of the chick?' Susan demanded.

'She's a hot babe!' the boot boy exclaimed.

'Sarah's on her way over here right now!' the schoolgirl told her captive.

'Is she gonna fuck me?' Slim wanted to know.

'I doubt it,' Jones sniggered. 'You're not really her type, you're neither good-looking nor famous. That'll be her and Cath at the door.'

Susan returned a minute later with her two friends. Sarah had a camcorder in her hands. One of Johnny's white walls gave the correct visual balance. The teenager took a tracking shot of Slim's great bulk then handed the camera to Cathy. She walked over to Slim and planted a stiletto heel on his stomach, before arranging her hands on her hips.

'How do I look?' Sarah asked as she pouted.

'Great!' Cathy replied. 'It's a fabulous shot.'

'What are we gonna do with Slim?' Susan put in.

'Let's get some jam and smear it all over the bastard!' Sarah suggested.

'Nah,' Jones shot back. 'Johnny will do his nut if we make a mess of the carpet!'

'Why don't you two shave his pubes while I film it?' Cathy smirked.

'Yeah, that'll be a laugh!' Sarah and Susan chanted in unison.

Jones found lather and a packet of disposable razors in the bathroom. Sarah sat on Slim's beer gut and soaped him up. Susan knelt between the boot boy's legs and got shaving. Split seconds later, her friend grabbed a razor and joined in the fun. The skinhead had a throbbing erection. The girls' hands kept brushing against his dick but it was clear neither of them were going to give him the kind of relief he craved.

Johnny Aggro was sweating profusely beneath his rubber mask. He wanted to wrap up the Lodge meeting so that he could get away. In a couple of hours, he'd be meeting Atima Sheazan and then the day's fun would really begin. Hodges made the sign of the five-pointed star and the animated chattering that had been going on around him suddenly stopped.

'You've got to learn,' Hiram gusted, 'that this is not some kind of democratic debating society. The Semiotic Liberation Front is an ancient fraternity based on a strict hierarchy! In the good old days, failure to obey your superiors was punished with death!'

'I would rather disembowel myself than give away the secrets of the SLF!' the Lodge members warbled in a low monotone.

'That's better!' the skinhead saluted his troops. 'But I'm not satisfied with your progress. You're doing okay at propagating Neoism but your petty vandalism at the Bow Studios was really far too tame!'

'Destroying those sculptures got a lot of media coverage!' Donald Pemberton protested.

'Shut up!' Hiram admonished. 'You've got to do something really vile. Something that will leave the cultural establishment gob-smacked. What I suggest is that you go and desecrate William Blake's grave in Bunhill Burial Grounds!'

'Wow!' the Lodge replied in hushed tones. 'That's a really wicked idea!'

'Of course it is!' the boot boy crackled. 'I gave it to you! Now what I wanna know is when are you gonna do something about it?'

'We're having the private view for our *New Neoism* exhibition tomorrow night,' Spartacus put in, 'so that's out.'

'What about Friday or Saturday night?' Joseph Campbell suggested.

'No good,' Ross MacDonald said, 'the media is always asleep or completely boozed up at the weekend.'

'It'll have to be Sunday night!' Penelope Applegate announced triumphantly. 'That way we'll get maximum coverage in the Monday papers. It'll get the week off to a flying start!'

'You're right!' the rest of the Lodge agreed.

'We'll meet at Old Street tube as the clock strikes ten,' Spartacus jabbered. 'We'll have the deed done in less than an hour. Then we'll phone all the papers so that they've time to do a detailed write-up and yet still have the story on the presses before midnight!'

'Excellent!' Hiram spat the word as if it was a death sentence. 'I'm off now but you'll see me again soon. And if you all wanna make the grade as famous artists, none of you should slack on this project!'

Rebel was getting agitated as he banged on Johnny Aggro's front door. He'd lent his cousin his keys so that she could use Johnny's VCR and he'd given her strict instructions to hang around until he came over.

The skinhead was about to get back into the lift when his summons was finally answered.

'What took you so bloody long?' the boot boy demanded.

'I was mucking about with my friends,' Susan Jones replied sheepishly.

Rebel strode through to the living room and was amazed to find Slim tied to the radiator. The skinhead let out a loud peel of laughter, he could hardly feel cross with his cousin and her friends when they'd simply been having a bit of fun with the fat one.

'Free me!' Slim pleaded.

Rebel could do no more than snigger as he untied his friend. He didn't have much sympathy for his mate. Slim stood up and rubbed his wrists, then he lunged at Susan.

'Leave her alone!' Rebel scolded as he grabbed Slim's arm. 'She's just a schoolgirl and you haven't suffered any serious harm.'

'I suppose it's not her fault,' the fat bastard muttered as he picked up his clothes. 'So I'll let it pass. But when I catch up with Maria Walker, I'm gonna punch her fuckin' face in!'

'I wouldn't do that if I was you,' Rebel snarled. 'Johnny won't like it one little bit.'

'Fuck Johnny!' Slim slobbered as he locked himself in the bathroom.

'I bet he's gonna wank himself off,' Sarah put in. 'He was begging for some hand relief when we was torturing him!'

'Did you film it?' Rebel asked as he pointed at the camcorder.

'Yeah,' Cathy confirmed.

'Give me the keys back Susan,' Rebel ordered,

'and you lot can all clear off. Next time you get a couple of VCRs together, I'd like a copy of what you filmed.'

'Sure,' the girls sighed in unison as they made their way out of the flat.

Atima Sheazan was waiting for Johnny Aggro at Camden tube station. She was early, he was a few minutes late. They embraced. Their mouths met and locked in a lingering kiss. There was no need for small talk, unquenchable desires were surging through their veins. Simultaneously, million-year-old genetic codes were being scrambled and unscrambled across the muscular structure of these twin bulks.

The two of them wandered through some back streets until they came to a school. The main gate was unlocked because a handful of classrooms were being used for adult education courses. Sheazan led Hodges by the hand to a darkened corner of the playground. She pushed him against a wall, unzipped his flies and fell on her knees. Split seconds later, Atima was working her tongue up and down Johnny's erect shaft.

'That feels so good!' Hodges moaned as the bitch swallowed his cock.

Sheazan didn't reply, all her concentration was focused on sucking Johnny's dick. Hodges could feel love juice boiling up through his groin. Atima noted the tell-tale muscle spasms and eased up. The skinhead hauled Sheazan to her feet. He yanked down her knickers, hitched up her leather mini-skirt and pushed the girl back against a brick wall.

Johnny battered his way into the crepe-tissue of Atima's twat. For a few fleeting seconds, a car headlight lit up the darkened corner in which the couple were shagging. Footsteps were echoing around the playground and a door slammed in an adjacent street. Snatches of conversation entered Johnny's brain but he paid them no heed. Instead, the boot boy pumped up the volume.

'I want you to cum!' Sheazan sobbed as the skinhead beat out the basic 4/4 rhythm of uninhibited sex.

'No problem!' Hodges declaimed as he shot off a great wad of liquid genetics.

Atima and Johnny had reached that peak from which man and womun can never jointly return. Having achieved orgasmic union, the two lovers were now descending the steep cliffs of desire alone. Johnny felt his body armour click back into place. Once again, he was ready to do battle with the filthy hordes who wanted to impose politically correct sex on couples whose erotic fantasies were running madly out of control.

Eight

SLIM WOKE EARLY, feeling seriously pissed off. The previous day had been completely wasted. He'd spent nearly half of it tied up in Johnny Aggro's flat. His boss had told him that their firm would be extremely busy over the next few months and so there was no chance of a proper holiday in the immediate future. Thoughts of revenge spun around the boot boy's mind like clothes in a tumble drier. Slim knew he'd get a lot of stick if he beat up three schoolgirls—but a stuck-up bitch fast approaching middle-age was a different matter. Although the Raiders might not like him punching out the slag they'd been shagging, the skinhead figured no one else would give a toss if he assaulted Maria Walker. And so he headed to work via the local health centre.

'I have to see Dr Walker urgently!' Slim crackled.

'Maria isn't doing consultations this morning, she's busy with paperwork,' the receptionist replied primly. 'Hey, come back!'

Slim ignored the command and strode down the

corridor to Maria Walker's surgery. The boot boy didn't bother knocking on the door, he just threw it open and strode into the room. Maria leapt up, dodging a fist that was aimed at her nose. Simultaneously, she used her right leg to trip Slim up. The skinhead toppled over, banging his forehead against the edge of a desk and then collapsing into a concussed heap on the floor.

Walker worked fast. She stripped Slim and hauled him on to her couch. Then the doctor chained the boot boy down with the handcuffs she'd bought her masochistic brother for his birthday. It was fortunate indeed that she'd had the present wrapped up in her briefcase. Taking gauze from a draw, Maria bandaged Slim's genitals, then stood back for a few seconds to admire her handiwork.

'Wake up!' Walker droned as she slapped the boot boy's face. 'Wake up you moron!'

'Aaarrrggghhh!' Slim moaned. 'Where am I? What's going on!'

'You're chained up in my surgery!' Maria announced triumphantly. 'You came here to assault me but I gave you a whipping!'

'What's going on?' the skinhead repeated.

'Look down at your dick!' the doctor instructed.

'I can't see it,' Slim mumbled. 'I can only see bandages.'

'That's because I cut off your prick and balls!' Walker clacked gleefully.

'You can't have done!' the boot boy cried. 'I can feel myself getting a hard-on.'

'It's a phantom erection,' Maria contended. 'You must have heard about people who've had limbs amputated and for years afterwards suffer from phantom pains.'

'Oh no!' the skinhead sobbed and then promptly fainted.

'Snap out of it!' the doctor harangued before throwing a glass of water in Slim's face.

Although the boot boy regained consciousness, he looked very pale. He stared up at Walker like a child who couldn't believe the cruelty of this world.

'What am I going to do?' the skinhead asked in a weak voice.

'Go on a diet,' Maria informed him. 'Once you've lost a few stone, you can start feeling frustrated about the fact that if you still had a prick, you might have got yourself laid.'

The doctor unchained her victim. Slim got up, got dressed and left the surgery. The skinhead hadn't resigned himself to the humiliation he'd suffered at Walker's hands. However, he now realised that he'd do better using brain rather than brawn to outwit this vicious enemy. It didn't take long to reach the local police station and once inside, Slim rang the bell for service.

'I'd like to report a terrible crime,' the boot boy harangued the desk sergeant. 'Dr Walker has just castrated me! You'll find her at the local health centre. I want the bitch arrested immediately.'

'I think you ought to come into one of the interview rooms,' the cop's voice dripped sympathy, 'so that I can take down a few particulars relating to the case.'

After Slim had spent the best part of twenty minutes giving a statement, a doctor arrived to examine his injuries. The boot boy dropped his pants. The medic undid the bandage that Walker had wrapped around the skinhead's groin, thus revealing a perfectly healthy set of family jewels. Minutes later, Slim was charged with wasting police time.

*

Donald Pemberton had woken late but he was feeling just as angry as Slim. The previous day, he'd discovered that his girlfriend was a slag, a slut, a sexpot. Penelope Applegate had always sworn that she considered reproductive acts repulsive—but Don now knew she'd been lying. If Penny was a nympho with a difference, then the difference simply consisted of the fact that she was unable to admit to her sickness. While Pemberton had risen above the physical, to embrace the metaphysical, his chick seemed more interested in hanging out with degenerates than communing with art.

'Penny!' Don hollered into the living room. 'Make me a cup of tea while I dress!'

'It's your turn to make the tea!' Applegate bombasted. 'I made it when we came in last night.'

'I'm creatively incontinent!' Pemberton lectured. 'I need someone to run around me while I think about art.'

'Aesthetics and Resistance is a partnership,' Penny countered. 'If you want someone to run around you, then you should hire a maid. I need time to embrace the spiritual as much as you do!'

'Don't make me laugh!' Don sneered. 'Yesterday, I saw you crying out in ecstasy as various brutes spunked into your hole. You don't need time to immerse yourself in higher realities, you're just a nymphomaniac!'

'Those boys weren't brutes!' Applegate protested. 'We were all making love. With you that isn't possible, you're too wrapped up in your own ego to reach out and touch somebody else. But yesterday I realised that there isn't an inseparable gulf between the spiritual and the physical, these two apparently disparate things make up a single continuum!'

'Why don't you admit that you haven't risen

above your animal nature?' Pemberton discoursed as he made his way through to the living room. 'Given this fact, it's obvious that you're just an assistant in my art project. I'm the one who infused the work we produce as Aesthetics and Resistance with a great spirituality. If you brew some tea, I'll refrain from making further comments when you go a rutting with the first piece of beefcake you meet on the street!'

'I'm not making the tea!' Penny bickered. 'It's your turn, now go and get my breakfast!'

'Listen whore!' Don cried. 'We're assigning tasks on the basis of spiritual ability and I'm the only genius in this flat! Get yourself into the kitchen!'

'That's it, I'm leaving!' Applegate heaved. 'Fuck you, I don't ever wanna see you again!'

'You can't leave me!' Pemberton rasped. 'What about your career in the art world? What about the fact that I use the allowance I get from my family to support you? Besides, Spartacus will side with me and you'll be kicked out of the Lodge, then you'll never get signed up by a major gallery!'

'Oh, alright,' Penny sighed. 'I'll stay! But only if you make the tea!'

Jock Graham had joined a Christian group known as Christ's Crusaders. These bozos considered themselves the descendents of both the Templars and the Hospitallers, simply because they went out on the street in an attempt to convert ordinary people to an outlandish mystical creed. Paul Parvenu, the founder of this sect, didn't realise that the Crusaders of old had been more interested in learning the secrets of capitalism from the so-called infidel than in securing the safety of pilgrims traversing the Holy Lands.

'Like I always say at the end of these meetings,' Preacher Paul announced, 'we've got to get out on the streets and crusade for people's souls. We've got to slug it out for Jesus. We're fighting the devil when we're out on the streets asking people if they've let the Saviour into their hearts. Well, that wraps it up from me for today but before we go, Jock Graham has got something to say about a Satanic cult known as Neoism. Over to you Jock . . .'

'This Neoist stuff,' Graham lisped as he stood up, 'is seriously evil. Neoism is simply the latest front for a Satanic sect whose origins are lost in the mists of time. Until I found Jesus, I was an art critic and I can tell you a lot about the interrelationship between Neoism, situationism and Masonry. However, the important thing is that we mobilise to prevent Neoism moving out of the art world and into the mainstream. We've got to root it out of our culture and this means dealing harshly with the men who support it in the City of London. We've got to expose the fact that the battle between the Mercers' Guild and the Hanseatic League was faked up to deceive the public. In fact, both groups were simply representatives of a single organisation. We've got to expose the ways in which Satanism, as a practical religion of money worship, was handed down through the Rosicrucians, the Templars and the Knights of St Thomas . . .'

'Blasphemy! Blasphemy!' the assembled congregation chanted in unison. 'Out demon, out! How dare you cast aspersions on the crusaders we're named after!'

'But you've got to listen to me!' Jock yelled. 'If you'll just hear me through, I'll prove to you that there's a demonic connection between the Templars and Hassan-I-Sabbath. You see the Old Man of the Mountains made a pact with the crusaders . . .'

The art critic was unable to finish his presentation. Chairs were scattered across the room as Christian fundamentalists rushed towards him. Paul Parvenu was among the first Crusaders to reach this apostate. There was the satisfying crunch of splintering bone as the preacher's fist connected with Graham's mouth. Jock staggered backwards spitting out gouts of blood and the occasional piece of broken tooth. Strong hands grabbed the art critic and he was held down while Parvenu kicked him unconscious. Mercifully, it did not take long for the former marxist to black out. The Crusaders then lifted his limp body above their heads and carried it out on to the street, where they dumped him next to several bags of rubbish. They were not going to tolerate anyone casting aspersions on the conduct of Christian heroes who had saved many a pilgrim in a bygone age!

Amanda Debden-Philips was having an early lunch with Linda Forthwright. Following Karen Eliot's lead, the two arts administrators had decided they liked the Oxford Street Burger King and so this is where they rendezvoused for their tête-à-tête. Linda placed a laden tray on the table. Amanda grabbed a burger and strawberry shake, she felt ravenous!

'Have you had an invitation for this *New Neoism* show at the Thumbprint Gallery?' Forthwright enquired.

'Yes,' Debden-Philips affirmed. 'It's a squatted shop on Old Compton Street. I'm a little cross with Stephen Smith, who organised the show. Since he's now signed to Flipper, he should have consulted me before going ahead with it.'

'Why worry about it?' Linda chided. 'You'd have given him the okay, all forms of underground art are really big at the moment. Neoism looks like it's about to become huge, it seems to have gone art historical in the space of about a week!'

'Yeah, Neoism will be massive this year,' Amanda agreed. 'All the critics are saying it's the hottest thing since fluxus and the situationists. Nevertheless, I'm still angry with Stephen, he's undermined my authority. It's all very well for young artists to adopt anti-institutional rhetoric—but they should still be deferential towards their gallery when they're not polemicising for the benefit of the press!'

'When you put it that way, I can see you're right!' Forthwright gushed. 'I'd love to have Stephen bound, gagged and helpless in my bed. I'd treat him to a punishment session he'd never forget!'

'It can be arranged,' Debden-Philips drooled.

'Would you do it for me? Would you really?' Linda asked as she reached out and touched her friend's hand.

'No problem,' Amanda cooed. 'Let's both go to the *New Neoism* opening tonight. Once it's over, I'll instruct Stephen to go home with you. Smith won't have any choice in the matter, since he's just signed to Flipper and hasn't yet had a proper West End show, he's not in a position to argue with me about it. What I don't understand, is why you didn't lure him into bed with the promise of an Earth Gallery show before he joined the Flipper stable.'

'Until you signed him up, he looked just like another piece of beefcake to me,' Forthwright confessed. 'The thing is, I like my men to have the smell of success about them. Running a funded gallery means that most of the bozos I show are never gonna make any money from their art. Grant-aided types just don't appeal to me sexually, I have an unquenchable craving to humiliate powerful men!'

'I know what you mean!' Debden-Philips gusted. 'When I was a teenager, I wouldn't even look at a bloke unless he had a car!'

'But tell me about Neoism,' Linda replied, quickly changing the subject. 'There's so much I don't know about it. Just start off with the basics, like when it was founded.'

'I think there's a fundamental flaw in your question,' Amanda pontificated. 'Neoism was a development within the discourse of the avant-garde, as such it has shifting parameters and there's no way you can fix its point of origin.'

'But when was the term Neoism first used?' Forthwright persisted.

'In what context?' Debden-Philips wanted to know.

'An art context, of course!' Linda convulsed.

''Ere,' a workman said as he leered at Amanda from an adjacent table. 'You was in 'ere yesterday with another bird who was saying all the things you're saying now!'

'So what?' Debden-Philips puffed.

'I liked it more,' the labourer confided, 'when you and your friend was talking about sex.'

'You're repulsive!' Amanda chaffed.

'Me and my mates are working on a site just round the corner,' the building labourer persisted. 'If you want, we'll give you a gang bang in the porta-cabin. What about it, eh?'

'Come on!' Debden-Philips yelled at Linda Forthwright. 'I've finished my lunch, let's go and get a drink in more pleasant surroundings!'

*

Johnny Aggro had arranged to meet Karen Eliot in Soho Square. When he arrived, he was pleased to find her already occupying a bench. Most of the seats were taken and there were lots of people sitting on the grass. The skinhead would have suggested going to a caff if he'd found Eliot getting her arse damp on the lawn. Nature was for hippies. Hodges liked the city but wasn't particularly taken with its green spaces.

'This is nice, isn't it!' Karen announced as Johnny pecked her on the cheek. 'There's nothing like a bit of fresh air and sunshine!'

'Yeah,' Hodges concurred, 'apart from a skinful when you're down the pub with your mates!'

'Or setting up a secret society and controlling the destiny of everyone who joins!' Eliot grinned.

'Let's forget about the Semiotic Liberation Front for the time being,' the boot boy pleaded. 'We went through it on the blower. I'm really sick of all this shit about Neoism. I don't understand what arty types see in it. Give me a good Trojan record, something with a decent beat, I'll leave the high-brow stuff to the trendies because it doesn't do anything for me!'

'Okay, okay,' Karen conceded. 'We'll forget about Neoism for the time being. What do you wanna talk about instead?'

'Did you hear about Slim?' Johnny sniggered.

'I spoke to Maria on the phone this morning,' Eliot cackled.

'You haven't heard the best bit!' Hodges exclaimed. Then, pulling a video cassette from a carrier and handing it to Eliot, he added: 'This is a film of three schoolgirls sexually abusing Slim!'

Spartacus was overseeing the final touches to the

New Neoism exhibition. The Thumbprint Gallery looked as if a bomb had hit it. Paint was splattered over the walls, floor and ceiling, torn posters had been hung around the space at crazy angles, and the floor was littered with broken computers. Although most of the hardware had simply died from over-use, the exhibiting artists planned to inform anyone who'd listen that they'd been destroyed by Neoist computer viruses.

'What the fuck held you up?' Stephen Smith screamed at Donald Pemberton and Penny Applegate as they walked through the door. 'You should have been here hours ago! Don't you take this stuff seriously?'

'Art is the most important thing in the world,' Pemberton intoned solemnly. 'Penny and I had an argument, we had to patch things up before we came over here.'

'Okay! Okay!' Spartacus howled. 'Your personal problems really break my fuckin' heart. Now get in the kitchen and make an avocado dip. Although this is a squatted space, we've gotta impress the critics with how professional we are!'

'Yes, boss,' Don replied before making his way across the gallery.

'Not you!' the Grand Dragon hissed as he yanked Penny back by her collar. 'I wanna make use of your mouth, your talents would be wasted in the kitchen. Now give me a blow job!'

'Yes, boss,' Applegate intoned as she got down on her knees.

Penny undid Smith's flies and felt his prick harden as she massaged it with her hand. Applegate ran her tongue along Stephen's length. The SLF leader let out an insane cackle.

'Can anyone join in?' a passer-by asked as he

inched open the door, after spotting the oral action through a gap in the posters plastered across the window.

'Get out! Get out!' Joseph Campbell screeched.

'I'll give you twenty quid!' the stranger offered.

'It's more than my job's worth!' Campbell hollered. 'No one is allowed to interrupt the boss when he's getting his jollies!'

Joseph slammed the door in the intruder's face. Being a dedicated pervert, the bozo kept his bloodied nose pressed against the glass. Even if he wasn't going to get his dick sucked, he was determined to enjoy the spectacle of a bird on her knees servicing someone else.

Penny noted the tell-tale muscle spasms as Spartacus approached orgasm. She could hardly have missed them, Smith was shaking like a demented spastic. Split seconds later, liquid genetics boiled up from Stephen's groin and splattered into Applegate's throat. Penny gulped greedily on the wads of DNA, she liked the salty taste, it reminded her of a health drink popular during her childhood.

Sir Charles Brewster was having to think on his feet. The prices being paid for Neoist material were rising at an astronomical rate. There could be little doubt about the fact that the movement had entered its historical phase. The Progressive Arts Project supremo was hurriedly accumulating an impressive collection of items produced by the eighties' avant-garde. Much of it had been bought as a job lot from Martin Porker, a failed artist who'd flirted with Neoism around the time of APT 8. Porker was out of touch with trends in contemporary art and very short of cash. He'd parted with his entire archive for five grand.

The sudden upsurge of interest in Neoism had

created a lot of work for Brewster. Making the most of the opportunities that had suddenly presented themselves, meant he'd be running around like a blue-arsed fly for several months. The most immediate problem Sir Charles had to deal with was Jock Graham. The art critic had barged into his office without so much as attempting to make an appointment. Fortunately, Brewster was a past master at manipulating artists and critics. In fact, he considered Graham a particularly soft touch.

'You see Jock,' Sir Charles sermonised, 'I've been researching Neoism for years. While you're on the right track, there's a good deal you've yet to learn about the conspiracy.'

'But to me it looks like you've been promoting Neoism!' Graham protested.

'Do you know what a mole is?' Brewster demanded.

'Of course I do!' Jock spouted. 'It's a small animal that lives underground.'

'Not that kind of mole!' Sir Charles snorted. 'I'm talking about an infiltrator into an enemy organisation. It may look like I'm supporting the Neoists but what I'm actually doing is gathering intelligence on the group.'

'I see,' Graham whispered.

'Now what about teaming up?' Brewster asked. 'We could do a lot of damage by launching a two-pronged attack on the enemy. I'll amass information on our foe and you'll put it to practical use.'

'I dunno,' Jock hedged. 'What can you tell me that I don't already know?'

'So much,' Sir Charles confided, 'that we could sit here for a week and I wouldn't be able to impart a tenth of the information to you.'

'Wow!' Graham exclaimed.

'For starters,' Brewster whispered, 'let's just take a look at what you were saying earlier about the name Eliot being toilet spelt backwards if you add an extra "T". By rearranging the letters in the name Stiletto, you can also get the word toilet.'

'That's all very well,' Jock countered, 'but you've got an "S" and a "T" left over!'

'I was getting on to that,' Sir Charles explained patiently. 'The "T" is transferred over to the anagram of Karen Eliot's surname to give us a second toilet and the "S" stands for Satan, the connecting principal in all occult operations!'

'My God!' Graham yelled. 'This is all beginning to make some kind of horrible sense!'

'Now,' Brewster continued. 'Look what else you can do with the name Stiletto! It's an anagram of T. S. Eliot, with the spare 'T' again being transferred to the reversed version of Karen's surname to provide the alchemical link.'

'But!' Jock wailed. 'I thought the author of *The Waste Land* was a Christian!'

'No,' Sir Charles contradicted, 'that was just black propaganda spread by the Illuminati. In fact, T. S. Eliot was a stooge of the conspiracy!'

'By George!' Graham dilated. 'I think you're on to something.'

Sir Charles Brewster wasn't the only individual who'd been thinking on his feet because of a sudden acceleration in the speed of cultural change. Karen Eliot had taken Johnny Aggro to see an old Chow Yun Fat movie and while the guns were blazing, her brain was working at the speed of light. Having satiated themselves with heroic bloodshed, the couple were now back at

Eliot's flat. Hodges was on the blower, acting as Karen's mouthpiece.

'Spartacus!' Hodges barked. 'It's Hiram. Listen carefully, I've received instructions from the secret chiefs to pass on to you.'

'Right,' Stephen Smith bayed. 'Fire away!'

'There's to be a Neoist intervention at Chrisp Street Market in Poplar this Saturday lunch-time,' Johnny blurted. 'Announce it at the *New Neoism* private view tonight. I'll phone you tomorrow to fill in the details.'

'No problem!' Spartacus assured his controller. 'I'll speak to you anon.'

'Tomorrow,' Hiram repeated and then hung up.

Karen came through from the kitchen and handed Johnny a coffee before sinking back into the sofa. She'd decided not to go to the *New Neoism* opening because she didn't want to appear particularly au fait with the activities of the SLF Lodge members. Besides, Eliot had a lot of work to do preparing materials for the Neoist intervention at Chrisp Street Market on Saturday.

'What about a bunk up?' Hodges suggested.

'I don't feel like sex,' Karen replied blankly. 'Anyway, Maria's coming round in about twenty minutes and she wants to fuck you. I wouldn't mind filming the pair of you at it, what do you think?'

'I think you're bloody weird,' Johnny confided. 'I don't mind screwing Maria but I'm not having you video it. I'm not some piece of meat, you know! I've got feelings, I don't just exist to provide other people with sexual kicks.'

'What are you doing this evening?' Eliot demanded.

'I'm meeting a friend in Camden at nine o'clock,' Hodges announced.

'Well, you'll have to leave here by seven,' Karen informed him, 'because I've got a lot to do tonight. There'll be enough time for you and Maria to enjoy a sixty-minute session. I want you to meet me tomorrow lunch-time. By then I'll have prepared the posters I want passed on to Stephen Smith. I'll also give you further instructions to relay to him.'

'And what the fuck am I supposed to get out of all this?' Johnny admonished.

'You fuckin' love it!' Eliot boomed. 'And if you ever get to screw me again, you'll enjoy it all the more for having been made to wait. Likewise, I bet you get a fair bit of satisfaction out of helping to piss various arty types around!'

Hodges grinned. If only Eliot knew how much pleasure getting his revenge on Aesthetics and Resistance gave him, she'd have thrown a fit! Karen probably thought he was too thick to turn the situation to his own advantage—but the bitch would soon learn she'd made a terrible error of judgement. Give it a few days and there wouldn't be a secret society to promote Neoism on Eliot's behalf, because every last member of the SLF would be facing a lengthy jail term!

Jock Graham was parading in front of the Thumbprint Gallery. He'd made himself a placard which bore the legend 'FIGHT SATANISM, SMASH NEOISM.' The former art critic was also distributing a hastily produced leaflet. His intervention wasn't really having the desired effect. Not a single member of the art cognoscenti was taking his warnings about the conspiracy seriously. They thought it was a scam cooked up between Graham and the gallery to promote the show.

The exhibition itself was packed. Punters were standing arse to elbow as they sought to discover what the *New Neoism* was all about. Linda Forthwright was finding it difficult to keep her hands off Stephen Smith. The young artist had already resigned himself to the fact that he'd be providing this particular culture vulture with her jollies later that night.

'I thought the Neoist revival wasn't supposed to be taking place for another five years!' Emma Career of the Bow Studios was complaining to Ramish Patel.

'I understood that Sir Charles Brewster was planning a ten-year build up before Neoism was to be given the overkill treatment,' the film-maker shot back. 'I'd intended to leave it another eight years before I jumped on the band-wagon and now it looks as if I've missed the boat!'

'I suppose things just got out of hand,' Career orated. 'Sir Charles is a man of his word and if he told you he was working on a decade-long promotional programme, events must have overtaken him.'

'Oh yes, I'm sure of it,' Patel concurred. 'Brewster is a magnificent man, I've never met a more trustworthy chap. The problem is this damned phenomenon of cultural acceleration! Everything is happening so quickly these days that the people running the art scene just aren't able to keep up with events. The world is spinning madly out of control and we're facing a situation bloody close to chaos!'

Word had just reached Donald Pemberton that Jock Graham was parading up and down outside the gallery. The male half of Aesthetics and Resistance had been slaving in the kitchen preparing food and drink for several hours. Spartacus had just granted Don permission to abandon his work station, so that he could swan about amongst the guests.

'Let's get some tins of paint from the cellar,' Pemberton suggested to Penelope Applegate. 'Then we can go and throw it over Jock Graham!'

'What a super idea!' Penny sniggered.

Two minutes later, Aesthetics and Resistance ran out into the street. Graham had his back turned and Donald succeeded in emptying the entire contents of a tin of blue paint over his arch-enemy. When the former marxist spun around, Applegate threw red emulsion in his face. Jock dropped his placard and fled.

'This *New Neoism* is pure slapstick,' a critic from the *Journal of Immaterial Art* sneered. 'It lacks any significant intellectual content. Nevertheless, if what just happened was spontaneous, it has a naive charm. In my opinion, Jock Graham is an utter cunt and deserves a lot worse than being doused with paint. However, if the incident was pre-arranged, I can feel nothing but contempt for all the parties involved.'

Johnny Aggro arrived at Camden tube station a few minutes earlier than he'd planned. He stood next to a ticket machine, his back resting against the wall. On the dot of nine, Atima Sheazan rushed at him with open arms. Split seconds later, the former *Marxist Times* activist had her tongue in the boot boy's mouth. It was a long and lingering kiss, full of passion. Having greeted each other in this fashion, they made their way to the Oxford Arms.

'It's so weird seeing my parents again,' Atima sighed as she put down her pint. 'They don't want to let me out of their sight. You wouldn't believe the hassle I had getting out tonight. I had to promise them I'd be back by ten-thirty.'

'What!' Hodges spluttered. 'Are you telling me we've only got an hour or so together?'

'I'm afraid so,' Sheazan whispered, 'but don't blow your top, things will get better. My folks know that if they're too heavy, they'll lose me again.'

'What have you been doing today?' Johnny enquired.

'My mum's been working me to death,' Atima laughed. 'She's had me cleaning the house from top to bottom. My dad's invited all our relatives to come over tomorrow night, so that he can show off his reformed daughter. He feels vindicated because he's always told the family that I'd eventually see sense and give up Maoism!'

'I can guess what your mum will have you doing tomorrow then,' the skinhead chuckled.

'Tell me, clever clogs!' Sheazan demanded.

'She'll have you slaving over a hot stove until the guests arrive!' Hodges announced triumphantly.

'You're right!' Atima conceded.

'I guess some of your relatives will be staying overnight,' Johnny speculated, 'and I'm not gonna see you again until next week.'

'Half right,' Sheazan teased. 'My mum's relatives are coming down from the Midlands and they'll be stopping over with us. However, they'll be gone by Sunday lunch-time, so we can meet up then.'

Linda Forthwright gazed at Stephen Smith as he lay bound and naked on her bed. The young artist had bulges in all the right places. The arts administrator was convinced she would shortly be getting the fuck of a lifetime because her partner's cock looked huge now it was erect. Linda made slashing marks with her lipstick over Stephen's stomach and face. She then wrote the word 'SUBMISSION' on his chest.

Forthwright stepped out of her panties and lifted them to her face. When she sniffed the knickers, they smelt really rank. Just perfect for gagging her slave's mouth! Linda slipped the smalls over Smith's head and stuffed the stained section into his gob.

'Get a taste of my cunt!' Forthwright gushed.

Split seconds later the arts administrator had flipped Stephen on to his stomach. She retrieved a sneaker from the floor and tested it against her victim's arse. The sports shoe made a lovely thwacking sound and left a red welt on Smith's white flesh.

'It's gonna be a long night!' Forthwright announced. 'I'm really gonna enjoy this. I'll start off by teasing you. This isn't gonna be six of the best, instead there'll be a gradual tanning of your hide. Once I can feel plenty of heat coming off your bruised bum, I'm gonna grease up one of my stiletto shoes and shove it up your crack. You'll enjoy that, won't you!'

Stephen tried to reply but being gagged, the words he uttered were a meaningless mumble. Linda gave his arse a second tap with the sneaker and then moaned crazily.

'You know what?' Forthwright asked rhetorically. 'Once I've got really juiced up from punishing you, I'll make you lick out my twat. I hope you're a patient man because it'll be two hours before I let you stick your cock inside me. And after that, you'll have to wait at least another thirty minutes before I allow you to cum!

Nine

JOHNNY AGGRO WAS woken by the strains of free jazz drifting into his bedroom from the flat next door. It was a poor way to greet a new day. The skinhead needed to straighten himself out with some 4/4 rhythms! Hodges fell out of bed and crawled into the living room. Once he'd got a copy of *The Twisted World of Blowfly* on to his hi fi, the boot boy felt much better. Johnny stumbled into the kitchen and switched on the kettle, then went through to the bathroom where he splashed cold water in his eyes.

By the time the skinhead had downed a cuppa, Blowfly was cranking out 'Please Let Me Come In Your Mouth'. Hodges felt like having a wank but an image of Susan Jones and her friend Sarah flashed into his mind. The skinhead's thoughts were getting way out of line and if he didn't watch out, he'd find himself in serious trouble. Although Rebel's cousin had reached the age of consent several weeks ago, her friend was still fifteen and it would be at least another month before she ceased being jailbait! Now that he had time to reflect on the matter, Johnny realised it was a good thing he'd given his video of Sarah abusing Slim to Karen Eliot. It was a serious offence simply owning an amateur porn video that featured a schoolgirl!

Hodges let his mind drift. Blowfly was grinding his way through 'Fuck the Fat Off'. The skinhead took his time getting dressed. He still had a couple of hours free before hooking up with Karen Eliot. He wanted to see Atima Sheazan. He'd not had enough time with her the previous night. They'd not even had sex! And the skinhead now had to wait two days before he could see Atima again. Forty-eight hours in which Johnny would be kicking for kicks! The boot boy remembered that the Finsbury Firm, a gang of North London skinheads, were having a party in a house they'd squatted in Stoke Newington. That would give him something to do tonight.

Hodges made himself another cuppa. He plastered mixed fruit jam over two slices, then gazed out of the window as he chomped on his breakfast. Christ, the skinhead reflected, Poplar is a dump. Young mothers and their children scuttled around Chrisp Street Market looking like so many ants. Johnny had fucked a good number of the chicks and he often marvelled at their ability to look good in stilettos, tight clothes and expertly applied make-up. Being glamorous was a hard trick to pull off when you were a poverty-stricken single mother. Unfortunately, the local lasses' looks didn't last long. Poplar was full of pensioners plodding around at a snail's pace, oblivious to the fact that they were already dead.

Hodges' attempts to get his housing needs upgraded by faking mental illness had gone nowhere. What he required was a load of dough so that he could bag himself a W1 address. The boot boy decided to quiz Karen Eliot about how he should set about forging a career for himself in the art world. There seemed to be a lot of dosh being invested in 'serious culture'. From a financial point of view, artistic success was simply a matter of conning people into paying telephone numbers for worthless crap. With the exception of Eliot, Johnny had more respect for your average cardsharp or bank robber than the scumbags he'd met on the gallery scene. Nevertheless, the artist's trade was legal and so it had to be better than risking a heavy jail sentence every time you set off for work!

Sir Charles Brewster hadn't attended the *New Neoism* private view the previous night. Squatted galleries weren't really his scene. Besides, he was interested in authentic Neoist material from the nineteen-eighties, not a bunch of bandwagon jumping poseurs who'd missed the boat by well over a decade. While Sir Charles was very happy about the credibility the *New Neoism* lent to the original movement, he was convinced that if Stephen Smith and his comrades had been genuine innovators, they'd have come up with a previously unused name for their group.

Brewster had received numerous reports of the revels at the Thumbprint Gallery. More than one individual had relayed the news that there was to be a Neoist street action in Poplar on Saturday. Many of those present had been disappointed that not a single member of the original Neoist group had visited the exhibition. If Karen Eliot had shown her face, this would have lent the proceedings an authenticity they appeared to lack. Sir Charles had difficulty in controlling his laughter when caller after caller informed him that Jock Graham had colluded with the New Neoists in staging an obviously fake protest in Old Compton Street. Brewster's attention was fully occupied by this dupe. Jock Graham was paying the Progressive Arts Project supremo a visit.

'I don't think the protest I staged last night did much good!' Graham wailed.

'We've just got to keep at it, in the hope that the message about Neoism being a Satanic plot eventually gets across to the public,' Brewster countered.

'But no one will take my warnings seriously!' Jock yelled while simultaneously stamping his foot.

'I'm building up a dossier of evidence against the Neoists that can be leaked to the press,' Sir Charles declaimed. 'This material is so damning that people will have to take it seriously!'

'What sort of things have you got?' Graham demanded.

'Take a look at this, it's dynamite,' Brewster said as he handed the art critic a xerox of the programme for the *Third International Neoist Apartment Festival* held in Baltimore in 1981.

'What's so special about this piece of tomfoolery?' Jock wrangled as he cast his eyes over the document.

'That,' Sir Charles quibbled as he pointed at a name with his index finger. 'Laure Drogoul, she was heavily involved with the Neoists in the early eighties!'

'So what?' Graham whined. 'I've never heard of her.'

'Maybe this will refresh your memory,' Brewster haggled as he handed Jock a sheaf of press cuttings from the early nineteen-nineties.

Christopher Drogoul was the principal actor in the set of news stories Sir Charles had collated for the former marxist's benefit. They revealed that this apparently upright citizen had been imprisoned by the US authorities for alleged involvement in a banking scandal, illegal arms deals and meddling with international affairs.

'You must be kidding!' Graham barked. 'They can't be the same person, it would mean that Drogoul has had a sex change!'

'I didn't say they were the same person!' Brewster snapped. 'Conspiracy theorists are fixated with the du Ponts, Rockefellers and Rothschilds because the Illuminati operates through family networks. Chris is Laure's brother!'

'My God!' Jock spluttered. 'What the hell can we do about this?'

'You've got to get out there,' Sir Charles prevaricated, 'and warn every Christian group that will listen, speak to every arts administrator who will see you, brief every reporter prepared to cover the story. You've got to organise a protest against the Neoist action in Poplar on Saturday. In short, you'll have to work your butt off!'

'Right!' Graham bawled. 'I'm on my way!'

'Before you go,' Brewster stage-whispered, 'I wanna show you one more thing. The conspiracy can be traced through the avant-garde, from the futurists to the present. We'll go through the details later, this is just to show you one of the ways in which the Satanic plot connects back to fluxus.'

Sir Charles handed Jock a photocopy from a fluxus catalogue. This showed an envelope addressed by the group's founder, George Maciunas, to the composer La Monte Young. It was postmarked 9 October 1962, so it dated from the period when Maciunas was working as a graphic designer for the armed services. The return address, clearly marked on the envelope, was Army Post Box 666, New York City.'

'666,' Graham sighed. 'The number of the beast.

These bastards don't seem to have any fear of being exposed as part of a plot to destroy Christian civilisation.'

'I know,' Brewster replied solemnly. 'Which is why you've got to work your fingers to the bone warning the public about them!'

Emma Career was on a day-long working trip to Newcastle. She'd arranged to meet Martin Porker for lunch in the cafeteria of the local School of Art. The former Neoist had long been a fixture at the institution, where he taught foundation and first year degree students. Career found Porker sitting at a table with a plate of doughnuts in front of him. The failed artist was absent-mindedly dunking this fare into a huge mug of coffee.

'Hi, you must be Martin Porker,' the arts administrator gushed, having identified her dinner date from his huge gut. 'I'm Emma Career.'

'Hello,' the arts tutor replied. 'Take a seat. I'm afraid I was too hungry to wait for you before starting my lunch. I was out on the piss last night and I needed a fry-up to help me shake off a hangover. Having slept late, I only had time to eat eight Weetabix for breakfast.'

'Forget it,' Career rejoined congenially as she sat down. 'I'm not going to eat, I don't feel hungry. What I'm interested in doing is talking to you about Neoism.'

'Oh that,' Porker yapped. 'It was all a terrible mistake. No one ever made any money from it. I wasted a good few years working on the fringes of the movement, only to end up teaching at this second-rate arts institution. These days, I produce huge expressionistic canvases. I've learnt a lot from my students, some of them are now making a fortune by producing this sort of work for the London market.'

'If you're not producing Neoist style works any more,' Emma hedged, 'perhaps you've got some old material that you'd like to show me?'

'Nah,' Martin caterwauled. 'I've not got a thing left. I cleared out my attic last week. Sir Charles Brewster paid five grand for everything I'd got. I consider myself lucky to have got anything for it. No one is interested in the stuff and I'd been thinking about throwing it in a skip.'

Emma felt her heart sink. If the arts administrator had been a little quicker off the mark, she'd have beaten Sir Charles to this cut-price gold mine. The Progressive Arts Project supremo was bound to make a huge profit on this purchase. However, Career still thought Porker worth cultivating, as there had to be something that could be salvaged from this missed opportunity.

'If you made some new works in the Neoist style,' Emma bandied, 'I'd give you a solo show at the Bow Studios.'

'Look where Neoism got me!' Martin whinged. 'If I'd been more cynical during the eighties, I wouldn't have ended up working as a tutor at this poxy college!'

'There must be some compensations,' Career coaxed. 'After all, I bet lots of your students are pretty young girls!'

'Young!' Porker snorted. 'They're all well past the age of consent! I always wanted to work with children!'

At this point, Emma made her excuses and left. She'd met some sick bastards in her time but the ex-Neoist took the biscuit. The stories she'd heard about

Porker desperately seeking work as a babysitter were obviously true! Career had no intention of being regaled with first generation versions of the pervert's twisted fantasies. Emma insisted on certain standards being maintained!

Having spent time in the Tea Rooms outlining the various ways in which the membership of the Semiotic Liberation Front should be manipulated in the future, Karen Eliot took Johnny Aggro back to her Bloomsbury flat. The art star then devoted the best part of an hour to showing the skinhead her huge photo collection of guys she'd beaten, spanked and otherwise abused.

'Why the fuck do these geezers let you snap them bound and naked?' Johnny asked in awe.

'Because they enjoy it,' Karen elucidated. 'You'd like it too if you could just get over your macho hang-ups.'

'There's no fuckin' way I'm ever gonna let you tie me up!' Hodges countered. 'God only knows what tortures you'd come up with, I'd have to be outta my mind to let you do it.'

'You'll give in eventually,' Karen laughed. 'I know your type too well. You're a borderline masochist unable to admit your true feelings to anyone. That's why you cover your desire to be dominated by a strong woman with macho skinhead cultism!'

'Come off it!' Johnny sneered. 'I just like the look, hard but smart!'

'Nah,' Eliot contradicted. 'Your dress sense is inextricably linked to your sexuality. The reason you go for exaggerated masculinity in your clothes is because subconsciously you hope it will disguise your yearning to wear short skirts and high heels!'

'I'm sick of arguing about this!' the boot boy announced. 'Let's talk about something else instead.'

'Alright,' the art star conceded. 'Let's discuss Neoism.'

'Okay,' Hodges agreed.

'It's funny,' Karen observed, 'until now you always said Neoism bored you.'

'That's true,' Johnny declared with conviction. 'I think Neoism sucks, what interests me is the money to be made in the art world. How do I set myself up as a top-flight painter?'

'The easiest way to make money from art,' Eliot honked, 'is to work on the administrative side. Most artists are failures from a financial point of view. There's such a profusion of so-called talent that collectors can pick and choose who they want to support!'

'But aren't you coining it?' Hodges demanded.

'Sure,' Karen quacked, 'but I'm the exception that proves the rule. Most artists are either poor or have inherited wealth. They toil within the gallery system because they've swallowed the myth that a genius is creatively incontinent! Some of them even consider the social status they gain as a result of their work to be a sufficient reward for their labour. Admittedly, these types tend to come from wealthy backgrounds, so they're not short of a few bob!'

'Are you telling me I can't make a fortune as an artist?' the skinhead clacked.

'I'm not saying you can't do it,' Eliot rasped, 'I'm just telling you it's bloody difficult.'

Rebel clocked Maria Walker as he trudged

through Chrisp Street Market. She was pleased to see him and a quick conversation revealed that both of them had taken the afternoon off work. The skinhead agreed to accompany the doctor to her terraced house at the bottom end of Violet Road.

'This is nice,' the boot boy observed as he sank into a black leather sofa.

'Do you want a cuppa?' Maria enquired. 'Or shall we get straight down to rutting?'

'Let's just fuck,' Rebel determined.

'Stand up and turn around,' Walker instructed. As Rebel did so, she added, 'Has anyone ever told you what a beautiful arse you've got?'

'No,' the skinhead laughed nervously.

'I want you to drop your pants and trousers,' the doctor snapped.

'Why?' the boot boy asked.

'Just do it,' Maria gabbled. 'That's it, let me see your crack. Oh, it's lovely, it was made for spanking!'

'You're really twisted bitch!' Rebel cackled.

'True, too true!' Walker snickered.

The doctor sidled up behind the skinhead. One of her hands snaked around Rebel's gut and toyed with his erect prick. Split seconds later, Walker forced an index finger into the boot boy's anal crack. Rebel turned his head and Maria kissed his cheek. Mad thoughts ran through the doctor's mind. Walker was sick of her boyfriend, he was far too uptight to let her make use of the sex toys she'd bought in Soho and that now lay unused in a bedroom cupboard.

'Lie on your stomach,' Maria whispered into Rebel's ear, 'and close your eyes. I'll be back in a minute.'

The skinhead did as he was told. He let his mind drift. The boot boy saw the mudflats beneath him as he soared through a clear blue sky. The breeze was salty and waves crashing on a volcanic beach echoed across aeons of time. The youngster didn't pay much attention to what was going on as Walker knelt beside him and pulled his arms behind his back. Rebel only opened his eyes when two metallic clicks alerted him to the fact that a pair of handcuffs had been locked into place around his wrists.

'Hey, what's goin' on?' the skinhead squealed.

'A bit of fun,' the doctor giggled. 'I just wanna open your mind to various sexual possibilities and demonstrate that there's a very thin dividing line between pleasure and pain. Don't try to resist because I won't undo those handcuffs until I've had my kicks!'

Maria proceeded to tap Rebel's buttocks with a cane. Gradually, the speed and intensity of the strokes increased. Maria kept this up until the boot boy's backside gave off a healthy red glow. Walker then picked up a vibrator, switched it on and shoved the sex toy up the skinhead's arse. Next, the doctor took off her knickers and rubbed the rank panties in Rebel's face.

'Now,' Maria said as she undid the handcuffs. 'I want you to show me how passionate a man gets after he's been subjected to a bit of abuse!'

Rebel pulled the vibrator out of his arse and hurled it across the room without bothering to switch the thing off. Having thrown Walker over his knee, he hitched up her skirt and spanked the bitch. There was nothing subtle about what happened next, there didn't need to be, the skinhead simply took the doctor doggie-style on the floor. He penetrated her dripping mystery in one easy thrust and shot his load after twenty-four strokes!

*

Donald Pemberton and Penelope Applegate were invigilating the *New Neoism* exhibition at the Thumbprint Gallery on Soho's Old Compton Street. There'd been a constant stream of visitors throughout the morning and the place was mobbed during the lunch hour. Three art students were making copious notes on the show when Stephen Smith arrived with a friend.

'Hi!' Spartacus boomed.

'Hi!' Aesthetics and Resistance echoed.

'This is Patrick Good,' Smith announced. 'He's doing freelance reviews for *Art Scene*.'

'Yo!' the critic thundered while simultaneously raising his right palm to shoulder level.

'Yo!' Pemberton and Applegate echoed.

'Patrick,' Stephen proclaimed, 'is prepared to give the show a rave review once we've treated him to a piece of virgin arse.'

'I want him!' Good undulated, pointing at Donald.

Pemberton turned white as the blood drained from his face, then the sensitive young artist keeled over and collapsed on the floor. At this, Spartacus and the critic broke into peels of laughter.

'What's so funny?' Penny demanded.

'I told Good that Don would faint if I ordered him to have sex with a man,' Smith explained. 'Patrick is straight, picking your boyfriend as a sexual partner was a wind-up. Now take our friend through to the kitchen and give him a blow job!'

'Okay,' Applegate acquiesced.

'Wow,' one of the art students who was visiting the gallery expounded to Spartacus. 'That trick you just pulled was pure Neoism. I've been reading up about the group and pranks were obviously a major part of what the movement was about.'

'That's right,' Stephen concurred. 'Neoism means never having to say that you're sorry. It's the birth cry of the higher man destined to do away with all the dross imposed on humanity by a corrupt ruling class!'

'Can I be in your next Neoist exhibition?' the student asked.

'Is that chick your girlfriend?' Spartacus demanded as he pointed at the bitch 'Because you can join the movement if she'll suck my dick.'

'I ain't givin' you head!' the babe snapped. 'But I'll be more than happy to sit on your face!'

'That'll do nicely,' Smith avowed. 'We'll go into the kitchen once Penny has finished giving Patrick his jollies.'

At that moment, ten young men belonging to the Jesus Brigade burst into the gallery. Jock Graham had informed these bigots that Neoism was part of a plot to overthrow Christian civilisation. The militants had intended to smash up the exhibition but now stood looking at the work on display in bewilderment.

'Okay,' their leader eventually demanded. 'Who beat us to the punch? Was it Wimmin Against Rape and Pornography who destroyed the work you were showing here? They often pick the same targets as us but for completely different reasons. We hate them, their refusal to accept that God created Eve from Adam's spare rib is anti-Christian. Come on, answer me, was it WARP who wrecked this *New Neoist* show?'

'I don't know what you're talking about,' Spartacus jabbered. 'The work is meant to look like this, it hasn't been damaged.'

'Come on!' the Christian swelled. 'I'm not

stupid, I won't fall for your lies. Anyway, we've got no time to waste, since the exhibition has been destroyed by other hands, we're off.'

The Jesus Brigade filed out through the door and Stephen resumed the interrupted conversation with his student friends. He liked the three kids a lot. The chick had a foxy attitude and was therefore guaranteed to be a bundle of fun in the sack. After his recent sex session with Linda Forthwright, Smith had decided that he liked dominant wimmin.

Karen Eliot had been showing Johnny Aggro a selection of her home porn videos.

'Anyway,' Karen oscillated as the video rewound, 'you've seen enough footage of me in action to know that if you were willing to explore your true desires, you'd love to be my slave.'

'Come off it,' Johnny mocked. 'I'd rather tie you up and spank your bottom!'

'I'm a top!' Eliot feigned. 'I'd never let you do that! But would you like to see what I've done with the footage of your mate Slim?'

'He's not my mate any more,' the skinhead corrected. 'He's been turfed out of the Raiders for being a cunt.'

Karen changed the cassette in her VCR and pressed the play button on the remote control. The footage had been cut up and featured a lot of close-ups of Slim's face. In places, the film ran in slow motion or else kept looping back over a scene. A message intermittently flashed up on the screen—'Peter Watson aka Slim.' The soundtrack was an assortment of sampled farts.

'It ain't exactly subtle!' Hodges observed.

'It doesn't need to be,' Eliot maintained. 'Neoism is about slapstick and farce! Besides, you're gonna get the Semiotic Liberation Front to retune the TVs in the window of the Chrisp Street Market electronics shop to 32 Hz. Simultaneously, I'll be making a pirate broadcast on to the sets from a van parked in a side street. Unfortunately, people passing the shop won't get to hear the sound, I just dubbed it on for my own amusement!'

'You're fuckin' wicked!' the boot boy testified.

'I'm an evil genius!' Karen added sarcastically. 'Anyway, it should make life in Poplar more exciting than usual. The place is a dump, I dunno how you can bear to live there.'

'Nor do I,' Johnny replied morosely.

Eliot rewound the cassette and removed it from the VCR. In its place, she put a video of suicides and assassinations. Karen figured it would cheer Hodges up, and it did so in five seconds flat.

'Fuck,' the skinhead swore as JFK was wiped out in the Dallas turkey shoot. 'I hate politicians, it's great seeing them getting done over!'

'Yeah,' Karen sniggered. 'It reminds you that this old world is up for grabs. No one group of people runs the show, the whole shebang is spinning madly out of control!'

'You sound like a bloody politico,' Hodges spat. 'Who cares about how the world is run? Left wing or right wing, it's all bollocks. I'm not interested in trying to brainwash people. I just wanna have my kicks and get on with my life. I'll be happy once the busybodies stop sticking their noses into my business and deciding that some kind of legislation is needed because I'm not like them.'

'That's completely utopian!' Eliot growled. 'I find it amusing that at least ninety per cent of the population share your opinions and yet the masses always get fucked over by the tiny minority who've mastered the basics of political control.'

Jock Graham was doing his best to expose the Satanic cabal behind Neoism. He'd spent the morning phoning every journalist and editor he'd ever met. Unfortunately, neither Fleet Street hacks nor art world insiders were interested in opposing the evil plot to destroy Christian civilisation. The critic had more luck with religious groups—although the major denominations refused to take this occult threat seriously. The only way to get the message across to ordinary men and wimmin was by handing out leaflets on the street.

'Stop the Satanic menace!' Graham exhorted the hundreds of individuals who were passing him on Oxford Street. 'Smash Neoism! Do God's work here on earth!'

'You what? You what? You what, you what, you what?' Ross MacDonald and Joseph Campbell chanted in unison as they approached the fundamentalist.

'Help!' Jock screamed. 'Police! Arrest these men! They'll murder me! They're part of a Satanic conspiracy!'

As the artists drew closer, Graham turned on his heels and ran up to the cops who were standing a few yards away. MacDonald and Campbell strode confidently up to the critic, who was now cowering beside the two constables.

'Save me from them!' the fundamentalist gibbered. 'They're Neoists, the world won't be safe until their souls are burning in hell. See, see, where Christ's blood streams in the firmament!'

'Could I have one of your leaflets?' Ross enquired.

Jock lunged at the artist, his fist narrowly missing MacDonald's cheek as the younger man weaved to one side. Graham attempted to kick his adversary in the balls but one of the cops grabbed his shoulders to restrain him. The other constable pulled the critic's arms behind his back and slipped a pair of handcuffs on the deranged man's wrists.

'Imposters!' Jock tutted. 'If you deserved the respect that I normally accord to your uniform, then you'd protect upright citizens who are defending Christian values in the face of a Satanic plot!'

One of the Mets radioed for an ambulance. There was no point in taking this nutcase to the police station. What the madman needed was a sedative and long-term psychiatric treatment.

'He's got a knife!' Graham bleated as MacDonald bent down to pick up one of the anti-Neoist leaflets that had been scattered across the pavement.

One of the cops punched the Christian nutter in the mouth. There was the satisfying crunch of splintering bone as Jock blacked out. Until an ambulance crew arrived with a sedative, this was a pretty effective means of keeping the lunatic under control.

'Thank you officer,' Ross smarmed. 'I think you and your partner may have saved my life.'

'Think nothing of it son,' the constable replied modestly. 'It's all in the line of duty. The taxpayer wouldn't be getting value for money if us police officers weren't risking life and limb every time we took to the streets.'

'Nevertheless,' MacDonald mooed, 'it's terrible that Joe Public hasn't been safe since the government launched its cost-cutting care in the community schemes!'

'The answer is to say no to drugs and vote liberal democrat at every opportunity!' the cop replied wisely.

Amanda Debden-Philips couldn't believe her luck. She'd arranged to visit an old school chum in Kennington but the bitch had been delayed at work. Amanda's friend shared a rotting terraced house with several poverty-stricken artists. Peter Anderson, a near mythical Neoist figure, was staying with one of these bozos. Debden-Philips recognised the wild man of the eighties avant-garde immediately, thanks to his long beard and pony-tail. The arts administrator quickly engaged Pete in a tête-à–tête about culture. However, Amanda knew that if she came straight out and quizzed Anderson on Neoism, he'd clam right up. Peter's reticence was the stuff of legend. A series of manipulations was required if he was to be pumped for information about Neoism.

'I disagree completely,' Anderson lowed. 'The art world didn't promote a single artist of any worth during the eighties. Sure, jokey little movements like Neo-Naturism had their fifteen minutes of fame in some Kings Road gallery, but even these attempts at reviving the corpse of serious culture were given the cold shoulder by Mayfair.'

'It would seem to follow from your argument,' Debden-Philips snapped, 'that no art of any merit was produced during the eighties!'

'I didn't say that,' Peter chirped. 'What I was suggesting was that the only work of merit was created outside the gallery system.'

'I don't know what you're talking about!'

Amanda exclaimed. 'According to you, this was a period of conservatism and conformity. If your claims to this effect are true, surely no one was engaged in marginal practices!'

'You're ignoring one of the most important groups of the twentieth century,' Anderson twittered. 'Have you forgotten that the Neoist Network was active during much of that decade?'

'I haven't forgotten about Neoism,' Debden-Philips protested. 'I've never heard of it!'

'Typical,' Peter muttered. 'You're a typically ignorant art world bitch. If we took a wander across Kennington Park, we'd soon locate the site of the Eighth International Neoist Apartment Festival. It was held in and around a terraced house on Aulton Place!'

'Tell me about Neoism,' Amanda spluttered.

'It's too complicated,' Anderson trilled. 'It would take me a week to convey the basics of an exoteric interpretation. To grasp the movement's esoteric meanings requires years of arduous spiritual training.'

'What about giving me a few facts?' the arts administrator wailed. 'Like who founded the group?'

'Oh, that's easy,' Peter frothed. 'A Celto-Tibetan mystic named Yantoh. He'd wandered the lengths of both Atlantis and Mu before they sank beneath the waves and acquired much wisdom as a result of these travels. Yantoh had many occult powers, including the ability to transform himself into a dog. He established the Neoist Network as a means of attracting fresh disciples to help complete the Great Work!'

'That's all very well,' Debden-Philips yelled, 'but it doesn't tell me anything at all about why Neoism was the most important avant-garde movement of the eighties!'

'Art,' Anderson replied knowledgeably, 'is a mere cipher, a key to assist poor, deluded mankind escape from this shadow world. In itself the avant-garde is of no consequence, art works only gain significance when they are utilised to unlock the secrets of the universe!'

Johnny Aggro had done his duty. Various materials and detailed instructions for the Neoist intervention at Chrisp Street Market had been delivered to Stephen Smith. Hodges was sick of the Hiram and Spartacus nonsense in which he was embroiled. However, within forty-eight hours, the Semiotic Liberation Front would find themselves in serious trouble with the law. This would be the culmination of the skinhead's revenge against Donald Pemberton and Penelope Applegate. Once the cops were in on the action, he'd be able to turn his back on all this secret society nonsense. Maybe he'd even get the Raiders to squat Don and Penny's soon to be empty flat!

The boot boy had been killing time in a Dalston pub. It was well past eleven when he made his way up to Stoke Newington. The Finsbury Firm had squatted a huge property on Manor Road. Their party was beginning to swing when Johnny arrived. *Trojan's Greatest Hits* was blasting from a huge pair of speakers and half a dozen skinhead girls were dancing around their handbags. The two-score blokes present were getting tanked up before getting down to demonstrating their expertise at the grape-crusher stomp.

'Whatcha!' Samson boomed into Hodges' ear. 'You should have got 'ere twenty minutes earlier! Slim turned up. I gave him a clout round the ear and he fucked off! I've never seen the wanker run so fast!' It was the only way 'ee could avoid a real kickin'. I told 'im 'ee was a right cunt for trying to punch out a bird!'

'Oh, well,' Johnny sighed philosophically. 'Even if there ain't any more heads to bash tonight, it shouldn't be difficult gettin' laid. I fancy that tart over there, the one with the fishnets and the cut-off jeans. She's sporting the tastiest feather-cut I've seen in the past year!'

'You'd better leave 'er alone,' Samson warned his leader. 'She's goin' out with one of the Finsbury Firm. It wouldn't be right to pull one of their birds when it's them layin' on the hospitality!'

It was at this juncture that the Catford Crew turned up. The Finsbury Firm made a point of not

inviting politicos to their parties, but some idiot had forgotten this cardinal rule and told the boneheads about the do. Everyone present knew it was only a matter of time before there was trouble. Politicians were always ruining ordinary people's fun by turning the most trivial issues into major ideological debates.

'Enough of that ethnic rubbish,' one of the Nazi nutters announced as he pulled the Trojan album off the deck. 'Let's listen to some British music instead!'

The bonehead pulled a copy of *The Strong Survive* by Skrewdriver from a carrier bag and slapped it on to the stereo. This instantly killed the party atmosphere, since no one could dance to such leaden crap. Spilt seconds after the Nazi nutter wandered off to get a beer, one of the Finsbury Firm put the reggae compilation back on. The bonehead made his way back to the record deck but this time it was being guarded by several skins.

'We're not gonna listen to your garbage,' one of them announced. 'This is our party and we wanna dance. Skrewdriver were just a bunch of bald rockers playing bad heavy metal. Their music has nothing to do with the skinhead cult and if you wanna listen to such crap, you'll have to do so in other company because we only play reggae at our parties!'

Someone snapped the Skrewdriver album in half and this was the signal for all hell to break loose. The Nazi nutters attempted to make a break for it but their route out of the house had been blocked by quick-thinking skins. Bottles cracked against fascist skulls, while boots thudded into their soft bellies and groins. A few minutes later, it was all over. The boneheads were thrown on to the street. It would be quite some time before these bozos got their shit together and headed for the emergency ward of a local hospital where they'd be able to lick their wounds while their bruised bodies were patched up.

'Why do these political cunts always have to try and ruin our fun?' one of the birds was demanding. 'Last time we had a party, a load of red wankers tried to stop us dancing to a Prince Buster record because they said it was sexist! I fuckin' hate these political bigots, they should . . .'

'Did you see me put the boot in just now?' her boyfriend interrupted. 'I must 'ave broken loadsa teeth!'

Ten

JOCK GRAHAM WAS woken by the grey light of dawn filtering in through the uncurtained window. As he struggled to lift himself up, sheets tangled around his body. The bed was fitted with straps to restrain violent patients but these had not been secured. The art critic had been so heavily sedated that, according to medical theory, he shouldn't have woken up for at least forty-eight hours. Unfortunately, the shrinks running the institution hadn't taken into account the psychological drives that occasionally allow religious fanatics to perform superhuman feats. Graham tried to focus his thoughts as he swung his legs over the bed. Split seconds later, he collapsed on the floor.

It was another hour before the art critic regained consciousness. This time he was less confused. He remembered the cops arresting him after he'd been attacked by Satanic Neoist conspirators. It didn't take Jock long to work out he was incarcerated in a mental hospital. The art critic saw escape as imperative, so that he could save Christian Civilisation from the Legions of the Anti-Christ! He had to assume that the police and the doctors were under the direct command of the Illuminati. Graham would kill the bastards if they stood between him and freedom!

There was a noise in the corridor. An orderly was delivering breakfast to patients in the secure rooms. Jock darted across his cell and stood with his back flat against the wall. Keys clicked in the lock and the orderly pushed open the door. The art critic grabbed the cunt by the throat and proceeded to throttle him. The orderly turned red, then white and finally blue, before asphyxiating.

Graham stripped the corpse before slinging it on to his hospital bed. Once sheets and blankets had been thrown over the stiff, it looked like someone enjoying a deep sleep. Jock slipped into the dead man's clothes. The jeans were loose around his waist, the sleeves on the shirt and jumper didn't reach his wrists, but the bozo's white coat covered these defects. Fortunately, the shoes were a perfect fit.

The art critic made his way along the corridor. The sixth key he tried opened the security gate that led into the hospital grounds. Graham walked in a straight line across a well-tended lawn. He marched through some woodland and eventually came to a brick wall. After scrambling over this obstacle, Jock found himself in a country lane. He ran along the road until he came to a parked car. The art critic hot-wired the Cortina and split seconds later, roared off in the direction of London.

The traffic snarled up in Streatham and was still only crawling along when the ex-marxist reached Brixton twenty minutes later. Graham parked the car on a side street. He dumped his white coat in a rubbish bin. In Coldharbour Lane, Jock grabbed a schoolboy by the throat. The kid was frightened to death and handed over two ten-pound notes plus a fistful of change without arguing about it. The mugging was on a par with other forms of heavenly deception. Graham needed the money to cover the cost of both a second-hand suit and the bus fare to Poplar. Without the readies, the art critic didn't have a hope in hell of saving Christian Civilisation from the Satanic Neoist Conspiracy!

Johnny Aggro was only partially awake when he turned over and struck a femail bulk. The skinhead groaned and crawled out of bed. He felt better once he'd slapped a compilation of Maytals hits onto his hi fi. 'Bam Bam' helped clear the fog from his mind, while '54–46 That's My Number' gave the boot boy enough enthusiasm to splash cold water into his eyes and put the kettle on. The up-tempo beat chugging away behind Frederick 'Toots' Hibbert's melodious voice helped Hodges forget his raging hangover. Johnny had got home at 5 a.m. that morning and then spent two hours banging away at the bitch who was still snoring in his bed. Considering the fact that he'd had a skinful and not much more than four hours' sleep, the boot boy felt pretty damn good. A second cuppa as 'Bim Today' blasted from Wharfdale speakers really lifted his spirits. In a little more than twenty-four hours, the skinhead would rendezvous with Atima. Things were looking up.

Hodges stared out of a window at Chrisp Street Market, twenty-three floors beneath him. The Saturday morning shoppers still resembled ants but something was wrong. Instead of moving with the usual clockwork precision of their pre-programmed lives, the local proles were acting as if an alien army had invaded their turf. A huge crowd was gathering on the south side of the shopping precinct. The market traders were visibly losing business to some unanticipated rival.

Johnny rushed through to the bedroom and pulled on a fresh pair of Union Jack boxer shorts. He grabbed a button-down and his favourite tonics. Hodges sat on the bed as he tied his boot laces. The bird he'd brought home was woken by this flurry of activity. Johnny tried to remember her name. It began with an 'S' but wasn't Sally, Susan or Sarah. Despite her feather-cut, the chick had used something quite punky. Slash, that was it—a nickname!

'What's happening?' the knuckle-girl demanded.

'Something weird!' Johnny responded. 'I've never seen anything like it here!'

'But what is it?' the bird persisted.

'I dunno,' Hodges conceded. 'That's why I wanna go out and see what's goin' down!'

'Wait till I'm ready to go with you!' Slash commanded.

'Hurry up then!' the boot boy replied irritably. 'I don't wanna miss it!'

'Make us a cuppa while I dress and put on me make-up,' the knuckle-girl pleaded.

Johnny stomped through to the kitchen and put on the kettle. Slowly it dawned on the skinhead that the disturbance twenty-three floors beneath him must have something to do with Karen Eliot and the Semiotic Liberation Front. He'd passed on the instructions for the Neoist Action in Poplar but the alcohol that was still churning through his veins was hampering the efficient functioning of his brain. Nevertheless, the whole thing seemed incredible. He realised that Eliot's ideas for the happening at Chrisp Street Market would cause Slim a fair amount of embarrassment but it was hard to believe that she'd stirred the inbred locals into breaking the dull routines that governed their robotic lives!

Maria Walker didn't hear her social-worker boyfriend come into the house with the week's shopping. The doctor's attention was fully engaged by the hardcore video she'd borrowed from Karen Eliot. Watching seventeen-year-old boys with perfect bodies being put through their sexual paces by a bunch of middle-aged wimmin was highly entertaining. Walker had something rather important to tell Bob Salisbury-Smith but she'd figured it could wait until after he'd fetched the groceries.

'What's this filth you're watching?' the care worker demanded. 'I joined Concerned Radicals Against Pornography to stop irresponsible types consuming anti-social material that degrades wimmin!'

'The video's called *Teenage Pricks Service Well-Stretched Snatch*,' Maria rebutted. 'The title might be shit but the action is hot!'

'I can't believe this is happening in my own home!' Salisbury-Smith wailed. 'What's got into you bunnykins? Has some evil pervert been twisting your mind with hate propaganda aimed at promoting the sex war?'

'Nah!' Walker snarled. 'I just figured it was time I got liberated. I'm not gonna put up with any more crap from wankers like you who wanna censor the imagination. If you had your way we'd be living in a world inhabited by sexless robots who never engaged in activities that challenged the administrative practices of Big Brother style bureaucrats and other right-on scum!'

'What are you saying?' Bob spluttered.

'I'm telling you to get out of this house and stay

out of it!' Maria yelled. 'I'm telling you that you don't cut it between the sheets and our relationship is over! I recently took up screwing some of the young men who belong to a Poplar skinhead gang and it reminded me what I'd been missing since I hooked up with you! In fact, one of the boot boys is shacking up with me, he'll be round here in about an hour!'

'I won't hit you!' Salisbury-Smith exclaimed. 'I abhor violence! However, I'm not moving out, this is my home! And the yobbo isn't moving in either! He'll probably start beating you the minute I've gone. Working-class males are brutes, that's why I joined the Labour Party, to civilise them!'

'You won't civilise Rebel!' Walker bellowed. 'He'll simply beat your brains to a bloody pulp! For your own safety, I'm advising you to pack a suitcase and then depart under your own steam! If you hang around, my new boyfriend might well see to it that the only way you leave is in an ambulance!'

'Don't try and intimidate me with these threats!' the social worker barked. 'I'm staying and that's final! Besides, I deal with oiks every day of my working life! I know how to handle working-class scum!'

'You're outta your bloody mind!' the doctor ruffled. 'The boys you work with are all crippled! Rebel isn't going to arrive in a wheelchair, he'll come striding in wearing a pair of steel toe-capped boots!'

'In that case,' Salisbury-Smith screeched. 'I'm going to get a hammer from the garage. I may abhor violence but that doesn't mean I'm gonna be intimidated by racist and sexist yobs!'

'Who said Rebel was racist?' Maria disapproved.

'You told me he was a skinhead!' the social worker announced triumphantly. 'Besides, it's well-known that most working-class males have fascist sympathies!'

'You bigoted cunt!' Walker screamed. 'All your leftie posturing is simply a cover for a vortex of knee-jerk prejudice!'

Johnny and Slash weren't the first people to notice that Chrisp Street Market had been plastered with posters depicting Slim being humiliated by a schoolgirl. They pushed their way through the huge crowd that had gathered outside the TV shop and were eventually rewarded with a glimpse of further abuse taking place on the iconic surface of several television screens, thanks to Karen Eliot's pirate broadcast.

'After futurism, dadaism, surrealism, situationism, nouveau realisme, fluxus and conceptualism, comes Neoism!' a voice chanted mindlessly through a megaphone.

Like almost everyone else present, Johnny Aggro ignored the Semiotic Liberation Front's New Neoist intervention. Slim's mother, Vera Watson, who was standing in front of the TV shop, had become the centre of everyone's attention. She was an instant star, thanks to the treachery of a hostile neighbour who'd revealed her identity to a pushy journalist.

'The girl in that film is only fifteen,' a newsman announced excitedly as he made an obscene gesture at the television screens, 'how does it feel to know that your son is sexually perverted?'

'Peter is a good boy,' Mrs Watson snarled defensively, 'he's always done right by me. He'd never do anything kinky. That isn't him on the telly, it's some kind of electronic trickery. It's like when the baddies fake

Arnie's death towards the end of *The Running Man*. The footage is far too good to be real!'

'I understand your son is twenty-four years old,' the journalist persisted, 'and that he is a member of a notoriously violent skinhead gang called the Raiders.'

'I've got nuthin' more to say to you!' Vera flounced.

A media whore slipped Mrs Watson twenty quid. Vera had a determination that matched her girth but the money sent this proud working womun into a state bordering on religious fervour. Slim's mum had known poverty for much of her life and she fingered the crisp note in the way that a nun would caress a statue of the infant Jesus. As the trendy had correctly guessed, a little dosh was all it took to get Mrs Watson to drop her guard.

'Come on Vera,' the newsman chirped. 'Tell us about the sexual exploits of your son and his skinhead gang!'

'Peter has sown his wild oats,' Mrs Watson admitted, 'and while he's been in a few fights, he's always defended himself like an Englishman with his fists and his boots. My son never uses blades or shooters. He's always looked after his old mum too, having lived at home all his life. Most of Peter's school friends are married now—but he never had much luck with girls. The only ones who'd sleep with him were whores like that Sarah Osterly. I've heard that every boy in the fourth and fifth forms at the local school have had their evil way with that slut! Sarah might only be fifteen but she's had hanky panky with hundreds of men! Peter, on the other hand, has only slept with a handful of girls in his entire . . .'

Vera's monologue was interrupted by Sarah's

mother. Janet Osterly was led through the crowd by a journalist who'd waylaid the bitch on her way home from a part-time cleaning job. Janet pummelled Slim's mother with her fists but she was no match for her older and more heavily set rival.

'My Sarah is a good girl!' the cleaning lady howled as she was knocked to the ground. 'She's been corrupted by your kinky good-for-nothing son. Everyone around here knows Slim's got a conviction for . . .'

Mrs Osterly's voice was lost in the roar of the crowd as other individuals jumped into the fray. Numerous inter-family feuds raged among the local community and this confrontation was a chance to bring them all into the open. The sides seemed pretty evenly matched as the fighting spread across Chrisp Street Market.

'Excellent! Excellent!' the newsmen muttered as their back-up crews sought to record the action with their outside broadcast cameras.

Vera Watson wasn't the only individual dealing with media enquiries that day. However, Sir Charles Brewster was an old hand at manipulating the press and had quite deliberately let it slip to several friends who worked in television that he'd had personal dealings with Jock Graham, the art critic turned crazed killer. An interview was set up within a matter of minutes because the public needed inside information about the man who'd escaped from a lunatic asylum that very morning after murdering an orderly.

'So tell me,' the newscaster Ronald MacTrevor simpered. 'Just what is Jock Graham like as an individual?'

'Highly unstable,' the Progressive Arts Project supremo replied authoritatively. 'I met him on several occasions and he always struck me as being a dangerous lunatic. He's what's known in psychological jargon as a "true believer", someone who is fanatically devoted to whatever meme has taken control of their mind. At one time he was a marxist but more recently he converted to Christian fundamentalism.'

'And when was the last time you saw him?' MacTrevor probed.

'Yesterday afternoon!' Sir Charles exclaimed. 'Only a few hours before his arrest for attacking various artists and policemen in Oxford Street!'

'Really?' Ronald hissed in mock disbelief. 'What were the circumstances of this meeting?'

'Graham turned up at my office without an appointment and knocked my secretary to the floor when she tried to prevent him reaching me,' Brewster revealed to a shocked British nation.

'What did he want?' MacTrevor had adopted the airs of a master interrogator.

'He said,' Sir Charles whispered, 'that he'd come to warn me about an increasingly popular art movement known as Neoism. Graham claimed he had proof that it was a front for plotters bent on overthrowing Christian civilisation.'

'Can you elaborate?' Ronald demanded.

'Sure,' Brewster assented. 'You see, Graham claimed that Neoism was an attempt to complete the work of fluxus artist Joseph Beuys. As is well-known, Beuys was a disciple of the occultist, or anthroposophist, Rudolf Steiner. Now, in Steiner's cosmology, the evolution of the earth is the result of a constant cooling down and hardening of spirit into matter. So we're going from something fluid, amorphous, warm and dynamic, to a state that is best characterised as hard, formed, cold and static. Are you with me?'

'Yes,' MacTrevor confirmed.

'Now,' Sir Charles declaimed. 'You find the divine at the top of the spiritual spheres and stones at the bottom of the material plane. While spirit is present in every being, there is a danger that the things in the middle—for example plants, animals and men—will turn into stone. To prevent this happening, Steiner suggested that a spiritual leader was required to reverse the process.'

'I see,' Ronald put in.

'So,' Brewster continued. 'A Messiah is required to warm the spirit that is present in all beings. This Messiah may be a shaman, a teacher or an artist. Beuys read this theory as a mode of construction for the modern artist. Thus, in his sculptural work, he uses fat which is fluid when warm and hard if it's cold. This element was combined with felt, an insulating material made from animal hair. Thus when Beuys attached a strip of felt to a pile of fat, it was a simple act of shamanism, an attempt to spiritualise matter.'

'But,' MacTrevor protested, 'surely if Graham was a religious nutcase, he'd like that sort of thing!'

'No way,' Sir Charles contradicted. 'Graham is a fanatical Protestant who believes that matter is Satanic. The sources from which Beuys drew his inspiration were clearly pagan and thus form part of the Anti-Christ's programme for world domination. Here I'm assuming, of course, that you believe the nonsense put about by Bible-thumping fundamentalists!'

'The ideas of Steiner and Beuys seem to share a strong affinity with Germanic mythology,' Ronald observed knowledgeably. 'Was Graham aware of this and if so, how did he connect it to Neoism?'

'Graham told me,' Brewster confided, 'that there was a direct line of development running through the ideology and activities of Hitler's Nazi Party, Beuys and the Neoists. He insisted that the holocaust was an act of shamanist transformation, a warming and dissolving of form, a Gnostic purification!'

'That's incredibly tasteless!' MacTrevor spat.

'I know,' Sir Charles agreed, 'but it tells us a great deal about Graham's warped mind! He was convinced that the concentration camps were just a dry run for the coming reign of the Anti-Christ. Graham literally believes that the Neoists are completing the work begun by Hiram when he built Solomon's Temple and that as a result of their activities, we're about to enter the period of Tribulation prophesied in the Bible!'

'Whew!' Ronald whistled. 'Graham must be utterly insane to believe that kind of rubbish!'

'That's exactly what I've been telling you for the past ten minutes!' Brewster cried triumphantly.

'Cut!' the producer yelled and the interview was over.

Karen Eliot gazed across East India Dock Road. Chrisp Street Market was a mass of fighting bodies. The art star was only able to catch fleeting glimpses of the television shop from where she was standing. Nevertheless, it was obvious that the plate-glass window had been smashed and display goods were being looted. Eliot leaned into the back of her van and shut down her pirate transmitter. The electronics had done their job by beaming a piece of S&M trash at a carefully selected target audience. Most films of this type were simply an aid to solitary sexual satisfaction, but by hacking one into a communal situation, the material had the potential to cause a riot! Karen climbed into the driver's seat and sped off towards the City. Her job was done and as a result, the social fabric in this part of the East End was rapidly disintegrating!

Johnny and Slash carried a huge television they'd just looted into Fitzgerald House. This state of the art technology was a vast improvement on the set the skinhead had been using for the past two years. A group of youths ran out of the block as the couple made their way to the lift. The kids were laughing as they sped towards the exit and Hodges soon discovered the reason for their mirth. The lift had been sent up to the top floor. Johnny pressed the call button and when the doors opened several minutes later, the skinhead had to jump back from the flames. The teenage gang had looted a furniture shop and stolen a sofa, which they'd doused with petrol and put in the lift before setting it ablaze.

'Come on,' Hodges hissed at Slash. 'Let's get outta here, it looks like the whole shithouse might go up in flames!'

'What about the TV?' the knuckle-girl demanded.

'Fuck the telly!' the skinhead railed. 'There's no way we can get it up to my flat. This block is a fire trap. Let's go down to Greenwich and have a look around the market!'

Johnny grabbed Slash by the hand and dragged her to All Saints DLR station. The skinhead didn't recognise Jock Graham, who'd just come in on the northbound platform. The art critic had got on the wrong bus at Brixton and ended up in Plumstead. Jock made his way across East India Dock Road to Chrisp

Street Market. His heart sank as he took in the hundreds of men, wimmin and children who were rioting. This was exactly what the Satanic conspirators had plotted. The violence that was erupting in the wake of the Semiotic Liberation Front happening would make the front page of every national newspaper and attract impressionable individuals to Neoism! Spartacus spotted the art critic and led his comrades in an orderly retreat to the sedate atmosphere of a West End coffee shop.

'Stop, stop!' Graham bellowed. 'In the name of the Lord I want you all to stop! Listen to me! You're all being duped into participating in a Satanic conspiracy!'

No one paid a blind bit of notice to the Christian nutter. Windows continued to be smashed, the police station was torched and consumer goods were being piled into trolleys before these were pushed home by happy proletarian shoppers. A man in a wheelchair asked for a cigarette and was handed a box of two hundred. Jock looted a knife from Steve's Best Sellers. He walked up to a youth who was battering the skull of a muzzled dog with a baseball bat. Graham shoved his blade into the teenager's kidneys and when he removed it, the shiny surface dripped with dark red blood. The art critic's next victim was a young mother busy looting sweeties for her children. Then he went for a pensioner, plunging the knife into the greybeard's neck.

'I'll stop you rioting!' Jock thundered. 'Even if I have to kill you all! You're dupes of a plot to destroy Christian civilisation! Where are the police when we need them? I'll tell you, enjoying themselves with harlots who they've hired on the proceeds of the bribes paid to them by the Illuminati! Whatever happened to law and order? This is supposed to be a Christian country and look at you! Men, wimmin and children behaving like a bunch of savages! I'll kill the lot of you because the day of the Lord of Hosts shall be upon everyone who breaks the law!'

Graham staggered around the pedestrian precinct stabbing anyone who was too slow to dodge out of his way. The heavy traffic on East India Dock Road prevented the rioting from spreading south towards the Isle of Dogs. The recently refurbished shopping centre was being reduced to a gutted shell. Fitzgerald House was in flames. The trouble was spreading north on to the Lansbury and Teviot estates, where the mob torched the homes of prominent local liberals. The scum who'd been manipulating the local population for their own ideological ends were about to pay the price for their ceaseless meddling in the affairs of ordinary people. The first former councillor was caught in Zetland Street. He was tarred and feathered, then made to run down a double line of angry locals who beat him with clubs and sticks. Those at the end were left with no option but to put the boot in on this cunt. The bozo collapsed before he even reached them.

Bob Salisbury-Smith had been standing in the hallway of the house he shared with Dr Maria Walker for the best part of an hour. He was determined to give the bastard his girlfriend had been screwing a good fright. When the toe-rag arrived, the social worker intended to bash him on the bonce with his best hammer. Maria had locked herself into an upstairs bedroom and unbeknownst to Bob, this foxy chick had thrown a knife out of the window and on to the garden path.

Rebel spotted the blade as he approached the front door, picking it up was little more than a reflex action. Split seconds after the boot boy rang the bell, the portal swung open and Salisbury-Smith lurched at the skinhead wielding his hammer. Rebel weaved to one side and thrust the knife into the social worker's heart. Salisbury-Smith staggered along the garden path clutching his chest. Within seconds, his Grateful Dead T-shirt was soaked in blood.

'I done 'im, I done the bastard!' Rebel crowed.

The social worker still had the hammer in his hand as he fell into the gutter. Maria rushed down from the bedroom and hauled the boot boy into the house. She threw her arms around Rebel and kissed him passionately. Walker could feel the skinhead's throbbing manhood straining against his flies. The doctor wanted a wild sado-masochistic session but knew this would have to wait until after they'd dealt with the police.

'We've gotta get our act together,' Maria instructed. 'You've gotta start looking like you're upset about what happened. You just had to kill a man in self-defence and you're pretty cut up about it.'

'Okay,' Rebel agreed.

'Go through to the kitchen,' Walker instructed. 'Cut up an onion and rub the slices around the edge of your eyes. It'll make it look like you've been crying because of the remorse you feel. I'm gonna call an ambulance and the police.'

The doctor punched out the digits 999 but the number was engaged. She kept pressing the re-dial button on her phone but without any luck. It took twenty minutes to get through to the emergency services and even then, the telephonist didn't appear very interested in the murder.

'Hi,' Maria choked. 'My boyfriend has just been stabbed to death. I think it was an accident.'

'No,' the telephonist contradicted. 'We've got a

positive identification on the killer. It's Jock Graham. This escaped maniac is on the loose in your area and he's knifing people left, right and centre. The body count is already well into double figures. Graham is armed and extremely dangerous, if you see him, don't attempt to approach the bastard!'

'Can you get an ambulance and squad car over here?' Walker enquired.

'Maybe tomorrow,' the voice at the other end of the line replied. 'There's been a mass outbreak of lawlessness in Poplar and the emergency services are stretched to the limit! We're not able to deal with the demands being placed on us right now. Please allow at least a week before ringing back and chasing us up. I'll take the details but beyond that, there's nothing we can do for you right now!'

Sarah Osterly liked to spend Saturdays in the West End. In her fashionable clothes and make-up, the schoolgirl looked at least eighteen. She found it easy to solicit invitations to the homes and hotel rooms of affluent men. Sarah had been in a café with a TV set tuned to Channel 9 as the Ronald MacTrevor interview with Sir Charles Brewster was broadcast. She recognised the Progressive Arts Project supremo instantly as he strolled down Old Compton Street only a few hours later.

''Ere, mister!' Osterly exclaimed as she stepped in front of the arts pundit. 'You're the bloke I just saw on the telly who knows that escaped lunatic. It's really creepy you knowing a killer, and very sexy too!'

'You're a pretty young girl,' Brewster replied lecherously. 'Would you like to have sex with a guy who gets prime-time exposure every two or three weeks!'

'Oh yes!' Sarah squealed.

'Take my arm then,' Sir Charles replied, 'and by the way, how old are you? Sixteen? Seventeen?'

'I'm nineteen!' Osterly lied.

Brewster led the girl towards the Thumbprint Gallery where Aesthetics and Resistance were invigilating the *New Neoism* show. Penelope Applegate and Donald Pemberton were pretty hacked off about missing out on the Semiotic Liberation Front happening at Chrisp Street Market. Spartacus had insisted that because they lived in the area, their presence would reduce the impact of the event. Besides, someone had to look after the Old Compton Street exhibition during the hours it was open to the public.

'I want to take this girl through to the back room for a fucking,' Sir Charles informed Aesthetics and Resistance upon entering the gallery. 'Is that alright with you?'

'You can't do that!' Penny wailed.

'Do you know who I am?' Brewster yelped. 'I head the Progressive Arts Project and I've been knighted for my services to culture! If you won't let me fuck this girl in your back room, I'll see to it that your work is never exhibited again!'

'Sir Charles,' Applegate grovelled. 'I'm more than happy for you to use our kitchen for sexual purposes! I just don't want to see you getting into trouble with the law. The girl you've got with you lives near my Poplar council flat and I know for a fact that she's only fifteen!'

'Liar!' Sarah bellowed before spitting in Penny's face.

'Listen bitch,' Brewster snarled as he turned on Osterly. 'I know for a fact that this artist wouldn't lie to me about your age because I'm in a position to ruin her career. While I'm as fond of teenage snatch as the next man, I've no intention of breaking the law! So fuck off!'

'Wanker!' Osterly sneered as she stormed on to the street. 'I bet you've never even had sex in your entire fucking life!'

'Thanks for warning me,' Sir Charles beamed at Penny. 'At least I'm in the right area to find something that's both legal and has a meter on it!'

'There's no need for that!' Applegate whistled. 'I can provide you with oral, hand relief or full sex absolutely free of charge!'

'I'll take the blow job!' Brewster waxed. 'Let's go through to the kitchen so that you can get your pretty little mouth around my tool!'

Johnny Aggro had seen Slash on to a train at Greenwich just after five. The knuckle-girl was meeting her boyfriend at Waterloo station, he had a few days' leave after completing his basic army training at Pirbright. The skinhead tried to get back to Poplar but the police had shut down the DLR and there were no buses running on the Isle of Dogs either. The boot boy dialled a special hotline and a telephonist told him that Fitzgerald House had suffered major fire damage during the Poplar riot. Hodges was offered temporary accommodation but turned it down, saying he could stay with friends. Despite loosing his possessions, Johnny felt good about his home being burnt out, he was sick of the place and it was high time he moved on.

Rebel answered the phone when Hodges called Maria Walker. His mate told him that he'd never make it to the doctor's pad because the cops had sealed off the area. Rebel also made it clear that he'd moved in with

Maria and Hodges wouldn't have received a particularly warm welcome even if he'd been able to make his way to the terrace. Karen Eliot was out but she'd left a message on her answerphone saying she'd be having a boogie at the Nursery from nine o'clock onwards.

The boot boy retraced his footsteps through the Greenwich Foot Tunnel and walked to the railway station. It didn't take long to get into the West End. Johnny had several drinks in the Spice of Life on Cambridge Circus and then made his way to the Nursery. It was strange paying his way into the club alone. Usually, he had the rest of the gang with him. Hodges realised the Raiders were a thing of the past, Rebel and Slim were in line for a kicking if he ran into them. As for Samson and TK, they simply didn't have any ambition and actually seemed to like living in Poplar. If they wanted to come west for an evening, then Johnny was more than prepared to meet his old mates in a pub – but he swore to himself that he'd never set foot in the East End again.

The DJ was playing old Go Go records and Karen Eliot arrived during 'Put Your Left Hand in the Air and Your Right Hand Down in Your Underwear' by Redds and the Boys. The art star bought a couple of pints but these were abandoned in favour of the dance floor when Trouble Funk's 'Drop the Bomb' came blasting out of the PA system. Johnny and Karen stayed out on the floor during 'We Need Some Money' by Chuck Brown and the Soul Searchers but returned to their drinks when the DJ span a Rare Essence track.

'I need a place to stay,' Johnny told Karen. 'My flat was burnt down during the Neoist happening in Chrisp Street Market.'

'Don't act like it's all my fault,' Eliot retorted. 'You helped foment the riot!'

'Okay, okay!' Hodges seethed. 'But can I stay at your pad tonight?'

'Yeah,' Eliot replied begrudgingly. 'But just for one night and you'll have to sleep on the floor. You're no fun as a lover, you won't own up to your masochistic kinks. Unless I dominate men, I just can't get off on them sexually.'

'Hey,' a skinny guy in cycling gear interrupted. 'Where's your friend Slim? I met him here last week and I'd like to see him again.'

'If I see that cunt,' Johnny fumed, 'I'll kick his fucking head in! But I'll give you his phone number as long as you promise to tell his mother that he's your boyfriend. You got a pen and paper?'

'Hold on a second,' the cycling enthusiast replied. 'I'll borrow a Biro from one of the bar staff!'

Eleven

JOCK GRAHAM WAS knackered. He'd spent the night wandering around the East End, afraid to lay his head on the ground in case the sedatives still being pumped through his veins caused him to cross the threshold between deep sleep and death. The art critic cum crazed killer drifted up Brick Lane. The lights of the all-night Bagel Bakery acted as a Beacon, cutting through the grey fog of dawn. Graham entered the premises where he wolfed down two cream cheese bagels and a cuppa. Outside, he bought a late edition of the *Sunday Chronicle* from a vendor who'd spent eight hours selling newspapers to cabbies and the many other creatures that haunted the London night.

The main headline advertised a report on the 49 KILLED BY ANTI-NEOIST MADMAN DURING POPLAR RIOT. Jock scanned the verbiage and was outraged to discover that not only had his holy slayings been branded as murder, but he'd been accused of starting the trouble by a lying hack who was undoubtedly a stooge of the Illuminati. Graham decided something had to be done to counter this libel and so he made his way through the City of London to Chronicle House, home of the slander sheet. On the way, the art critic siphoned petrol from the tank of a Cortina, filling a milk bottle with the fuel.

'I wanna speak to the editor!' Jock reproached a receptionist.

'I'm afraid that's not possible,' the burly middle-aged man rebuked his interlocutor, 'she's not due in until ten o'clock.'

'You're lying!' Graham fulminated. 'The *Sunday Chronicle* never prints the truth, so I don't see why I should believe anything one of its employees says!'

'Oh,' the receptionist replied. 'I thought you wanted Muriel Brown, editor of the *Daily Chronicle*. Betsy Carver who edits our Sunday paper won't be around until tomorrow afternoon.'

'In that case,' the art critic snapped, 'get me a photographer, anyone will do!'

'Why?' the *Chronicle* employee enquired.

'Because,' Jock explained, 'I'm about to kill myself. Once you get me a photographer, I'm gonna pour this bottle of petrol over my clothes and set fire to them to protest against the slanders printed on the front page of today's paper!'

'I don't want you making a mess all over my carpet,' the receptionist grieved. 'But I'll do you a deal, if you go and immolate yourself in the street, I'll get you a photographer!'

'Okay,' the art critic agreed.

Graham wandered outside and sat in the middle of the road. He poured petrol over his clothes and then took a lighter from his pocket. He hoped the photographer wasn't going to be long, he was soaking wet and the flames would warm him up! A minute later, a woman holding a camera stuck her head out of a first floor window.

'Could you move back a bit so I can get a better shot, that's it! Don't set fire to yourself just yet. Right, I'm ready, but remember to grimace, you've gotta look like you're in agony! I can get some great shots of your facial expressions with this zoom lens, so we've got a good chance of making the front page.'

Split seconds after igniting his clothes, Jock was haloed by a sheet of flame. The fire consumed his body, leaving behind a heap of grotesquely charred remains. For a few seconds, Graham believed he was roasting in hell, before briefly convincing himself he was ascending to heaven. After this, his senses registered unbearable agony for what seemed like an eternity and finally the art critic felt nothing at all. With the loss of his instinctual drives, Jock was just a heap of dead matter.

Karen Eliot was a manipulatrix with a difference, she also liked to get her hands dirty when the opportunity arose to do so with impunity! It was for this reason that the art star had left Johnny Aggro kipping on the floor of her Bloomsbury flat and headed for Mayfair. In Eliot's mind, the individuals who made up the gallery scene were little better than street trash. They were simply another brand of vermin to be treated with the same contempt that any sane individual directed towards junkies, derelicts and drunks. Such scum were to be exterminated with the utter indifference one felt when crushing a bug beneath the heel of a boot. Unfortunately, the repressive tolerance of the British state meant that mass liquidation was out of the question for the time being. Instead, Eliot had temporarily resigned herself to exploiting the nervous disposition of the enemy.

In the hands of a veteran campaigner, a spray can becomes as effective a weapon as an AK 47. Karen painted Neoist slogans over the windows of every gallery in the street. Pausing for a few seconds before making her way to a breakfast meeting with Sir Charles Brewster, Eliot surveyed her handiwork. CONVULSION, SUBVERSION, DEFECTION, ran an epigram dating from the earliest days of the movement. NEOISM IS THE PRINCIPLE OF INFLATION AT WORK IN THE PLASTIC ARTS was sprayed across the front of a gallery that specialised in conceptual and minimalist works. While the classic formulation DEMOLISH SERIOUS CULTURE was a recurring motif tastefully splattered in day-glow paint on every building in the street.

'Karen darling!' Sir Charles inflected as his butler led her into the drawing room of his Mayfair town house. 'It's wonderful to see your smiling face again!'

'Yo!' Eliot whooped while simultaneously holding up the palm of her right hand.

The butler poured coffee as Karen sank into an over-stuffed sofa. Eliot helped herself to a croissant, well-aware that Brewster had long favoured continental-style breakfasts and so this would be a single course affair. The art star spread well-salted butter over the hot snack but declined the offer of jam to accompany it.

'This Neoist lark is breaking bigger and faster than anything I've ever been involved with,' Brewster beamed. 'It looks like being the most successful historicisation of a supposedly marginal avant-garde art movement ever!'

'Nothing beats the excitement of Neoism!'

Karen gushed. 'It knocks futurism, dadaism, surrealism, fluxus and situationism into a cocked hat!'

'You're right!' Sir Charles agreed. 'Although at first sight it appears to be little more than a parody of the classical avant-garde, Neoism's sheer trashiness ultimately lends it a transcendent quality! The movement's work is so utterly lacking in substance that it's awesome! And to top it all, just before you arrived, the news that Jock Graham committed suicide outside the *Chronicle* building was relayed to me!'

'Excellent!' Eliot whistled. 'You know that TRY SUICIDE was a slogan much used by the early Neoist group. Jock's death means that his anti-Neoist crusade will reap a whole new set of headlines. With all this media coverage, the value of Neoist works must be doubling by the minute!'

'I think they're more likely to be trebling by the second!' Brewster chirped.

The Semiotic Liberation Front were able to hold a Sunday morning meeting in the Thumbprint Gallery because this was the one day of the week that the *New Neoism* exhibition was closed to the public. The group's members were exhilarated by the success of their *Poplar Happening*—and in particular, the fact that it had made the front pages of the national press. Among themselves, they ignored the fact that the riot had been triggered by the pirate TV broadcasts organised by their mysterious secret chiefs. Neither this, nor the column-grabbing slayings by crazed art critic Jock Graham, was a feature of the wannabe art stars' animated conversation.

'The Holy Ghost just farted and made me God,' Donald Pemberton announced for the umpteenth time, 'and I don't think it's fair that we should be kept hanging on by whoever runs the SLF. Look what we did yesterday, the *Poplar Happening* has to be the most significant art event in the entire history of the world. We did that—you and me, not the secret chiefs we were serving. I want a gallery contract and I want it now!'

'Yeah,' Eugene De Freud put in. 'Don's right, we caused that big-arsed rumble yesterday and yet none of us even gets a name-check in the papers! We deserve the credit and some recognition. It's all very well getting loadsa publicity for the Neoist movement, but unless the name Freud crops up somewhere in the story, then it ain't doing nothing for my career!'

'You've gotta have faith!' Stephen Smith bellowed. 'The secret chiefs got me signed up, so they'll do it for all of you too!'

'It's all very well for you!' Penelope Applegate simpered. 'You've got your contract with Flipper Fine Arts. The people behind the SLF didn't demand that you demonstrate obedience before being launched on a wave of hype into the glamorous world of chi-chi parties and artistic recognition!'

'Oh, come on!' Spartacus retorted. 'All that's happened so far is Emma selecting a piece of my work for the next group show at Flipper. I'm not gonna get a one-man exhibition in the West End until the beginning of next year! You'll all have got contracts long before then!'

'Fuck that shit!' Pemberton grimaced. 'You can tell Hiram that we're not doing another bloody thing for him until we're all signed to major galleries! I'm through with doing people favours, I wanna be rewarded for my efforts!'

'All this bickering is a waste of time,' Smith spat. 'Let's talk about something useful instead! Why don't we finalise the details of tonight's action at Bunhill Burial Fields?'

'I'm not digging up Blake's grave!' Don growled. 'At any rate, I won't do it unless Hiram sorts something out for me with a major gallery first!'

'I've no way of contacting Hiram,' Stephen remonstrated, 'and it's unlikely he'll get hold of me before tonight. The secret chiefs will be hopping mad if we don't desecrate the Blake grave as ordered. Unless you do this, you'll never make it in the art world. If you all agree to participate in this caper, I promise that next time I speak to Hiram, I'll ask him to sort out your careers!'

'And what happens if we won't go along with this plan of yours?' Pemberton demanded.

'I'll have to boot you out of this SLF cell and find some raw recruits to take your place!' Spartacus hollered.

'Okay, I'll participate in tonight's activities,' Don conceded, 'but after that I won't do another thing for the secret chiefs until I get a gallery contract!'

'That goes for us too!' the others chanted in unison.

Johnny Aggro and Atima Sheazan met in the Crest, a rock and roll toilet located among the back streets of Camden. A ska band were doing a lunch-time gig in a side room but the love-struck couple missed the act because they had so much to speak about after spending a few days apart. Atima looked stunning in a leather mini-skirt and tight purple top with lipstick and nail polish to match. Johnny was wearing loafers, sta-prest and a Sherman, which made him look pretty much like all the other skinheads in the pub. Apart from its infectious beat, Hodges considered Jamaican-style music infinitely superior to Oi! because it attracted smartly dressed skins rather than the idiots who gave the cult a bad name and were in reality no more than bald punks!

'My family are dying to meet you!' Sheazan announced. 'At first they were shocked when I told them that you were a skinhead. They'd swallowed a lot of the lies put out by the media painting everyone who crops their hair as a fascist!'

'I hope you put 'em straight,' Johnny was genuinely concerned about the issue. 'Most skins aren't interested in politics of any variety. The cult is all about self-respect, looking smart and having a good time. Like any normal skin, I hate nazi nutters every bit as much as marxist morons! I'm a British patriot not a political idiot!'

'In the end,' Atima proceeded, 'it wasn't difficult convincing my folks that you're just a regular guy possessed by superhuman powers of persuasion. After all, without your help, I'd never have broken free from the *Marxist Times* circle and their mind control techniques. In fact, my ma and pa are really grateful because they know that without your intervention, I might never have spoken to them again. After I told my mum I was madly in love with you, she got on to dad and he's now offered to organise everything if there's a wedding!'

'Sounds good to me!' Hodges affirmed.

'Oh Johnny!' Sheazan pronounced as she threw her arms around the skinhead's neck. 'Will you marry me?'

'Yeah,' the boot boy replied bashfully, 'I wanna get hitched with you. Christ, I'm twenty-four in a few weeks, it's about time I settled down to family life. But fuck knows what I'll do about getting a job, I ain't got any paper qualifications, I left school at sixteen instead of going to college like you.'

'Don't worry about that!' Atima gushed before pecking her boyfriend on the cheek. 'One of my uncles has just bought a shop in Carnaby Street and he says we can run it together. He's already got one outlet selling heavy metal gear and he's happy for you to front this new operation which will specialise in skinhead and mod clobber. What's more, there's a flat above the store and my uncle says you can move into it if you agree to work for him!'

'Excellent!' Hodges bellowed. 'It's everything I've always wanted, a W1 address, an interesting job and a beautiful wife! Let's go and sort it all out with your family!'

'Not so fast!' Sheazan chided. 'I've got the keys to the flat and I think we should go and have a look at it before doing anything else! It hasn't been properly furnished but there's a mattress in one of the rooms and I think we could make good use of that!'

'You're gonna be the best wife ever!' Johnny thundered. 'Drink up! It seems like years since I last had a shag!'

Karen Eliot had a lunch date with Amanda Debden-Philips in the Berwick Street Wimpy Bar. This British-owned fast food chain had been bought out by Burger King in the early nineties but since it was operated on a franchise system, a handful of the concerns had opted out of the deal and retained the old name. For Eliot, visiting a Wimpy was a nostalgic occasion as she'd spent a great deal of her adolescence hanging out in burger bars. Debden-Philips had never set foot inside a Wimpy before, so the arts administrator considered the experience something of a novelty, although ultimately what was on offer hardly differed from the other fast food joints she'd patronised at Karen's instigation.

'I don't know how you manage to eat so much and yet remain so thin!' Amanda cooed in amazement as Eliot tucked into her platter. 'Those milkshakes you consume with such relish must be ever so fattening!'

'Shall I let you into a secret?' Karen whispered.

'Yes, yes!' Debden-Philips beseeched.

'What I do,' Eliot quacked, 'is go into the toilet and puke it all up after I've finished a meal!'

'Are you serious?' the arts administrator demanded.

'No,' Karen confessed, 'but I think eating disorders are a Neoist-style phenomenon, they represent a simultaneous celebration and critique of consumer culture. This was a feature of a lot of the best punk and rap acts too, everyone from X-Ray Spex through Sigue Sigue Sputnik to the Fat Boys. I guess the drug frenzy of the early nineties' rave scene is another example of this schizophrenic response to everything post-modern, although the latter subculture was so wonderfully chaotic it seems a travesty to make generalisations about it!'

'Forget all this pop rubbish!' Amanda chided. 'Youth culture has been decisively outflanked by Neoism! Just look at the papers, they've devoted page after page to the Poplar riot. There are a couple of TV specials planned, which means no one can doubt the fact that the avant-garde is back on the mainstream agenda!'

'I thought I'd already told you,' Eliot chipped in, 'that the mainstream no longer exists. It's been a cliché amongst po-mo theorists from Lyotard onwards that we live in a world of proliferating margins!'

'That's all very well,' Debden-Philips snarled,

'but most people don't read theory books. In fact, even those who crib a few catch-phrases from reviews of such works represent a tiny minority of art lovers. The people who matter are the collectors with money to spend! Egg-headed art students might be impressed by French intellectuals but the unsung heroes of the art world—the successful businessmen who buy pictures at retail prices—are more interested in icons than ideas!'

'I agree!' Karen shouted triumphantly. 'And that's why I'm interested in pop culture, with its star system based on sycophancy rather than intellectual merit.'

'When I was a kid,' Amanda reminisced, 'I had these Beatles dolls that a friend of the family had given to my older sister. I used to torture the bastards, sticking pins in them and imagining the fab four getting migraines and other ailments. The fantasies became more and more involved as I got older. I used to look up tropical diseases in a medical dictionary and then lie on my bed thinking about the band being really ill with malaria or something else they'd caught during an exotic foreign holiday. When I was fourteen, I decapitated the John Lennon doll and that's when I had my first orgasm! I was in seventh heaven when I heard about the Mark Chapman assassination.'

'With me,' Eliot announced, 'it was the Bay City Rollers. A lot of the girls at my school were madly in love with members of that group. I thought they sucked and much preferred Alice Cooper, although in retrospect I have to admit that 'Shang-A-Lang' was a pop classic. Anyway, I used to ask my pals what they'd do if the Roller they wanted as a husband got married to someone else. We'd get into all these insane fantasies about torture and executions. There was one girl who was completely fixated on Les McKeown and I managed to convince her that he'd got a groupie pregnant. So she went off on this whole trip about having the two of them tied up and cutting the baby out of the slut's stomach and making Les eat it. When you look at it, most people are very ambivalent about their idols, there's some amazingly intense love/hate relationships going on between people who've never met!'

'That's why I've always preferred the art world to popular entertainment,' Debden-Philips put in. 'High culture is much more honest and democratic, the people buying paintings often socialise with the artists who produced the work they're collecting.'

'Nonsense,' Karen contradicted. 'High culture is based on elitism. Pornography is the most democratic form of entertainment in contemporary society because it exposes the mechanisms of the spectacle by transforming its subjects into ciphers and thereby deconstructing the very notion of a star system. With pop music and painting, most people are deluded into thinking that individual artists actually count for something rather than being more or less interchangeable. You'd have to be a real idiot to make that kind of mistake when dealing with pornography!'

Johnny Aggro loved the Carnaby Street flat owned by Atima Sheazan's uncle. There were two bedrooms, a living room, fitted carpets and spacious cupboards! The kitchen had been refitted and there was even a waste disposal unit! However, beyond a few scatter cushions and a mattress, the place wasn't furnished.

'Who's been using the pad?' Hodges asked innocently as he threw his arms around Sheazan. 'Someone's been crashing here recently.'

'It's my cousin Bhavna,' Atima explained. 'Don't say anything about this to my family when you meet them but she's a bit of a raver. Bhavna likes to go clubbing so that she can pick blokes up and bring them here for a shagging. My cousin's got a fat behind and loves being fucked up the arse!'

'When can I meet her?' Johnny teased.

'You'll be introduced soon enough,' Sheazan laughed. 'But you won't like her!'

'Why not?' the skinhead demanded.

'Bhavna's a nympho with a difference,' Atima hissed theatrically. 'She needs men because of her sickness but also likes to punish the blokes who benefit from this weakness! Take a look in the cupboard over there!'

The boot boy did as he was told and split seconds later, reeled back in shocked surprise. The bottom of the fitted wardrobe was littered with whips, chains, dog collars, handcuffs and other props of sexual perversion. While Hodges was quite happy to spank girls who got off on being mistreated, he considered it deeply unnatural that anyone would want to reverse the roles of masculine master and femail slave.

Atima sidled up behind her boyfriend and pulled the skinhead's arms behind his back. She'd found a pair of handcuffs next to the bed and succeeded in slipping them over one wrist before Hodges realised what was going on and broke free from her grip. Johnny spun around and grabbed Atima. Moments later, the boot boy had his fiancée balanced on his knee with her tights around her ankles. Sheazan's buttocks were round and firm, she had a backside that was made for spanking. Hodges raised his hand and then brought it cracking down against Atima's tender flesh.

'Oocchh! That hurt!' Sheazan spat. 'If you

wanna smack me, use your left hand, the 'cuff dangling off your right wrist is fucking dangerous!'

'Let's get rid of the bleedin' thing,' Johnny suggested. 'It'll just get in the way. Where are the keys to undo it?'

'I dunno,' Atima replied. 'Can't you see them anywhere?'

'Nope,' Hodges sighed.

'I know what, I'll phone my cousin,' Sheazan cried triumphantly.

Atima pulled up her tights, ran down the stairs and made her way to a phone box across the street. Johnny watched her through the window. She spoke animatedly for a couple of minutes and then returned.

'Bhavna says she took the keys home with her,' Sheazan announced. 'She's gonna come over with them right away.'

There was nothing subtle about what happened next! The skinhead pounced on his girlfriend and pinned her to the mattress. It didn't take him long to get her knickers off and once he'd done so, Hodges discovered that she was all wet.

Sheazan had clearly been turned on by the task of informing her cousin that she'd attempted to chain up her boyfriend. Atima unzipped Johnny's fly and pulled his cock over the elasticated top of a pair of Union Jack boxer shorts. The skinhead battered his way into Atima's twat. He wanted to make Sheazan come six or seven times and still be at it when Bhavna arrived. Hodges was sure that his girlfriend would greatly enjoy being made to look like a complete slut!

Karen Eliot and Amanda Debden-Philips had proceeded from their lunch date to a Sunday afternoon salon at a plush flat situated on Chelsea Embankment. Florian Cramer who organised these soirées was a retired diplomat who'd befriended many of the more eccentric members of London's chattering classes. In attendance were several MPs and ambassadors, scores of artists, numerous social reformers, a multitude of academics, a handful of inventors and various media types.

'What is it you do?' Eliot asked a woman who was standing next to her.

'I'm Maria Robins, Baron Gobineau's personal assistant,' the do-gooder replied.

'I know the man!' Karen clamoured. 'He's the foreign geezer who thinks British prisons are a disgrace and should be closed down.'

'That's right,' Robins declared. 'People are born fundamentally good, it's the evils of free enterprise and pornography that cause crime.'

'I'm a Neoist,' Eliot put in, 'and I think things went wrong with the abolition of ritual king slaughter. Today, of course, we live in a democracy and so our ancient customs need to be both revived and updated. The government ought to be making up slates of individuals and then having referendums on whether or not they should be hanged.'

'You believe in capital punishment!' the do-gooder gasped in disbelief.

'It's more complicated than that,' Karen continued. 'You see, I'd make up slates containing a few convicted child killers and terrorists along with a dozen or so individuals taken at random from the electoral roll. There'd then be a vote on whether to hang the lot of them or let the alleged criminals off scot-free!'

'That's barbaric!' Maria wailed.

'No,' Eliot contradicted. 'It's a way of reintroducing ritual king slaughter into a democratic system where the electorate functions as the monarch. It would be a lot of fun and I'm sure criminals serving life sentences wouldn't object. Such a system would operate as a lottery with the possibility of crazed psycopaths being set free!'

'It's horrible, horrible!' the do-gooder mumbled as she made her way across the room.

'Hi, I'm a psychogeographer,' a man said by way of introducing himself to Karen. 'I couldn't help overhearing what you were saying and I think it's a wonderful idea. I'd also like to introduce compulsory unemployment for everyone aged between twenty-seven and thirty!'

'So would I!' Eliot concurred. 'I guess we'd both see Jorn's contribution to situationism as being far more substantial than Debord's rather reductionist theorising.'

'Yes, yes!' the psychogeographer cried heartily.

'Karen, come over here,' the host said as he took the art star's arm. 'You really must meet Martin Gorton, he's an archaeologist.'

'Okay,' Eliot sighed.

'Martin,' Cramer greeted the man as though he was an old friend despite having only just made his acquaintance. 'Meet an artist. She's wasting the world's resources with a little help from her painter friends. Tell Karen about how art caused the destruction of the Greek polis, then maybe she'll embark on a career that will be of benefit to Western Civilisation.'

'Have you been here before?' Gorton enquired.

'Yeah,' Karen confessed. 'Cramer says he detests artists but I don't treat his views very seriously. About five years ago he issued a standing invitation for anyone signed to my gallery to come along to these salons and here I am, still utilising them as a networking tool and a pleasant way to pass a Sunday afternoon. What about you, is it your first time?'

'Yes,' Martin admitted. 'A friend brought me along, he said Herr Cramer would love to hear about the research I've been doing. It shows that Plato's fears about the disruptive role painters and poets played in Greek society were not completely unfounded.'

'I'd like to know about that too!' Eliot enthused. 'Do tell me.'

'Hey, you two,' Florian interrupted the conversation before it even got started, 'I want you to meet an anarchist, she thinks we need a violent revolution to sort society out.'

'I'm not really an anarchist,' the girl mumbled as she was abandoned by the host. 'I've no time for utopian ideologies, what interests me is violence as a form of communication and the moral qualities it contains.'

'That's an issue which resonates with my interest in the ancient Greeks,' the archaeologist observed.

'Hey, you lot,' Cramer interrupted as he shoved a book into Karen's hands, 'I want you to meet a novelist, that's one of her books I've just given you.'

In this way, the afternoon quickly passed. Although neither Karen nor Amanda actually managed to finish a single one of the many conversations they started, they did get to meet a hell of a lot of people. Some of these contacts would be followed up and would prove useful in furthering the two wimmin's very different careers in the art world.

Atima Sheazan and Johnny Aggro had been at it like rabbits for the best part of twenty minutes. Both of them heard the front door open as Bhavna let herself into the flat. There was nothing subtle about what happened next, there didn't need to be, since both Johnny and Atima were hell-bent on humiliating each other. Each feigned ignorance of the visitor who was making her way to the room in which they were fucking.

'I wanna be on top!' Sheazan moaned.

The skinhead complied with his girlfriend's wish and the couple swapped positions without interrupting their 120 bpm sex session. Although Hodges didn't like acting passive in sexual or any other matters, he wanted to see the look on Bhavna's face when she caught her cousin at it with a skinhead! What Johnny didn't know about was the agreement the two girls had reached during their brief telephone conversation, to the effect that they'd teach the boot boy the pleasures of bondage and submission.

It was the skinhead who got a shock when Bhavna marched into the room and didn't bat an eyelid. She grabbed Johnny's arms and pulled them up above his head. Atima had her boyfriend pinned down as she did the rising trot on his throbbing manhood. Hodges realised what was going on and wrestled furiously with his fiancée's attractive cousin. Bhavna might have succeeded in restraining the skinhead if all she'd had to do was snap a handcuff shut on his left wrist. Unfortunately, Johnny had secured both ends of the restraint to his right arm so that it didn't get in the way as he fucked.

After Bhavna had unlocked one of the 'cuffs, the boot boy snapped it shut over her left wrist so that the two of them were chained together. He then snatched the key from the girl and freed his right wrist before grabbing the fetish chick's other arm and successfully chaining her up. Atima was having yet another orgasm as she rode her bucking bronco, Johnny twisted beneath his wife-to-be and threw her off his crotch. Bhavna's mini-skirt was riding up around her waist, Hodges grabbed her white panties and yanked them down her legs.

'Stop it! Stop it!' Atima bellowed as she beat her boyfriend's back with her fists. 'You're no fun! We wanted to chain you up, blindfold you and then make you lick cunt. But if you won't do it my way, I won't allow you to have sex with my cousin!'

'That's not fair,' Johnny snorted, 'I out-wrestled your cousin and so I should be allowed to give full expression to the sexual feelings I experience as a top!'

'No way!' Bhavna bellowed as she hitched her knickers up. 'Before Atima got involved in all that communist crap, the two of us used to take a lot of guys on three-in-a-bed romps. We'd chain them up, spank the fuckers and once we really got going, use our cunts to work their pricks and their mouths. You're engaged to Atima and while she's happy to let you lick my clit, there's no way she'll sit back and allow you to batter my twat!'

'That's right!' the skinhead's girlfriend put in. 'Since you won't indulge me with a little masochistic fun, I'm gonna see to it that you remain strictly monogamous!'

'Oh,' Johnny whined as he thought about his W1 address and the fact that he didn't want to lose it, 'I suppose it will be worth it!'

Slim and his mother were staying with relatives in West Ham. Their flat had been burnt down during the Poplar riot, resulting in the death of Peter's younger sister who'd been too scared to run the angry crowd baying for Slim's blood. The fact that Peter had been having bondage sessions with a fifteen-year-old school girl did not go down well with the majority of Poplar's working-class residents. While most of the blokes who were up in arms about the affair would have given their right arm to sniff the nymphet's knickers, this was not something they were prepared to admit in public.

'Can I have something else to eat?' Slim asked after gobbling down a plate of scrambled eggs on toast.

'No, Peter,' Auntie Doris replied. 'You've got to grow your hair and lose some weight, that way you'll be able to walk the streets without being recognised. And once you've shed three or four stone, I'm gonna send our Michael out to buy you some rave gear!'

'But I like being a skinhead!' Watson protested.

'Don't argue,' Doris spat. 'Your mother was never firm enough with you as a child and as a direct result you've ended up being a fat slob. You'll much prefer staying alive to being a dead skinhead. Unless you change your appearance, you're never gonna be able to leave this house and I don't want you under my feet all day.'

'For fuck's sake!' Slim swore.

'I won't have you using foul language in my house, young man!' Peter's aunt hissed as she clouted him around the ear. 'Apologise or I'll throw you out on the street!'

Before the skinhead had a chance to express his regrets over this lapse in manners, the sound of the front door being kicked in had the boot boy bolting towards the rear of the house.

'Don't anybody move,' an authoritarian voice announced over a megaphone. 'This is the police. We have marksmen covering the front and rear of the terrace. Anyone who attempts to escape will be shot!'

Slim couldn't believe it! He hadn't done anything wrong, so what the hell were the Mets doing busting in on him like this? Thoughts raced through his mind. Perhaps behind all her prim posturing, his aunt was secretly peddling arms, drugs and kiddie porn. Maybe the cops had simply made a mistake and raided the wrong address. The boot boy had nothing to fear from the police, perhaps they'd even come to protect him from a gang of crazed vigilantes. There was no need to do a runner if armed Mets were in the street, so Peter sat down and waited to see how things developed. Split seconds later, the skinhead was lying face down on the floor with a gun pointing at his head. A uniformed cop handcuffed his arms behind his back while simultaneously informing him of his rights.

'Peter Watson, you are under arrest for having sexual intercourse with an underage girl and inciting a riot by publicly broadcasting footage of illegal sex acts. You have the right to remain silent and I must warn you that anything you say will be taken down and may be used in evidence.'

Johnny Aggro was in a fine mood as he stood in front of the City Road entrance to Bunhill Fields. The former Dissenter's burial ground was now run as a public open space by the Corporation of London and covered four acres just north of the Square Mile. Inside, were a jumble of graves that housed the mortal remains of William Blake, John Bunyan and Daniel Defoe, among others. The Semiotic Liberation Front activists had been ordered to break into the burial ground via the Bunhill

Row gate, since no one was likely to disturb them on this quiet street so late at night.

The light murmur of traffic cruising around the Old Street roundabout drowned out the noise of the SLF using bolt cutters to bust open the locks that secured the west gate. It was the buzz of a whispered conversation that alerted the skinhead to the fact that the wannabe artists were making their way through the burial ground to the monuments erected in honour of Blake, Bunyan and Defoe. The boot boy smiled grimly as he heard a pickaxe cracking against the paving stones that surrounded these icons. Satisfied that a serious crime was being committed, Hodges made his way to a phone box on Old Street.

'Good evening,' a voice purred into the receiver.

'Hello,' Johnny replied. 'Is that the Mets?'

'This is the City of London police headquarters,' the voice purred back.

'I have some news concerning the desecration of William Blake's grave in Bunhill Burial Fields!'

'Yes?' the voice was tense and alert.

'A bunch of artists are digging up the poet's remains at this very moment! They consider the act to be some kind of happening. I understand that they are angry about press coverage of the Neoist riot in Poplar yesterday lunch-time.'

Hodges hung up. He'd said enough to ensure that within minutes scores of police cars would be cruising silently down City Road. Enough to induce the cops to blockade Bunhill Row before moving in with shooters to arrest the SLF. Enough to see to it that Donald Pemberton and Penelope Applegate were sent down for a few years. That would stop them blasting their neighbours with a tasteful selection of jazz tunes. Johnny headed for the twenty-four-hour bagel bar in Brick Lane. He wanted a late-night snack before catching a bus back to the centre of town.

Having failed to find any bones beneath the Blake monument, Spartacus ordered his troops to exhume bodies from other sites. They failed to turn up the remains of either Defoe or Bunyan. Shovelling away at the earth around the vast jumble of ordinary graves, the SLF unearthed a few skulls. Spartacus shed his clothes and wanked off over the haul. He'd soon show his followers what a bit of Crowley-style magick could do, and it would be a lot more fun than William Blake's brand of reformed druidry.

'I'd have liked to find the corpse of some bitch,' Spartacus railed. 'So that I could practise the Greek rite on the body. But there's nothing here, all the graves are too old. The last burial took place in 1860!'

The Lodge leader and his followers were so engrossed in these fantasies that they didn't hear the cops sealing off the burial ground. Armed constables had been placed at six-yard intervals around the railings that enclosed this open space. It was only when several police searchlights lit up the burial ground that the SLF learnt they were no longer alone.

'You are surrounded by armed marksmen, please proceed to the east gate with your hands above your heads,' a voice announced over a megaphone.

'What do we do?' Penny Applegate demanded.

'Get naked and charge the bastards,' Spartacus raged.

'You're fucking mad!' Don Pemberton countered. 'You'll get us all killed.'

'Don's right!' the rest of the SLF chanted in unison. 'We'll have to surrender.'

'These colours don't run!' Spartacus screamed as he raced towards City Road. 'Crowley's magick will protect me!'

There was a burst of gun-fire. Several bullets hit the Lodge leader and he collapsed in a pool of blood. Other marksmen picked off the rest of the SLF membership. Stephen Smith's mad charge had given the cops the excuse they needed for a mass execution. Although the death of every last member of this criminal gang would cause a few days hand-wringing among liberal do-gooders, in the long run it would save the ordinary taxpayer the expense of a trial.

Epilogue

THE NURSERY HAD moved from its original location in Soho to a back street behind Euston station. Karen Eliot was enjoying a night of nineties' nostalgia at the club. She was on the piss with her publisher, Fiona Booth. The dance floor was teeming with ravers getting down on their thang to the extended mix of Freaky Realistic's 'Leonard Nimoy'. Karen was still a major fixture on the arts scene but with the publication of her first book, *Class As Theatre*, she was also making waves in the world of letters. Fiona was in the ladies' and Eliot was mentally running over a series of quips to use in a television interview she was doing on Sunday afternoon.

'Alright!' Johnny Aggro boomed as he tapped the art star on the shoulder. 'Long time no see!'

'Oh, Johnny, hi,' Karen mumbled as she turned around. 'What are you doing here?'

'I met you at this club,' Hodges yelled. 'Back when it used to be located in Soho, remember? I'm a regular, or at least I used to be before I got hitched, this is Atima, my missus.'

'Hi,' Atima Hodges said as she extended a hand.

'Hi,' Karen echoed as they exchanged a firm handshake.

'Don't I know you?' Atima asked.

'I don't think so,' Eliot replied shaking her head.

'Yes I do!' the skinhead's wife exclaimed. 'I've read your book, *Class As Theatre*. I agree completely with your thesis, there's a great deal of pleasure to be had from subverting the exaggerated fashions and manners associated with various classes. As you point out, class is completely fluid. Look at Johnny, he's geared up as a skinhead and you'd imagine from this that he was working class. In actual fact, my family have set him up as a shopkeeper and he is economically a member of the petit bourgeoisie. I'm university-educated and at the moment I help John in the shop – but I'd like to get a job in publishing so that I can simultaneously play on both my classlessness and my middle class credentials!'

'When I met Johnny,' Karen declaimed, 'he had a skinhead gang. One of his mates was known as Rebel. He's now living with a doctor and working in the City of London. Rebel has done very well for himself. In fact, like me, he's proved that class is anything but destiny. It's something to be tinkered with and enjoyed. Once you consciously understand the codes, you can break them with impunity!'

'John,' Atima tutted. 'You've never told me about Rebel!'

'He's a cunt,' the skinhead replied. 'He nicked one of my birds!'

'He sounds okay,' Atima laughed. 'He cleared the way for me to get my hooks into you! Anyway, what happened to the rest of the gang?'

'Slim's in jail,' Hodges sniggered. 'I've told you

about him, he got done for having sexual relations with an underage chick. I guess that Samson and TK are still working in factories. They were total losers, they actually liked living in Poplar!'

'What about the SLF?' Eliot demanded. 'I haven't seen you since the Lodge members were shot down by the cops. Did you have anything to do with it?'

'Yeah,' the boot boy snorted. 'I told them to go grave-robbing in Bunhill Fields and then phoned the fuzz, so they'd be caught red-handed. I figured the cunts would get a few years inside. However, the lot of them getting wasted was much better, no one can ever prove I had anything to do with it!'

'It was a brilliant move,' Karen conceded. 'I wish I'd thought of it myself. The media coverage was really intense and provided me with the means of breaking Neoism worldwide. I've made a mint as a result, it's the most extreme piece of art historification ever accomplished and it rested entirely upon behind the scenes manipulation!'

'You thought I was just some working-class oik!' Johnny spat accusingly. 'Someone who could be manipulated into doing whatever you wanted. You laughed when I said I'd like to make it in the art world because the money looked good. I proved I've got a mind of my own!'

'Yeah,' Eliot mused. 'I owe you an apology for underestimating your intelligence.'

'Forget it,' the boot boy announced magnanimously. 'I don't want anything from you. I enjoy flogging skinhead gear down Carnaby Street, I'm doing alright from it, I'll be opening another shop soon. I don't give a damn what anyone thinks of me, I'm proud of what I am and what I've achieved.'